She scurr
door, and froz~

Oh, this is not good. This is not good at all.

A chair sat in the middle of the only room. Zip ties, a toolbox, a big jug of gasoline, and plastic were lined up next to each other on the floor. He meant to tie her up in the chair and torture her. And if help didn't arrive soon, that may still be her fate.

Her breathing accelerated and the room tilted. She forced her breaths to slow and her feet to start moving. She couldn't hide in the cabin. The front door was the only way in and out, a trap, and the huge drop behind the cabin, certain death. Gunfire continued to erupt. She spun.

David and Sheriff Hank were on opposite sides of Jon's truck in a standoff.

A red stain spread on Sheriff Hank's chest, and he fell to the ground.

Praise for Michelle Godard-Richer

Praise for Fatal Hunt from Author Fil Reid, "Fatal Hunt carries the reader on a roller coaster ride of tension that never lets up. With likable hero and heroine, with their cute little boy in tow, on the run from assassins sent by a gangster from the hero's past, it kept me on the edge of my seat until the very end."

Praise for Fatal Hunt from N.N. Light's Book Heaven, "Fatal Hunt is a spine-tingling romantic thriller I devoured…"

Praise for Fatal Hunt from Ind'Tale Magazine, ""Fatal Hunt" is a heart-pounding thriller that will have readers on the edge of their seats! With great character and plot development, Ms. Godard Richer does an outstanding job of engaging the reader…"

Praise for Fatal Witness from Author Trisha Messmer, "With edge of your seat plots, and protagonists you'll root for and villains you'll love to hate, Godard Richer crafts a tale with twists and turns so sharp you'll think you've figured it out only to have the rug pulled out from under you in the best possible way."

Fatal Witness

by

Michelle Godard-Richer

The Fatal Series, Book Two

Fatal Witness

Cover Art by *Diana Carlile*

The Wild Rose Press, Inc.
PO Box 708
Adams Basin, NY 14410-0708
Visit us at www.thewildrosepress.com

Publishing History
First Edition, 2023
Trade Paperback ISBN 978-1-5092-5026-4
Digital ISBN 978-1-5092-5027-1

The Fatal Series, Book Two
Published in the United States of America

Dedication

To my family for teaching me the power of unconditional love which influenced that key theme in my first thriller series.

Chapter One

A warm gust of wind lifted Jessica Miller's hair, obscuring her view of the sun making its gradual descent behind the Rocky Mountains, casting a golden hue in the sky.

She pushed her hair behind her shoulders and turned to peer up at her boyfriend, Jon, sitting behind her in the grassy field on his parent's ranch in Lewistown, Montana with his legs tucked around hers. She sighed. "I'm going to miss this."

He wrapped his arms around her and kissed her forehead. "What? The mountains?"

"No, silly." She rested her cheek on the soft flannel of his plaid shirt and inhaled his musky scent combined with the fabric softener his mother used. "You. I love you."

"I know. I love you too, Jess. I'll call you every day. It won't be the same, but we'll figure it out."

She fisted his shirt, wanting to hold on and never let go, and wanting to latch onto his optimism. But long-distance relationships were difficult, and they were in different phases of their lives. She would be starting an English program at the University of Calgary and intended to complete teacher's college afterwards. Four years her senior, he'd graduated college already and had been accepted into the FBI Training Academy.

Thousands of miles would separate them while they met new people and made new friends. And if they did manage to stay together, they'd spend most of their days with a heavy heart, living a half-life as they longed for each other. She couldn't and wouldn't condemn him to that. Her chest tightened at the idea of letting him go but setting him free was the right thing to do.

She shifted away and sat cross-legged facing him.

He frowned and his dimples disappeared.

Her throat thickened. She choked out a single word "No."

He took her hand. "No, what?"

"We can't make this work. I won't tie you down. I want you to meet new people and be happy."

"But I am happy with you. Aren't you happy with me?"

Tears filled her eyes and spilled down her cheeks. "I'm happy when I'm *here* with you, but I'll be miserable without you."

"We won't commit to each other right now." He wiped her tears away with his fingers. "But we'll keep in touch."

"Of course. I can't not have you in my life."

"I see where you're coming from. We're headed in different directions, for now. But after you finish school, we'll see where we're at." He patted the blanket in front of him. "Come back here. Let's enjoy this last night together, sweetheart."

"Okay." She turned and leaned against his chest.

The golden light around the mountains faded, and the sky darkened. As the day ended, so did a phase of Jessica's life. But when the sun rose a new one would begin.

****

Fifteen years later

In her bedroom cloaked in darkness, Jessica rolled over and squinted at the red numbers on the alarm clock. She groaned. *Two thirteen in the morning.*

Sleep evaded her night after night with the bed too empty beside her. In four short hours, she'd need to get ready for work and get her eight-year-old, Bryce, ready for school. Her nightgown clung to her damp, overheated skin and bunched underneath her side.

She climbed out of bed, then twisted the blinds open. Blinking as her eyes adjusted to the brightness of the streetlights, she lifted the window. She leaned on the sill and inhaled the fresh, cool breeze blowing in from the Rocky Mountains to her home in Cochrane, Alberta.

Something scraped on the asphalt off to the right, irritating her ears like nails raking across a chalkboard. She gritted her teeth. The neighbor's truck sat empty in the driveway beneath her window, yet the sound persisted. After a few seconds, it stopped, replaced by footsteps.

The lamppost shone on her neighbor, David as he came around the corner of his house. He wore a dark, long sleeve shirt, dark jeans, a black toque, and gloves. He lowered the tailgate of his truck and folded the tonneau cover back, then walked into the middle of the street with his back to her.

Fine hairs stood on Jessica's arms. David's presence always set her on alert, and this behavior only served to reinforce her belief—something wasn't right with that man. Jessica never understood what his wife, Sarah, saw in him. With her sweet personality and innocent looks, she could do so much better.

Jessica's instincts screamed: turn away, go back to bed, and forget this odd behavior. But curiosity froze her in place, eyes locked on the scene in front of her.

David pivoted and turned.

Jessica crouched beneath the window frame, not daring to move. The streetlight might illuminate her shadow and give her away. The last thing she needed to do was draw attention to her nosiness.

After a few long minutes of torture, his footsteps echoed on the pavement, coming closer and closer, then stopped in front of her house.

Air burst in and out of her lungs and stars clouded her vision. She forced her lungs to take in more air, expanding all the way, before exhaling.

His steps moved farther and farther away, then the scraping sound resumed.

Jessica stood and peered outside.

David came around the corner of his house with his back to her, hunched over, dragging something large rolled in a white plastic tarp tied with a rope around the middle. He dropped his load and then swiped at his forehead with his shirt sleeve. His thick arm muscles strained as he picked up whatever was rolled inside the tarp and dragged it along the driveway to his truck.

He hoisted the bundle over his right shoulder and grunted while using his momentum to flip it onto his truck. The truck bed bounced. A limp, bloody arm came loose from the tarp. The streetlight reflected off its white skin, illuminating a large butterfly tattoo on the inside of the forearm.

Jessica covered her mouth to stifle a scream. She'd recognize that tattoo anywhere. His wife lay wrapped in that tarp. Bile rose in the back of her throat. She swallowed it down. Her friend Sarah needed her help.

She grabbed a pen off the night table and scribbled the license plate number on her arm, then picked up her cell phone and dialed 911. The line remained quiet as the call went through.

David raised his tailgate, picked up a purse and a black duffle bag from the ground, and tossed them on top of Sarah without a second glance. He unfolded his tonneau cover and secured it, hiding her from view.

Jessica's called connected. The line rang once, then twice.

Hurry! Hurry! Please, answer!

She could do nothing to stop David as he rushed around to the driver's side and opened the door. If only someone would come on the line. Before climbing in, he turned back towards Jessica's house. She crouched under the window.

Her heart thudded hard against her ribcage, threatening to jump out of her chest. He'd almost caught her watching twice. She needed to be more careful. The truck door slammed shut, and the engine sparked to life. She kneeled and peeked over the edge of the window, clutching the phone.

A woman's voice spoke into Jessica's ear. "Police, ambulance, or fire?"

The phone jiggled in her fingers, but somehow, she managed to keep it in her grasp. "Police. 10 Branch Crescent immediately. My neighbor, David Hayes, assaulted or killed his wife. I saw him loading her wrapped in a tarp. Hurry!" She stood. "He's driving away in his new black Ford F150."

"Do you have the license plate?"

She read the plate number off her arm.

"All right, ma'am. I'm sending the information through to the RCMP detachment now. What's your name?"

"Jessica Miller."

"They'll send an officer to your house for a statement immediately."

"He can't know I called. Plain clothes, unmarked car."

"We can do that."

In a place of around thirty thousand people, just small enough to still be considered a town, David might recognize every officer on sight regardless of their street clothes, but it was a risk she had to take.

Sarah needed her.

Jessica's legs wobbled, threatening to give out. She dropped into a sitting position on the edge of her bed and buried her face in her hands. In this moment, she yearned for her husband more than ever. She forced herself to breathe slow and deep. Her heart rate dropped, and the queasiness passed.

She stood on steadier legs and tiptoed to the room next to hers. The metal hinges creaked softly as she eased the door open. Her son, Bryce, slept sprawled on his stomach, his blanket down by his feet where he'd kicked it off. She left him uncovered, yanked on the cord dangling from the ceiling fan twice to set it on high, then pulled his window down and engaged the lock.

Oh no! The doors! Did I lock them?

She sprinted past the guest room and down the staircase to the front door. Locked. Then the backdoor. Also locked. She shut the windows in the dining and living rooms, then bolted them.

No need to panic. We're safe.

Jessica sunk into the grey, chenille sofa in her living room and placed a hand on her heaving chest. *Deep breaths.*

As her pulse slowed, she shivered. She needed to change out of her damp nightgown before the officer arrived.

Rubbing her arms to warm them, she climbed the stairs to the washroom. She splashed hot water on her face, then pulled her hair back into a ponytail, disregarding the bags under her eyes. She dropped her damp nightgown in the clothes hamper on the way to her closet. Still cold, she pulled on jeans and a worn, pale blue, University of Calgary hoodie.

The coffee machine beckoned. Maybe a hot cup of coffee would help with the shock. She pushed the brew button on her machine. The familiar aroma of her favorite vanilla-flavored coffee wafted through the kitchen as liquid dripped into the carafe. She cradled a hot mug in her unsteady hands, unable to get warm, as she waited for the police to arrive.

Ten excruciating minutes later, a truck pulled into her driveway. Her husband's former partner, Tim, a man with salt and pepper hair, a round belly, and perpetually kind eyes climbed out. A sense of safety washed over her, easing the knots in her stomach.

She opened the door and waited for him to approach. "Hi. Come on in. It's good to see a familiar face."

"Good to see you, too. It's been a while." He followed her inside. "Other than tonight, how have you and Bryce been doing?"

She shut and bolted the door behind him. "We're good. Your family?"

"They're great."

Jessica fumbled with the rings on her left hand, the ones she couldn't bring herself to stop wearing. "Come sit in the kitchen. Would you like some coffee?"

"Yes, please. Black."

She got him a cup and sat across from him with her untouched mug.

"Thank you." He met her eyes and sighed. "Now, unfortunately, I have to ask you to tell me what happened from the beginning."

She studied the brown liquid in her mug, wishing coffee could make things better like it usually did, fully aware nothing could. "I figured as much." She described what she witnessed, in detail, as it played over and over in her mind like a movie reel.

He stayed silent and scrawled everything down.
When she finished speaking, he glanced up from his notepad. "Were you sleeping before you got up to open that window? Groggy at all?"

"No, I hadn't slept a wink." Jessica spoke firmly. "I saw what I saw. That streetlight makes the area in front of my house so bright—I need to close the blinds to sleep."

"Thought so, but I had to ask. Have to follow proper protocol, you understand. Did David see you?"

"He turned my way, and I ducked." Voices came through the walkie-talkie clipped to the belt holding up his jeans. "Can you check in with the station? See if anyone found David and Sarah, please?"

"Sure." He pushed a button on his radio. "Maureen, come in."

"Go ahead, Tim."

"Has David Hayes been apprehended?"

"Negative. They haven't located him yet."

"What happens if you can't find him? Sarah's poor family. They'll be devastated." Jessica's pulse pounded, and her stomach twisted. "She was definitely unconscious at the very least." She didn't want to think it, or worse, say it out loud, but her friend was most likely dead.

"I know. That's why I came here instead of going home to free up another cruiser. What more can you tell me about David and Sarah? How long have they lived next door?"

"I think they moved in about six months ago."

"Did you get to know them during that time?"

"Not David, but Sarah is—was talkative and sweet. Bryce loved her. We usually have coffee together at this table once a week. She just told me last Monday they were thinking of starting a family. I never noticed any indication of anything amiss before tonight."

"Did you ever have David over? Go to their house?"

Jessica shook her head. "I avoided him. It wasn't hard, considering he's hardly ever around. What Sarah saw in him, I sure didn't. David gives me the creeps. The way he stares at people for longer than what seems right, it makes me nervous."

"I noticed that about him as well. I don't have any more questions for now. We'll be driving through the area regularly until he's caught."

"The man living next door is violent and deranged. And I know how these things work. He'll be loose until you can get warrants and investigate. I live alone with

Bryce. Adam..." Her voice caught. "He isn't here to protect us."

Lines creased his forehead. "I miss Adam, too. Occasionally, on patrol, I turn my head to tell him something, then realize he isn't there."

She nodded and dropped her gaze into her lap, away from the pity in his eyes.

"I know this isn't easy. Christ, Jessica, you've been through enough for one lifetime. I'll do everything I can to help. Remember this, most murders aren't random. They're usually committed by someone close to the victim. David has no reason to hurt you."

"Most murders. Not all. I'm a witness. Witnesses tend to disappear too."

Tim nodded. "Which is why you were smart to ask for an unmarked car. Keep your doors and windows locked, and park in your garage. You'll have a locked barrier between you and the outside when you come and go. Here's my card in case you lost my number. Call me anytime."

She took the card, turned her back to him, and stuck it on the fridge with a magnet. She needed to get away from his sad eyes before she broke down. She couldn't grow accustomed to being pitied, no matter how much time passed.

In fact, she had pulled away from most of her friends, including Tim and his wife, because of those well-intentioned looks. They treated her differently, like a porcelain doll that could shatter if dropped. Didn't they realize what she needed most was to be treated the same as everyone else?

After ensuring her tears were suppressed, she turned to face him. "Thank you for handling this yourself. I appreciate it. Say hello to Peggy and William for me."

He stood and pushed in his chair. "I will. Call if he returns home or if you feel uneasy at all and get some sleep. You look like you're about to fall over. Don't forget to lock this door behind me." He pulled pepper spray out of his pocket and sat it on the table in front of her. "And you keep this on you at all times."

She picked up the canister and clutched it in both hands, then forced a polite smile through her grief. "I will. Thanks again."

Jessica shut the door and bolted it. Sleep wouldn't be easy, but she had to try. She climbed the stairs to her bedroom and shut the blinds — a pitiful barrier between her and the monster who lived next door.

Chapter Two

Her mind refused to cooperate and allow sleep to take over. The last conversation she'd had with Sarah played through her mind. They'd talked about babies and the weather. Nothing sinister stood out. She gave up and tried to calm her troubled thoughts with memories of happier times, like Adam lying on his side of the bed, holding her in his arms. But it was no use. Too soon the alarm clock chimed.

She showered and dressed in jeans and a flowy, floral print, shirt. Dark, puffy circles under her eyes betrayed her lack of sleep. She picked up a sponge and dabbed concealer over them. Hiding behind makeup would be easier than facing the barrage of questions from the well-intentioned people around her.

Jessica glanced at her alarm clock. *Time to wake Bryce.*

Her adorable boy slept in his usual pose on his stomach, butt in the air, mouth wide-open, oblivious to the world, and the darkness in it. She took deep breaths to calm her frazzled nerves. The idea of dropping him off at school with David on the loose churned her stomach. Only a few weeks remained in the school year. He could miss a day.

She sat on the bed, ruffled his dark hair, and shook his shoulder back and forth. "Wake up, buddy. Time to get dressed."

Bryce slept so deep, a bomb could go off beside his head, and he wouldn't know it. After a few minutes of shaking him, his eyes fluttered open. He rolled over, stretched, then lifted his feet in the air, anticipating socks. A morning ritual he hadn't outgrown yet.

She pulled socks on his feet. "Up you get. You can do the rest yourself."

Bryce groaned, then climbed out of bed and finished dressing. He clung to the railing as they descended the stairs to the kitchen.

She hurried to the fridge. "Do you want scrambled eggs and toast?"

He nodded, leaned his elbow on the table, and struggled to keep his eyes open.

She set plates on the table. In the time it took her to force down a few bites of eggs, Bryce had devoured his breakfast. He must've hit another growth spurt.

More alert from his food, he stood on steady legs. "Thanks, Mom. I'll pack my lunch while you finish your breakfast."

"That's nice. Thank you. You're coming with me to the preschool today. It'll be fun." Jessica labored through a piece of toast as Bryce took his lunch bag from the fridge and packed it in his backpack.

He said, "I'd rather go to school."

"It's just for today."

"Why?"

Because the neighbor probably murdered his wife last night, wasn't something she could say to her eight-year-old. Instead, she did something she abhorred and told her child an outright lie to protect him. "I need your help."

He grumbled, "Okaayyy."

"Good man. I'll let you pick out a chocolate bar after preschool."

"Yummy. You should have led off with that."

She smiled. "You're right. I will next time."

After they finished breakfast, she grabbed Tim's business card and slipped the pepper spray into her purse before they headed into the garage. She locked the doors after they got in the car, opened the garage door, and backed out.

David's truck dripped water in the driveway next door from a fresh car wash. A young officer she didn't recognize stood talking to David beside his truck. She averted her gaze to avoid making eye contact and clutched the steering wheel.

How could the police have let this happen? The evidence on the truck bed is gone!

She backed onto the street and drove away, distancing them from the darkness lurking next door.

Bryce asked, "Why are the police talking to David?"

"I'm sure they have their reasons. Promise me you'll stay far, far away from him."

"I always do. He's mean."

Jessica's eyes snapped to the rear-view mirror. "What makes you say that?"

"A few months ago, I saw him kick the neighbor's cat."

"Why didn't you say anything to me?"

He shrugged. "I was busy playing with my friends, and I sort of forgot until now."

"Is there anything else about David you forgot?"

"No."

They arrived at the preschool in a little strip mall a

few streets away, ending the conversation. She parked in the empty lot and scanned her surroundings. Her hands shook. The ringing in her ears made the news on the radio station fuzzy.

Pull yourself together. David should be in jail soon.

She forced a smile for Bryce's benefit with her hand on the door handle. "Let's go in and get things ready for the day."

"It's worth it for chocolate."

Jessica ran around the car to Bryce. Her back screamed as she hoisted him off the ground, but the pain was worth it. The best way to forget about the bad was to focus on the good, making her boy happy. One day soon, too soon, he'd refuse to let her play these games. But for now, he giggled as she made airplane noises, and ran the whole way inside.

She closed her eyes, leaned against the locked door behind her, and took a deep breath. Opening them, she took comfort in the familiar surroundings of her sanctuary. Cheerful, messy finger paintings hung on the walls of the little classroom. Chairs and desks were grouped together with name tags on them. Toys sat on shelves, waiting to be played with.

She loved her job. Nothing filled her soul with more joy than teaching children. The cloud of sadness, fear, and worry hanging over her lifted as she began prepping the day's lessons. Bryce built an intricate tower with colorful, wooden blocks in the corner as she worked.

The children and her assistants arrived an hour later. She did her best to put David out of her mind by concentrating on them. An hour ticked by with no updates from Tim, then another, and another. Each one chipped away at her defenses allowing worry to creep in. After the last child fell asleep during nap time in the afternoon, she locked herself in the bathroom and called Tim.

"Any news?"

"There's no easy way to say this. The bastard cleaned up after himself. Forensics have been through the house and truck with a fine-tooth comb. They found nothing, absolutely nothing. And would you believe not a single one of your neighbors has a doorbell camera?"

"But Sarah isn't there. And she won't have shown up for work at the Walmart or called in sick."

"He claims Sarah left yesterday, and he doesn't know where she is. Some of her stuff was gone, he even produced a typed letter, supposedly from her, saying she was going away for a while. We can't arrest him without any evidence."

She gritted her teeth to keep her voice from raising. Waking the kids wouldn't make things any better. "That's it? The department's giving up?"

"Of course not. We know you're telling the truth. Forensics collected an article of Sarah's dirty clothing. We're taking a cadaver dog out to the wooded areas around here. We found a car wash receipt from early this morning. Forensics swabbed the inside of the drain in the stall he used. With luck, we'll find Sarah, and some evidence to corroborate your statement."

"What am I supposed to do now?"

"Be vigilant, lock everything like I said last night, but act normal so you don't tip him off. Hopefully, he doesn't know you called the police. Other neighbors on your street could have made that call. Houses are squeezed together in those newer developments."

"You're right, we have a lot of neighbors, but how many have my view? How many could see into the truck bed with him backed into his driveway?"

"At the very least, the house to the right of his. I would even say a few more houses on either side of you. Hang in there. We're doing everything we can."

"Please call if there's a break. I'll be a basket case until he's locked away."

She hung up the phone. The occasional police drive-by wouldn't keep them safe. *What do I do now? Pack? Run? Give up everything?* Uproot her son who missed out on enough without a father in his life, let alone losing everything else he knew?

No, she wouldn't leave her home. She had friends on the force. If someone tried to break in, or threatened, she had pepper spray, and help would be a phone call away. For Bryce's sake they needed to get back to their normal routine.

After the last child had been picked up, she took Bryce to the grocery store near their house. The prices at Walmart were lower, but she couldn't face shopping in Sarah's place of work where reminders of her waited on every aisle.

Bryce didn't complain even though he would miss his usual tour of the toy department. He pushed the cart as they perused the aisles, content with keeping an eye out for his favorite snacks.

Chills ran up her spine on the cracker aisle. David came around the corner ahead of them and headed their way. He stared at her, through eyes so dark, they were almost black with his mouth in a thin line.

Oh my God! What do I do?

He towered over them. She felt like a field mouse facing a hungry barn cat. If only she had a hole to retreat to. She remembered Tim telling her to act normal. What should she do? Say hello and then bolt? How futile considering the daggers aimed her way, but what other option did she have? No one else shopped the cracker aisle.

Bryce grabbed her arm and stiffened beside her.

She patted his shoulder. "Buddy, go pick out a chocolate bar, then meet me by the bananas."

"Okay." Bryce took off taking care to go the opposite direction away from David.

She forced a smile and waved at her neighbor. "Hi, David."

He walked towards her without responding.

Her heart pounded in her ears, her palms resting on the cart grew slick from sweat, and trembled. She clutched the metal handle tightly, hoping her shaky hands wouldn't betray her fear.

He came closer and closer, then stopped beside her, his arm touching her shoulder.

Jessica suppressed the instinct to flinch.

His eyes bored into hers. He leaned into her, trapping her against the metal shelving, and knocking boxes off the shelf. The edge of the metal pressed into her arm.

She grimaced but refused to moan out loud and give him any satisfaction. "What the hell, David? Let me go."

David leaned his head in closer. So close, his minty breath and Old Spice aftershave penetrated her nostrils. He whispered in her ear. "You should have minded your own business."

She lied, "I have no idea what you're talking about, but if you touch me again, I'm calling the police."

"You stupid bitch. I know you already did."

A sour taste rose into her throat, and she swallowed it down, suppressing the urge to vomit all over him. Although, he deserved it and more.

A shopping cart creaked around the corner of the aisle. David released her and walked away.

At least Bryce didn't see that.

She rubbed her sore arm and turned to see which way David would go. He turned left. She steered her cart at a near jog to the opposite end of the aisle, then hurried to the banana display.

She'd sent Bryce there because the produce section was busy with open sightlines. Bryce waited wide-eyed as he searched for her, clutching his chocolate bar. She wheeled towards him as fast as she could without running into anyone.

"I'm here, buddy."

"You all right, Mom? David looked really mad."

"I'm in one piece."

She took her cell phone out of her purse and dialed Tim. The phone rang once, twice, then three times. *What do I do if he doesn't answer?*

"Hello?"

Thank God! "Tim, I need you. We're at the small grocery store around the corner from my house by the bananas. We had a run in with David."

"Run in? Did he hurt you?"

"A bit. It was more of an exchange of words."

"I'm on my way. Stay where you are."

She stuck her phone in her purse and clutched the can of pepper spray inside.

Bryce turned to her. "I'm glad you called him."

"Better safe than sorry, right? No need to worry. Go ahead and eat your chocolate. We'll scan the wrapper at the cash."

"Don't I have to eat dinner first?"

She ruffled his hair. "Not today. You've been an extra good boy." Sensing eyes on her back, she turned towards the exit.

David met her gaze with a satisfied, sadistic smirk on his face, then walked out the door as if nothing had taken place.

How could someone get so much enjoyment out of taunting a single mom with a son in tow?

Tim came in the entrance and strode up to them. "David pulled out of the parking lot. You should be fine to go home. We'll check out your groceries, then I'll follow you back to your place so we can discuss our next move."

Jessica stared at the stuff in the cart. Her attempt at maintaining a normal routine had failed dismally. Normal wouldn't happen as long as they stayed in Cochrane. She rummaged through the meat and boxed goods in the shopping cart.

"I don't think I'll need most of these after all. I'll leave the rest of this with the cashier." She chose a package of fresh chicken legs, three cobs of corn, and a liter of milk.

"Don't you need food?"

"Not after this. Will you stay for dinner?"

"Definitely. I'm not leaving you alone."

She inhaled a deep, cleansing breath. They couldn't stay in Cochrane. Her supervisor at the preschool would be angry, but their safety was more important.

Montana, here we come.

Chapter Three

Three years earlier

Jon hummed while whisking eggs. He inhaled the fruity, homey aroma of fresh ground Colombian coffee beans wafting through the small kitchen of his townhouse. Finally, he was home in Washington D.C. with his wife after wrapping up a six-month undercover assignment.

The shower shut off upstairs. Cynthia would be down in another fifteen minutes or so. They'd have a little time together before she'd head to the high school nearby where she worked as a resource teacher for special needs students. Her routine never changed whether he was home or away. Those kids needed her and gave her the balance in life he hadn't been able to, with being away so often. But that was all about to change.

Toast popped in the toaster as Cynthia's heels clacked down the hardwood stairs. Jon buttered it and dished scrambled eggs and sausage links onto two plates. He set them on the two-person table by the window in their kitchen.

Cynthia wrapped her arms around his middle. Her heels gave her the height she needed to kiss his cheek. "I missed you so much."

The raspberry, floral scent of her perfume drifted into his nostrils. "I know. Missed you too, darling." He patted her hands. "Sit. I'll get the coffee."

"You're overcompensating."

"I know. But I want to."

He poured coffee into mugs, brought them to the table, then sat across from her and watched her pile eggs on her toast. How he had missed these little things. The idea of absence making the heart grow fonder rang true. He loved everything about her.

She smiled. "Well, aren't you going to eat?"

"Eventually. First, I have something to tell you."

"You're smiling so it can't be bad. What?"

"I'm done with undercover work."

"You are?"

"Yes. I'm working as a field agent in D.C. from now on."

She laughed and bounced in her chair. "For good? Really?"

"They didn't like it. But yes. Enough is enough. It's time I settle down and focus on you."

"On me? Just me? Or are we growing this little family? We both said from the beginning kids were in our future."

"I'm ready to settle. Coach little league or go to ballet recitals."

"It's about time." She glanced at her watch. "Shoot. I gotta get going." She leaned over and kissed his cheek.

"You aren't getting away that easy." He stood and pulled her into his arms. Looking into her eyes, he said, "I love you, darling. More than anything."

"I know. I love you, too. You've made me the happiest woman in the world. We have to talk about this later. Something must've happened to get you to this point."

"Darling, that's in the past. I want to work on our future."

"I'll let it go. For now. You'll tell me when you're ready." She brushed her lips against his, collected her briefcase, and called, "goodbye," as she walked out the front door.

He loved Cynthia's intelligence and uncanny ability to see right through him. Memories of the past six months crept in, and with it, his guilty conscience. In the process of infiltrating a criminal enterprise, families were inevitably torn apart. Wives and children tied to criminal husbands and fathers always ended up as collateral damage.

Many of the men he had arrested were born and bred into criminal families. They never stood a chance. The only difference between him and them was their upbringing. Jon's heart warmed thinking of his family's ranch in Montana where he was raised, along with his brother, by the best parents anyone could ask for.

To a young man fresh out of college, a farm life held no appeal. He'd wanted the excitement of an urban lifestyle. But after just over a decade in the city, a simple life didn't seem that boring anymore. He craved home, the dry mountain air, and quaint little town, but Cynthia's family lived in Baltimore. She'd put up with him being away over half the year for almost a decade and deserved to be near her family when they had children.

Jon filled the sink with soap and water, then deposited their breakfast dishes. The old dishwasher crapped out a few months after he left. Cynthia, being on her own, hadn't seen the need to replace it. With him home full time, they needed a new one. In fact, maybe a whole new appliance package as a surprise was in order.

Out with the old. In with the new.

After he finished washing the dishes and sitting them on the rack to dry, Jon drove to a hardware store with a big appliance section. He wandered along a row of stoves, the most important appliance in any kitchen. He stopped in front of a gas range to read the description of its features.

His phone vibrated in his pocket. The number of Cynthia's high school flashed across the screen.

He smiled, swiped the screen, and put the phone to his ear. *I miss you already, too.* "Hello."

An unfamiliar female voice responded. "Hello. Is this Jonathan Kent?"

"Yes. What can I do for you?"

"I'm the secretary at the high school."

"Yes?" He waited for her to continue. Maybe Cynthia had forgotten something at home and was too busy to call herself.

"Would you happen to know where Cynthia is? She hasn't come in or phoned. I tried calling all her numbers and got voicemail."

His mind scrambled for any reasonable explanation. "No. That can't be. She left home at her usual time this morning."

"She isn't here."

He hung up, opened the browser in his phone, and searched for the dispatch number to the D.C. Police station closest to the high school, then called it.

"D.C. Police"

"This is Jon Kent from the D.C. FBI field office.

Were there any serious collisions this morning in your district?"

"No, sir. None."

Jon's heart pounded in his ears. He'd accumulated a long list of dangerous enemies over the years in his line of work.

Don't panic. Work mode. Keep it together. "Thank you."

He hung up and sent a message to his old point of contact Special Agent Reynolds.

—My wife disappeared this morning on her way to work between 7:30-7:45. I'm retracing her steps now. Contact me ASAP.—

He called Cynthia and got her voicemail as he moved past aisles crammed with people, searching for a fast escape. After five aisles and no clear path, he dodged around shopping carts and patrons to the doors. Once outside, he sprinted the rest of the way to his black sedan.

Wait. Her phone.

Jon took his phone from his back pocket and touched the find my device icon. He entered their password, then scowled at the circle on the screen as the GPS system booted. Ten long seconds later, it displayed two locations. One dot where he stood in the store parking lot, and the other showed Cynthia's phone a few blocks away from their townhouse.

Jon started his car, rammed his foot on the accelerator, and peeled out of the parking lot. A line of cars at a red light forced him to slam on the brakes. He glanced at his dash wishing he'd stopped by the field office on the way home the day before to get his siren installed.

"Come on. Come on. Turn green already."

Unbidden, his mind conjured images of Cynthia tied to a chair being beaten and tortured.

No, dammit! Don't go there.

As the light turned green, and the cars in front of him started to move, he remembered their kiss that morning, the happiness in her eyes, and the smile on her rose-colored lips.

I'll find you, darling.

He turned off the main road, choosing to detour through an industrial section that took him farther off course, but with far less traffic and stops along the way. He got to his neighborhood in half the time. He drove around the crescent twice past where Cynthia's phone appeared on the map and found no sign of her or her blue Honda Civic.

Jon pulled along the side of the road and reloaded the find my device application. Cynthia's phone hadn't moved, and his dot was beside hers. On a hunch, he walked to a small park across the street, eyes glued to his phone. He stopped when their locations overlapped and touched his screen to play a sound on her phone.

A pinging came from nearby. He followed the sound to a water drainage sewer a few feet ahead of him. He squatted in front of it and peered inside. A small flashing light shone in the shadows beneath. He used the flashlight on his phone to illuminate the darkness. Cynthia's phone lay at the bottom.

His phone vibrated in his hand and Agent Reynold's number flashed on the screen. He swiped it and put it to his ear. "Hello."

"Jon, I'm at your house. Where are you?"

"I'm a few blocks away at the neighborhood park. I

found Cynthia's phone at the bottom of a drainage pipe."

"I'm on my way."

Jon hung up and absently shoved his phone in his pocket.

The one chance I had at tracking her, gone.

If only the school had called when she was ten minutes late rather than waiting an hour and a half and giving whoever took her a decent head start. Instinct told him Cynthia was already long gone even though he'd kissed her goodbye that same morning. And even though he'd routinely spent half the year or more away from home, he'd never felt further away from his wife.

He searched around the drainpipe. The grass had been cut short, there wouldn't be imprints from a body or a struggle for him to find. On the flip side, short grass wouldn't hide blood or other physical evidence. He found no sign of either. That wasn't to say she hadn't already been restrained by someone elsewhere.

Putting himself in the assailant's shoes, if he had just kidnapped someone and wanted to dispose of their phone, he'd chuck it wherever he happened to be and bolt. The phone was most likely thrown out a window and landed in the drainpipe by chance. The longer you took to separate the phone from your victim, the higher the chance you'd be found.

A black SUV stopped along the side of the road behind him. Reynolds climbed out of the passenger side and jogged to him. "We'll find her, Jon."

Jon met his colleague's gaze and nodded. No words in a situation like this would suffice or convey the multitude of emotions and thoughts running through his mind.

"The CSIs are on their way to analyze the area and get the phone. If there are any cameras between your house and here, we'll get the footage. I have a team of agents going door to door."

Jon nodded, satisfied with that response. He would do the same in his colleague's shoes. "Then I assume we'll be looking at the area outside my house and checking my wife's computer and phone records?"

"Yes. You can be involved throughout the whole process. I won't hide anything from you, but you need to let me lead the investigation. You're too close to this."

Jon swallowed around a lump in his throat. "That's fair. I'll head home while you supervise things here in case Cynthia surfaces."

"Sure. Go ahead. Take a few minutes alone to wrap your head around this. You must be in shock."

Shock doesn't come close to covering it.

****

Jon searched through the clothes hanging in Cynthia's side of the closet and rummaged through her drawers. Nothing seemed to be missing and their luggage was still under their bed. He collected her laptop from their dresser and brought it to the kitchen table. He opened it and touched the power button. The main screen prompted him for a password. He typed in Skittles, the name of her childhood poodle, and was granted access to her main screen.

His gut churned. He hated invading her privacy this way, but it had to be done. He clicked on the message icon and discovered her phone was linked to the computer. Various conversations were open. The one she had with him was at the top as well as others with her work colleagues, family, and friends.

He found nothing out of the ordinary, no threats, and no indication she planned to leave. What he did find were her kind words of encouragement and offers of help. She genuinely cared about everyone in her life. Her selflessness was the thing he loved most about her.

Jon clicked on Cynthia's calendar and displayed her schedule. She had meetings scheduled for most of the day and a grocery list for later. Moving through the following days and weeks, he found similar things. She'd also developed lesson plans for each of her students for the rest of the month. Those weren't the actions of a woman planning to leave.

Someone must've taken her. Someone who hates me. It's my fault.

Chapter Four

Jessica preheated the oven after unpacking her one bag of groceries. Her stomach was in knots, but Tim and Bryce needed to eat. She shook chicken legs in breading then stuck them in the oven on a sheet pan along with potatoes and carrots to roast.

Tim leaned against the kitchen peninsula sipping from a glass of water. "Are you sure I can't do anything to help?"

She glanced into the living room. Bryce sat on the sofa with his tablet, wearing his headphones. "Actually, there is something."

"Name it."

"Can you keep an eye on dinner while I call my Aunt Debbie? If she'll have us, I'm heading south to Montana first thing tomorrow morning."

"I could go next door right now and arrest him for assaulting you. Your arm is badly bruised."

"Does he have a record?"

"No."

"There's no point. It's only one bruise. He'll make bail, then he might come after me again."

"You could come stay with me."

Jessica shook her head. "You work long hours. I can't put your wife and son at risk. Besides, what about when Bryce is at school, or I'm at work?"

Tim sighed. "You're right. But why Montana?"

"I have dual citizenship. My aunt lives in Lewistown. It's a small town. Only sixteen hundred people."

"Sounds like a good place to hide. You make that call, but on my phone. These things are too easy to trace nowadays. I'll keep an eye on Bryce and dinner."

"Thanks so much."

She took the phone to her bedroom, hauled a suitcase out of her closet, and opened it on top of her bed. She dialed her aunt's number, then hit the speaker phone icon.

After a few rings, her aunt picked up. "Hello."

The familiar, soft, soothing voice on the other end brought a smile to Jessica's lips. "Hi, Aunt Debbie. How are you?"

"I'm great. It's good to hear your voice. When are you coming for a visit? Bryce must have grown so much."

Jessica grabbed a few pairs of her favorite jeans, then stuffed them into the suitcase. "Bryce and I need to skip town. I was hoping I could stay with you until I find a place to rent in Lewistown or nearby."

"Of course. What happened?"

She filled her aunt in while rummaging through the bathroom vanity for essential toiletries and makeup and packing them.

"Oh Jess, that's horrible! How fast can you get here?"

"We'll head out first thing in the morning. With any luck, we'll arrive in time for dinner."

"Is someone there with you now? You can't stay there alone."

"Adam's old partner, Tim, is here. He's already

volunteered to sleep on my couch tonight."

"Okay, then. You'll be safe. Be careful now, you hear? Make sure you aren't followed."

"I will. Thanks, Aunt Debbie. See you tomorrow."

Jessica shoved Tim's phone in her pocket, then picked up a framed picture from her night table. She clutched the photo of her husband to her chest, and tears rolled down her cheeks. A photo was a poor substitute for being in his warm, strong arms.

A few weeks after the picture was taken, an armed robber had shot Adam in the head at close range during his shift. As Bryce grew older, he resembled his father more each day with his dark hair and facial expressions. He had a little bit of her in the shape of his face and eyes, but he was mostly Adam. She wiped her tears and focused on how lucky she was they'd had Bryce before he died.

The oven beeped. *Time for dinner.* She wrapped the frame inside her shirts and packed it in the suitcase.

****

After dinner, while Tim did the dishes, Jessica turned on Bryce's favorite show. She held him in her lap, breathed in the natural scent of his skin, and stroked his hair. He yawned when she turned off the television.

"Let's get you to bed, buddy."

"Can you read me a story?"

"Of course, I can."

She tucked him in, then read a chapter of his graphic novel out loud until he fell asleep. Brushing the dark hair away from his forehead, she kissed it, then whispered. "Goodnight. I love you."

Before leaving his room, she triple-checked the

lock on his window, shut the blinds, and turned off his lamp.

Please let him be safe until morning.

She headed to the basement, dragged out duffle bags, a hockey bag, and boxes. She could live without material things, but she sure as heck wouldn't expect Bryce to leave anything behind. He wasn't a spoiled child and treasured what he did have. His art supplies especially meant the most to him.

"Need any help?" Tim asked.

"No thanks. My stuff is packed. Bryce has mostly outgrown his toys except for his Lego. He spends most of his time doing art or on his tablet. I'll be left with a few things to grab from Bryce's room. Probably better to get them in the morning."

He settled into the reclining chair in the corner. "Don't forget the passports and birth certificates."

She opened a hockey bag and brought it to a white storage cabinet in the corner of the living room where they kept the art supplies. "You're right. I should get those out before bed. It hadn't even crossed my mind."

"Understandably so. You have a lot to deal with."

"Now I'm wondering what else I could be forgetting."

"Cell phones these days are like homing beacons for anyone who knows how to trace them. I can't see him following you out of town. But I would suggest turning your phone off until this blows over. Pick up a burner for emergencies on your way out of town tomorrow."

"Sound advice. Do you have any more?"

"Keep an eye on your mirrors while you're driving. If anyone's following, take a few turns. If you're still being followed, stop somewhere public, lock your doors, and call 911."

She shivered picturing David following her in his truck, or worse, slamming into the back of her car, forcing her into incoming traffic—*Stop it. Don't think it.* "Thanks, Tim."

"One more thing. Do not tell anyone where you're going. People talk. Word would get back to him."

An hour later, she finished packing the art supplies and Legos. After getting some blankets out of the linen closet and a pillow for Tim, she sat in her favorite recliner across from him with a cup of herbal tea. Her eyelids drooped. She forced them open.

Tim put his hand on the bottom of her mug as it slipped from her grip. "Jessica, go to bed. I'll be here. You're safe."

"No sleep last night is catching up with me. Thanks again."

****

The familiar rumble of an engine vibrated underneath Jessica tossing her from side to side. She opened her eyes. Stars twinkled in the sky above her.

Where am I?

She tried to sit up but couldn't move. Rope bound her hands and feet. A shovel lay to her right.

She bent her knees, pressed her feet flat against the aluminum bed, and tried to use her stomach muscles to pull herself into a sitting position. But without her hands free to keep her upright, the truck's forward momentum propelled her onto her back. She screamed over and over, hoping, praying someone would hear.

The vehicle took a right turn. The uneven surface of the road jostled and bumped her around. Dense woods surrounded her. Hope of being rescued quickly faded. She was on her own.

This can't be happening! Bryce needs me. I have to survive.

She used her bound hands to tug at the rope binding her feet, but the knot didn't give an inch. The truck stopped. The engine quieted. A door opened and shut. Footsteps came nearer, then the tailgate opened.

David shone a flashlight in her face and smiled. "Ah, you're awake. Perfect. You can watch me dig up Sarah's grave. I'm going to bury you alive beside her."

She closed her eyes and put every ounce of her strength into a loud scream.

A cold breeze enveloped her face. Her eyes flew open, revealing the ceiling of her bedroom. She bolted upright in bed with her quilt clenched in her fists and gasped air into her lungs. Her eyes darted around the room into the dark corners and shadows.

Empty. I'm alone.

"It was only a dream. Thank God." Her voice hitched. "I'm home with my baby. I'm all right."

Jessica leaned against her headboard and sobbed. Sleeping next door to David proved to be worse than staying awake. At least conscious, she could rein in her fear. Wiping her eyes, she glanced at her alarm clock. Four in the morning. Groaning, she tossed her quilt aside and climbed out of bed.

She discarded her sweaty nightshirt in favor of leggings and a loose-fitting sweater. After checking on Bryce, finding him asleep peacefully, safe and sound, she set out to make coffee.

On her way to the kitchen, she stopped in her tracks. Something white covered the window of her front door, obscuring the puddle of light on the floor from the lamppost outside. Maybe it was another flyer advertising a candidate running in the local election. She paused with her hand on the deadbolt. Anything could be hiding in the dark ready to pounce.

She'd wait until the sun rose, casting light upon any shadows. Turning towards the kitchen, she paused. *The exterior light.*

Jessica flipped the switch by the door, illuminating a sheet of paper taped facing the inside of the house: *No one can save you.*

Covering her mouth with a shaky hand, she stifled a scream. She fought the urge to open the door, grab the note, and rip the paper to shreds. David could be lurking nearby in wait. She sprinted into the living room where Tim snored on her couch.

Jessica grabbed his shoulders and shook him. "Wake up. I need you."

He groaned and rolled over to face her. "Jess. It's still dark. What's wrong?"

She switched on a lamp. "He taped a frigging note to my door." She relayed the written message.

He sat up, rubbed his eyes, and laced up his boots. "Son of a — pardon the language, but that takes balls. Got a freezer bag handy?"

"Yes. I'll go get it."

"I'll have the sheet of paper run for prints. Lock the door behind me. I'll knock when I'm done."

"Okay."

While waiting for Tim, Jessica made coffee. She set two full mugs on her kitchen table, then took a chair. As she cradled her steaming mug in her hands, she studied the main floor of her house.

She loved the focal point, her gas fireplace. Limestone surrounded the firebox filled with decorative logs and crystals. Over the mantel, hung a picture of Adam in his uniform on the day of his graduation from the police academy. Next to it, her favorite portrait of her and Adam together on their wedding day.

They'd taken their wedding photos at Lake Minnewanka. In the photo, they stood face to face, smiling into each other's eyes. Behind them, the Rocky Mountains reflected off the crystal blue water. One of the happiest days of her life alongside the morning Bryce was born.

Reminders of Adam lived all over the place; in the furniture they'd picked out, the walls they'd painted together, and the knickknacks they'd collected from vacations. A sinking feeling in the pit of her stomach said she wouldn't be seeing any of these things anytime soon once they left for Montana.

Ten minutes passed. Her first cup of coffee sat empty, and Tim hadn't returned. *Did he go to his car for something?* After another five minutes passed, she took the canister of pepper spray out of her purse and walked to the front door. The note was gone.

She pressed her face to the glass. Tim, her protector, lay face down on the porch, a stream of blood trickling out the back of his head. *No!*

She paused with her hand on the lock. If she unlocked the door, she could be at David's mercy, and no help to Tim. Not to mention her son slept upstairs. She dug her phone out of the waistband of her leggings and swiped the screen.

Tim sat up, reached behind his head, then stood carefully and wobbled slightly on his feet. He came towards the front door on steadier legs.

Jessica unbolted the door and pulled him inside. She engaged the lock, brought him to the kitchen, and sat him down at the table. She pressed a clean dish towel to the wound on his head. "We need to get you to the urgent care. You were unconscious."

He held his hand against the towel. "Head wounds bleed. It's only a small cut."

Her voice cracked. "This happened to you because of me. And instead of helping you, I left you to fend for yourself. What happened out there?"

"You did the right thing staying inside. I was bagging the note facing your front door. Someone must have come up behind me, hit me over the head with something, and took the note." He shook his head gently. "I never should have turned my back to the street. Should've known better."

"Someone? I think we both know who hit you."

"Yes, we do. But I didn't see him." He pulled the curtain aside and gazed out the living room window. "The houses are all dark. This early in the morning, there are no witnesses."

"Are you sure you won't let me take you to the clinic? You might have a concussion. Your elbow is scraped too."

"I've been knocked out before. I'm not dizzy, and I don't feel sick." He picked up his cold coffee and took a sip. "Delicious. This will help."

"I'll heat your coffee for you. If you start to feel sick, let me know."

David fooled Tim, a seasoned cop, so easily. *We need to get out of here.*

****

Jessica put a sheet pan of bacon in the oven and whisked eggs in a bowl as Tim peered out the living room window. "Is David gone?"

"Yes. His truck isn't in the driveway."

"Good. While he's nowhere near us, we can make our escape."

Bryce came down the stairs pale-faced and rubbing his eyes. His sleep must've been as troubled as hers. He asked, "Escape to go where?"

She smiled into his blue grey eyes, replicas of hers, and patted his shoulder. "Montana to visit Aunt Debbie."

"Okay." He ran into the living room and circled back to the kitchen. "Where's my toys and my tablet?"

"They're in the car."

"Is my police dog in the car?"

Bryce loved that stuffed toy, a police hero like his father. He hadn't outgrown it as he had his other stuffies. No way she'd leave him behind. "Yes, Bryce. Don't worry. He's in the backseat waiting for you."

Bryce frowned. "What aren't you telling me? Why was David so angry? And why did Tim stay here?"

She sighed. A bright child like Bryce wouldn't go along blindly without asking questions. She'd give him a less violent, watered-down version of the truth. "I can't get into specifics. David did something awful, and I saw him. That's why he's mad."

"Why don't the police arrest him?"

Tim said, "We're trying but we need to gather more evidence."

Jessica steered the conversation away from David. "Want bacon with breakfast?"

"Yeah! Bacon!" Bryce pumped his fist. "Can I

have nuggets and fries for lunch?"

"Yes. I promise we'll stop on the way to Aunt Debbie's house."

After breakfast, Jessica packed snacks for the road, then bagged the rest of the food in the house for Tim to take home. She walked into the living room and handed the bags to him where he stood by the window on lookout duty. "Any sign of him?"

"No. I'll follow you to the gas station by the highway, and we'll get you a burner phone. Then I'll trail you for another hour to make sure you get out of town safely."

"I don't know how I can ever repay your kindness."

"You don't owe me anything. Adam had my back for three years. It's only right I have yours now."

She touched his shoulder. "Thank you."

"You're welcome." Tim headed out to his truck with his bags.

Jessica hollered up the stairs. "Bryce. Time to hit the road."

****

After stopping at the gas station, Jessica took advantage of her police escort, and put the pedal to the metal. Even with Tim behind her, she couldn't overcome her sense of unease which increased after Tim took an exit to head back to Cochrane. She checked her mirrors every ten seconds. Once they arrived at the border crossing, she reasoned the physical distance should be great enough to relax her watch.

Chapter Five

Jessica took a familiar turn down the dirt road leading to her aunt's farm. Debbie's old but well-maintained two-story farmhouse came into view. The shutters and front door had recently gotten a fresh coat of yellow paint. Jessica drove up the rocky driveway and smiled.

Her Aunt Debbie sat in her glider on the front porch in her usual jeans and denim shirt with her hair pulled back in a bun.

We made it. We're safe.

Jessica shifted the car into park and struggled to fend off tears, praying her arrival would mark the end of her nightmare with David. Having to start over until David was behind bars wasn't ideal, but she'd been forced to when Adam was taken from her. She could and would survive again. Now wasn't the time to break down and give into the misery at the unfairness of her situation.

Debbie hurried over, then opened the back door. "Bryce, look at you. You've gotten to be such a big boy on us."

He smiled. "Got any cookies, Auntie?"

"Of course. Go ahead inside."

Jessica climbed out of the door and stretched her legs. "Hi, Aunt Debbie. Thanks for letting us come out here to stay on such short notice."

"Oh, Jess, dear. It's no trouble at all. I'm happy for the company."

"We brought a lot. I can leave most of our stuff in the trunk, so we aren't crowding your space. I wanted Bryce to have his things to help with the sudden move."

"Don't worry. I found you a place. Jon Kent has a house available on the ranch. Once he gets it cleaned up, the place is all yours."

Jessica opened her trunk and grabbed her old suitcase. "Jon Kent? I thought he lived in Washington with his wife. I haven't seen him around these parts in ages."

"He moved back a few years ago after he retired and went back to ranching. I invited him over to dinner tonight so you can get reacquainted."

Jessica extended the handle on her suitcase. "Thanks for finding us a place so quickly. Is he bringing his wife?"

"He's a widower like you."

"What? When did she die?"

"Cynthia disappeared on her way to work one morning without a trace. Her body was never found, but she's been declared legally dead. Don't mention her around Jon. He's only started acting more like himself in the past few months."

Tears prickled Jessica's eyes. "Poor, Jon. I won't. I'm sure he wants to hear mention of his wife as much as I want people bringing up Adam's name."

"The last thing I wanted to do was bring your mood down after all you've been through. Moving on." She took Bryce's bag. "Come on in. I'll get you some milk and cookies."

Jessica grabbed a duffle holding Bryce's clothes

and hung it over the handle of her suitcase. Shutting the trunk, she wheeled their stuff to the door. Overwhelmed by the need to lock the car, even though they were a mile away from anyone, she stopped, pulled her keys out of her purse, and pressed the lock button.

They settled Bryce in the living room, then took seats at the kitchen table over a pot of tea.

Debbie leaned across the table and held Jessica's hand. "How are you holding up?"

Jessica squeezed her aunt's hand. "I feel better now that I'm far away from Cochrane."

"Did you warn your parents in case he looks for you there?"

"Yes. Mom promised me she'd actually use the house alarm, and she said to thank you for being there for me when she couldn't."

"I'm glad they have an alarm system. When we were kids, your mom never wanted to shoot rifles with your grandfather and me. She preferred cooking and baking with your grandmother. Anyone else you can think of to warn?"

Jessica swirled her tea bag around. "No. Mom said she'd let my sisters know to be cautious. The worst was having to tell my boss what happened."

"Why? Did they give you grief?"

"It's a small preschool. I left them hanging. They can't promise they'll have a job for me when I get back, especially since I don't know when or if that will happen. I'll have to start over no matter how things shake out."

"Oh, I see. How are you going to pay a mortgage and rent?"

"I'll be fine. Knowing how dangerous his job was,

Adam had lots of insurance. The house in Cochrane is paid for in full. And the guys at the station set up a widow fund for us. I have more than enough to start over."

"You aren't registering Bryce in school for the few weeks left, are you?"

Jessica sipped her tea. "No, not until next year. I want to keep him close. And I don't want to have to tell anyone about David."

"Why not? You've known some folks around these parts your whole life."

"They'll treat us differently. I don't want their pity. I got enough back home to last a lifetime. I love how you've always treated me the same, no matter what."

"I understand. I hated how everyone was different around me after your Uncle Ted died. You should know, I already told Jon."

"If I'm living on his property, he deserves to know."

"You should freshen up before he gets here. He's coming at seven."

Jessica searched her jeans and khaki green shirt for stains or wrinkles. "What do you mean? I don't look *that* bad, do I?"

Debbie chuckled. "Now Jess, I know you and Jon had a thing. You were sneaking into the barn with him. Don't tell me you don't want to look your best."

Jessica rolled her eyes. *Aunt Debbie the consummate matchmaker.* "I haven't looked at anyone that way since Adam. And I doubt Jon has eyes for anyone but his dead wife."

"You both deserve happiness."

"Fine, I'll humor you."

Jessica climbed the narrow wooden staircase to the second-floor guest room and unzipped her suitcase. She didn't see anything wrong with her clothes. Touching up her makeup would suffice. She'd always been a t-shirt and jeans kind of girl. Jon wouldn't be expecting anything different. Besides, she'd be shocked if Jon wore anything other than jeans and a plaid shirt.

I wonder what he looks like now. Am I still going to get butterflies in my stomach at the sight of him?

She shook her head to snap herself back to reality. After touching up her concealer, and smoothing the eyeshadow caught in the creases of her eyelid, she went to the living room to check on Bryce. He was sitting cross-legged on the end of the couch with his tablet in his lap.

"Doing all right, buddy?"

"Yeah."

"Need anything before I help your aunt make dinner?"

"More cookies?"

She giggled. "I'm sure Aunt Debbie will let you have more after dinner."

He stuck out his lower lip. "Okay."

His pout got her every time. She pursed her lips so she wouldn't laugh and went back into the kitchen. The warm, spicy smell of taco seasoning wafted through the air, and her tummy rumbled. "What can I do to help?"

"Can you set the table then bring the toppings over? Does Bryce like tacos? I can make him something else."

"He eats almost everything. I'm sure it'll be fine. Besides, I told him if he ate his dinner, you'd let him have more cookies."

Debbie laughed. "Cookies usually do the trick."

A hard knock sounded on the door. Jessica jumped.

Debbie nudged ground elk around in a pan. "That must be Jon. Can you let him in?"

"Sure."

Jessica trembled the whole way to the front door. She wrung her hands, disgusted at her own fear.

I'm scared of my own shadow!

She glanced through the peephole. Jon stood on the porch in his usual plaid and denim, complete with a cowboy hat and boots.

Wow! Her breath caught and her fear evaporated. He was still hot— really, really hot, in a rugged way. He wasn't a boy anymore. His tall, lean body had filled out in a pleasing manner. His shirt sleeves cut into large, sculpted arms set apart by a wide chest, and his jeans clung to bigger, stronger thighs, but the same boyish, clean-shaven face remained, more refined with a few wrinkles.

His dirty-blond hair showed a few flecks of grey reminding her of how much time had passed since they parted ways. But his eyes and expression had changed. Those eyes were still the same shade of light blue but belied the carefree sense of happiness she remembered. Jessica recognized that haunted look, identical to her own gaze in the mirror.

Steeling herself, she opened the door. "Hi. Nice to see you again. Come on in. Aunt Debbie's finishing up the taco meat."

His eyes lit up and his lips curved into a smile, casting aside the haunted look. "Nice to see you, too. Your aunt told me about your situation earlier. How are you holding up?"

"I'm better now that you … whoops, I meant I'm here." *Get it together, Jessica.*

He pecked Debbie on the cheek. "Hello. I picked up cinnamon rolls from The Rising Trout for dessert."

"Great. Thanks, Jon. I'll take that. Come sit down. Want a beer?"

He pulled out a chair. "Sure. Thanks."

Needing time to recover, Jessica formed an exit strategy. "I'll get Bryce."

Bryce hadn't moved from the couch.

Jessica guessed it had something to do with her not limiting his screen time away from home. "Dinner's ready."

Bryce stood. "Then can I have more cookies?"

Jessica guided him towards the kitchen. "Yes. Then more cookies."

"Will our new house have a big yard like Auntie's?"

"I don't know. You can ask Jon. He's renting us the house."

Bryce climbed into the chair Jessica pulled out for him. "Who's Jon?"

Jon smiled and waved at Bryce from across the table. "I'm Jon, and you must be Bryce. Yes, your house does have a big yard. And you know what else?"

"What?"

"I live on the same property, and I have cows and horses. Maybe you can come over and ride with your mom sometime. You're old enough to learn."

Bryce unleashed pleading eyes. "Can we, Mom?"

His eager face always melted her heart. She couldn't refuse him. Besides, it wouldn't hurt her mental state to spend time with an old friend. Despite the baggage they both carried, he still churned her stomach, and raised her internal temperature. "I haven't ridden in a while, but sure we can."

"Can we go tomorrow?"

Jon laughed. "I need to clean your new house tomorrow so you can move in. Maybe after dinner if it's okay with your mom." He met Jessica's gaze. "Would you like to come over for a barbecue with Bryce?"

"We'd love to. Are you sure we aren't imposing? We're already making work for you with getting the house ready without notice. How about we meet there in the morning? I'll help you clean."

Debbie set a serving dish full of taco meat on the table and gave Jessica a secret wink. "I don't mind babysitting Bryce. He can help me around the farm. You two do what you need to do."

Jon said, "I'd be happy for the help, but I have to warn you, it's filthy. The last tenants did a fly by night three days ago instead of paying rent, and they didn't clean in their hurry."

Jessica filled a tortilla with meat and toppings for Bryce. "I've been a preschool teacher for years. I'm no stranger to messes."

"Well then, meet me there at nine. If I happen to be running behind, your key is under the doormat."

Jessica smiled. "I'll be there."

Debbie sat at the table. "Well, everything is ready. Dig in."

****

Soon after dessert, Jessica yawned. "The drive wore me out."

"I bet. Get some rest and I'll see you in the

49

morning." Jon pushed his chair away from the table. "Thank you for the wonderful meal, Debbie, and the new tenants."

Jessica stood. "I'll walk you out."

He followed her to the door, then tipped his hat. "I'll see you in the morning."

"Yes, you will. Goodnight."

He gave her one last lopsided grin before opening the door and walking out.

She shut the door behind him, put her eye to the peephole, and admired Jon's confident, assured, big strides all the way to his truck. After Jon drove off, the house was too empty. To distract herself from that train of thought, she stacked the dessert plates.

Debbie touched her arm. "Let me. You look beat. Go to sleep. I'll get Bryce to take a bath, then we'll watch one of his DVDs before bed. I'm up early. I'll take care of him if he wakes first."

"But…"

"No buts, Jessica Miller. Let someone help you for a change."

Jessica resigned herself to going to bed. Once Debbie decided on something, there was no changing her mind. "That would be nice. Thanks for everything."

"I'll always be here for you, Jess."

Jessica checked the locks on every door and window before retreating to the guest room, then dug a nightshirt out of her suitcase. She curled up in bed, full and content, then shut her eyes. Within seconds, her mind conjured the image of Sarah's body rolled in the tarp.

No. Don't go there. Happy thoughts.

Jessica flashed back to a warm summer evening

when she was eighteen years old sitting on a blanket nestled into Jon's arms with his legs cradling her body. In a field on the Kent Ranch, they'd said their goodbyes.

She'd loved him so much, but they were headed in different directions. Jon had left for Quantico for FBI training the next morning, and a few weeks later, Jessica had returned home to Calgary to start university.

Their promise to reevaluate their relationship after she finished school never came to pass. She met Adam during her first semester, and not long after, Jon met Cynthia. Adam was the sweetest, most considerate person Jessica had ever known, and she'd love him forever.

A loud thud came from outside. Her heart drummed like a heavy metal band as she jumped out of bed, opened the window, and stuck her head outside.

No person or animal wandered the fields outside the guest room window.

Where had the noise come from?

Aunt Debbie came around the side of the house and strode inside the barn, rifle positioned on her shoulder, ready to shoot.

My God, she's brave!

Debbie walked out a few minutes later with her rifle at ease, then stopped and gazed at Jessica hanging out the window. "There's no one in the barn. We're fine."

"Good to know. That noise shook me up."

Debbie laughed. "It gave me a bit of a fright, too. You never know what can wander in a barn around these parts. Goodnight."

Chapter Six

Jon whistled as he ran a brush along Daisy's back. Grooming his favorite horse in solitude usually calmed his mind and soul more than hers. On this night, nothing could chase away his troubles.

Jessica, his first love was in danger, and spending time with her after so many years made his head spin. The sizzling electricity binding them together like a rope, flooded him with warmth, yet guilt and grief tightened his chest at the same time. He missed Cynthia so much his stomach hurt and having feelings for Jessica felt like a betrayal.

Besides which, he couldn't risk getting close to Jessica. The FBI had wiped out all records of him in the area, and the locals wouldn't betray him, but what if someone found him in Lewistown? The same person that took Cynthia could do the same thing to Jessica and Bryce.

But his mind couldn't help but wander to a time years earlier when he'd finally gotten up the nerve to tell Jessica how he felt about her. After a lifelong friendship, they'd spent one amazing summer together. Back then they were carefree, vital, invincible, and clueless, ready to take on the world.

He assumed they'd still have a lot in common. Much like him, she'd experienced some horrible things. First losing her husband while her son was an infant, and now being chased out of her home. No one should have to deal with one let alone both of those things.

Unable to keep his strokes gentle, Jon stopped brushing Daisy. He hung up the brush, gave Daisy an apologetic pat, then fed her an apple. "I'll see you later, sweet girl."

He inhaled deep breaths of fresh mountain air on the way inside his house, detached from his personal connection to the situation, and switched into investigative mode. First things first, with his daily chores on the ranch and dinner behind him, he needed to get a better sense of the man who'd threatened Jessica.

He sat in front of his computer and typed David Hayes into an internet browser. Location wouldn't be relevant because he'd only moved next door to Jessica six months ago. Jon hit the images tab, then scrolled through various faces.

Three fit the physical description with the size and dark hair and eyes. One lived in England and had posted images in the past week. Another lived and worked in Australia which ruled him out. The third had a large social media presence on various sites for his accounting firm and a personal account full of images of his wife, not named Sarah, and five children.

Jon scrolled through the rest of the results from his search. He found no sign of the David Hayes who lived across the street from Jess in Cochrane, or his wife Sarah. In this day and age, having no social media sent up a red flag. People who acted in such a manner either valued their privacy or had something to hide.

And why threaten Jessica knowing the police couldn't arrest him anyhow?

Those weren't the actions of a stable person. Those were the actions of a man under strain or with serious anger management issues. A guilty man who'd murdered his wife and intended to kill the witness.

****

The next morning, Jessica stood on tiptoe and put her eye to the peephole. The sun shone on the empty porch swing and the planters of bright yellow marigolds flanking the steps.

She stepped outside, glanced left to right, then scoured the woods across the street for any signs of movement. Branches shifted along the edge of the woods.

Jessica sprinted across the front porch to her car, pressing the key fob in her pocket along the way. She climbed in, and locked the doors, eyes fixed on the branches continuing to sway. Her vision grayed a little, and her breaths came in pants.

A large buck's antlers pushed through the trees. He walked between them and grazed on the grass in the ditch.

Stars clouded the outskirts of her vision. She pressed her forehead to the cold leather on her steering wheel and took a few minutes to calm her breathing before starting the ignition.

I've got to pull myself together. David didn't follow me here. There's nothing to be afraid of.

Her hands quivered as she drove down the gravel laneway and turned onto the dirt road. She clamped her hands around the steering wheel to stop the tremors. If only her body would stop betraying her.

No other vehicles drove the back roads. Jessica had the road all to herself. She passed horse ranches, farms with rolling hills of grain, and dairy farms where cows wandered free, leading her fifteen miles away from town. Not a human in sight. Her hands relaxed.

The remoteness of the Kent Family ranch appealed to her need to be away from civilization. David would never find her here. Coming up on the right, a familiar black iron archway, with the Kent name inscribed on it, hung over the open gate leading onto Jon's property. She turned onto the gravel road and followed it past the main house. The road curved for a mile, leading past fields of grazing cows. Jessica spotted a short gravel driveway and turned. She parked, climbed out, and studied her new home.

The older, single story brick house had a chimney, likely for a wood-burning fireplace to compensate for the unforgiving Montana winters. The flower beds along the front of the house overflowed with weeds, and the lawn resembled a field of wildflowers rather than grass. But being unemployed, she had plenty of time to whip the yard into shape.

Best of all, dense coniferous forest surrounded her. The evergreens emitted their sweet-scented esters of spring and birds sung in nearby trees. At night, the owls would hoot, and the crickets would sing outside their bedroom windows. No more bright lampposts and exhaust fumes.

A wooden shed stood on the back right corner of the lot. Jessica unlatched the door. Clouds of dust kicked up around her, and she sneezed. A garden shovel leaned against the wall next to a snow shovel, a few bags of potting soil, and some empty planters. She snagged the garden shovel and turned over the soil to loosen the weeds in the flowerbeds.

When she finished, she leaned the shovel against the house and used her forearm to wipe beads of sweat from her face.

Jon still hadn't arrived. He'd said to go ahead inside without him, but the mess he described wasn't one she wanted to face alone. Especially on such a pleasant morning with the sun warming her skin.

Jessica climbed on the John Deere mower parked beside the shed intending to tackle the field that was the front yard, but the key was missing.

Strange. Jon always used to leave the keys to everything in the ignitions.

She retrieved the shovel and wandered back into the little shed, letting the door shut behind her. The light filtering in through the wooden boards illuminated the small space.

Jessica scanned the walls on either side of the door for a key hook. Not finding one, she stood on tiptoe, barely able to reach the dusty shelves on the back wall.

The door creaked open behind her. *No place to hide.* Sweat trickled in her eyes and down her back. *I need a weapon.* She threw the shovel over her shoulder like a baseball bat and spun to face the intruder.

Jon stood in the doorway with his palms held out in front of him.

The shovel weighed ten pounds more. Her cheeks warmed, and she glanced at her old sneakers.

Jon eased the shovel out of her hands and leaned it against a corner. "I should have knocked first."

"It's my fault. It's your house, your shed, and I almost swung at you with your own shovel."

He took her hand, then rubbed his thumb across her palm. "It's okay. No one can blame you for being jumpy. Let's start again, all right? Good morning. You look a lot more rested today."

She raised her head to face him and gazed into his eyes. Electricity flowed between their hands and warmth flooded her skin. "Good morning. I do feel a lot better after a good night's sleep. How are you?"

"I'm good. Shall we go inside and see your new home? Or was there something else you needed in here?"

"Do you keep the key to the John Deere in the shed?"

"I leave the key in the ignition. We're in the middle of nowhere. Why?"

"It's not there. I was in here looking for it."

He frowned.

"Hopefully, it's in the house somewhere. If nothing else, I'll drive my mower over later, if I can't find the spare key. So, ready to head inside?"

"Yes, please. I'm excited to see the house."

He led her to the front door, lifted the mat, and handed her the key. "This one is yours. I have mine on my key ring."

He unlocked the door. A cloud of dust stirred as he swung it open, then the permeating odor of rotten garbage assaulted them, and they hadn't even yet crossed the threshold.

Jessica held her breath, then stuck her head inside the door. Empty wrappers, bottles, cans, and dirty dishes covered every available surface and garbage overflowed from the can onto the kitchen floor.

She covered her nose with the back of her hand and suppressed her gag reflex. Her eyes filled with moisture to cleanse the filth. "You weren't exaggerating. This place is a wreck. And the smell—I can't think of anything nasty enough to describe it."

"Now I'm embarrassed. Told you it was bad. If you want to cut and run, I'll understand."

"No, I'll help." She grabbed a rock from the border around the flower beds and propped the door open. Clean oxygen to make the place livable was a must. "Are there garbage cans around?"

"Yes, they're kept in the other shed on the opposite side of the house to keep the wildlife out. I'll get one."

Jessica moved through the house opening every window. Once the stench eased to a more bearable level, she took stock of the place.

The furniture appeared to be in good condition under a thick layer of dust and dirty dishes strewn on every surface. A nice brick, wood-burning fireplace with a mantel acted as a focal point in the living room which opened into the dining room, making an efficient use of the small space. Once she finished decorating and putting her own stamp on the space, they'd feel more at home.

She returned to the kitchen and opened all the upper cabinets. They were empty except for a stray glass. The dirty dishes scattered all over the kitchen, coffee table, and dining room table were likely stored there once upon a time. In the lower cabinets, some non-perishable food items remained but no cleaning supplies. Not shocking considering the state of the place.

Jon whistled as he came in the kitchen with a garbage can in each hand. "We're in luck. I found empty garbage cans."

"Good. Have you seen any cleaning stuff around

here?"

"No, I assumed there would be, seeing as they left everything else."

"I looked in all the cupboards. No luck."

"I'll run home to get cleaning supplies and fresh bedding."

Her heart raced as his footsteps retreated. She locked the front door in the small mud room and the sliding glass door in the kitchen. She clasped her hands together as she stood in front of the living room windows, overwhelmed by the urge to lock them. The stench would become horrible if she gave in.

Until the episode in the shed, she'd been convinced of her safety. Why couldn't she shake the dread of impending danger?

Shoving aside the doom and gloom, Jessica took a garbage bag into the room Bryce would occupy. The floor was strewn with paper, food wrappers, and dirty mismatched socks.

She held up a drawing of a scribbled horse. A reminder of the children's artwork she used to hang in her little classroom. Tears trickled down her cheeks. She couldn't throw the drawing out. Instead, she set the horse aside on a dresser. She dumped the rest of the trash in the garbage bag.

The old, oak hardwood needed to be vacuumed and mopped, and the dressers wiped clean, but otherwise the room was ready for Bryce. She picked up the garbage bag and headed towards the kitchen.

Someone pounded on the front door. The garbage bag slipped from her hand and clunked on the floor. She headed towards the door, then paused a foot away. Another knock penetrated the buzzing in her ears. She leaned against the wall.

"Jessica, are you there? It's me, Jon. My hands are full."

She fumbled with the lock, then opened the door. "I'm sorry. I was cleaning up Bryce's room, and well…"

Jon shut the door, set his bucket of cleaning supplies and armful of bedding down, and rested his hand on her shoulder. "Jess, what's wrong?"

"I panicked. I assumed you would use your key. I feel like an idiot. I don't think David is the type to knock, looking for permission to come in."

"Don't you dare beat yourself up about this. It's natural to be afraid. You were taunted by a murderer. I would be seriously worried if you weren't scared. He's still on the loose. You have every reason to be vigilant."

"I came to the middle of nowhere to feel safe. But I don't."

"You only got here yesterday. This whole thing is fresh in your mind. It'll take time for you to get past all you went through. Trust me, I've been there."

"Been there? You've been threatened?"

"I've put a lot of people away. The FBI wiped all traces of my existence so I could retire. I'm constantly looking over my shoulder. But in time, you get used to living that way."

She covered his hand with hers and squeezed. "Thank you. I hope you're right."

"Do you feel better around me? Safe? You should. I can handle myself, and I'll be looking out for you."

"I do. More like myself." *Even though I'm a blushing schoolgirl again.*

"If the fear gets too overwhelming, and you need

me, call. I'll take you grocery shopping later if you'd like. Show you around town."

"Yes, please. The thought of a grocery store makes me cringe after my encounter with David."

"I know. Your aunt told me all about it."

Dwelling on her state of mind wasn't getting them anywhere. She needed to change the subject. "Great. Let's get to work."

****

After they finished overhauling the house, Jessica stood next to Jon on the front porch, holding a bottle of water, locked in his gaze. Pain flashed in Jon's eyes, and he turned to face the trees.

I know that look. Guilt. Loss.

His suffering mirrored her own. He'd loved his wife the way she'd loved Adam.

His eyes travelled back to hers again. "We make a good team, Jess. Your help saved hours of work."

"You've done plenty for me, and I'm very grateful. I should get Bryce and our stuff so we can move in."

"I'm heading home to check on things, then I'll come back to mow the lawn."

"You don't have to do that."

"No, I don't, but I want to." He locked the door. "Come, I'll walk you to your car."

"Okay."

After she pushed her key fob to unlock her car, he held the door open while she climbed in, started the ignition, and put the windows down.

He leaned to peer in. "I'll see you in a bit."

"If we don't cross paths before dinner, what time should we come over?"

"About five. We'll be able to finish dinner in time

to ride during the sunset."

He smiled, tipped his hat, then walked away.

She followed his progress in her rearview mirror. Through his suffering, he remembered the sunsets and wanted to provide comfort. His heart and desire to do good remained.

Adam would've liked him. Too bad they never got to meet.

Jessica sighed, then put her car in reverse, backed onto the street, and drove to her aunt's farm.

Aunt Debbie stood on the front lawn and dipped her old bubble wand in a large container filled with soap. She waved the wand in the wind, and a massive bubble drifted through the air. Bryce ran through the bubble laughing.

Jessica got out of the car.

A soaked Bryce ran over and hugged her, covering her in soap. "Hi, Mom. Come play with me and Auntie."

"Sure. For a few minutes. We'll play, load our stuff in the car, then I'll show you our new house."

****

Jon ensured his lead ranch-hand, Chip, had things under control before heading across the fields to Jessica's house. He reached in his pocket and pulled out the spare key for the lawn mower he'd found at home. Noticing the overturned soil in the flower bed, he made a mental note to get Jessica flats of flowers from the hardware store. Gardening had always been one of her favorite past times in the summer. She'd need busy work to keep her mind in a healthy place.

He continued past the house to the John Deere parked beside the shed. He climbed on and went to stick the spare key in the mower, but he couldn't. The original key dangled from the ignition.

That's odd.

Jessica had said the key was missing, and she'd never been the flighty type, but she'd had a few hellish days.

Jon jammed the spare key in his pocket, then started the mower. He steered towards the edges of the property along the edge of the forest and scanned the trees for movement. In a spot sloping downhill, moisture pooled, creating a large swatch of mud.

He parked, climbed off the mower, then kneeled to examine two large, fresh footprints unmistakably pointed in the direction of the house. They appeared to have been made by a man's size twelve hiking boot. A full size bigger than Jon's foot, and very unlike the usual footwear worn around the property. His staff all wore cowboy boots, and they had no reason to be on the rental property on the back corner of Jon's land.

Adrenaline surged through his veins as two possibilities became clear. The first, a hunter wandered onto his property tracking game, or the second far more ominous, David followed Jessica to Lewistown. The discovery of the key made the second possibility far more plausible.

The incident in the grocery store, and the note David taped to Jessica's front door, indicated an enjoyment of psychological torment. Taking a key, then replacing it, would fit with that modus operandi. If Jessica found the key, she'd think she'd lost her mind.

Jon followed the muddy footprints through the woods. The trail ended at a dirt road running along the edges of the Kent property line. Fresh tire tracks, unmarred by dust or rain headed north towards a rural road.

Not a ranch hand.

He finished mowing the lawn, parked the John Deere beside the shed, and used his key to let himself in the house. He searched every square inch including the closets, under the beds, and the unfinished basement for intruders and found none. Nothing was disturbed, but he wasn't taking chances. He closed and locked every window and door.

Poor Jessica.

He'd have to share his suspicions with her, but not until she had a good meal and a relaxing evening. Maybe he'd persuade her to stay the night and put off telling her until he had time to investigate further. For now, he'd linger out of sight in the woods and keep an eye on her. His presence would act as a deterrent.

Chapter Seven

Jessica glanced in her rearview mirror and chuckled. Bryce's face was smooshed against the car window, as they drove up to the house.

She opened his door. "Want to check out your new yard, buddy?"

"Wow! I've always wanted a yard like this." He breezed past her and sprinted around the square outlined in the freshly mowed grass.

She breathed in the heavenly, sweet aroma of the fresh clippings. *Thanks, Jon.* She smiled. Old memories flooded back of other small gestures, like fixing her beat up old car, and the flower bouquets he'd picked every time she visited Lewistown over the years.

Bryce ran to her. "I love it! It's so big!"

She ruffled his hair. "I'm glad, buddy. Let's go inside and check it out."

After settling Bryce into his new room with toys and unpacking the rest of her suitcase, she took a long, hot shower to wash away the grime from cleaning, and contemplated what to wear. Since they would be riding, jeans and a cotton button-up shirt were her best bet. She left a few buttons open at the top, straightened the natural waves in her hair, and applied makeup.

"Bryce, time to go to Jon's. Come put on your shoes." She walked to the tiny mud room off the living room, opened the front door, stuck her head out, and scanned the woods on either side of the house for movement.

"What are you doing, Mom?"

Looking for David. "I'm making sure there are no wild animals around like coyotes, wolves, or bears."

His eyes grew wide. "Bears?"

"Don't worry. They usually don't bother people unless we bother them or go too close to their babies. Besides, the coast is clear. Let's go."

Jessica led Bryce along the winding gravel road past a huge field of cows. The path forked ahead. To the left stood a red and white, well-maintained barn with horses grazing nearby. She went in the opposite direction toward the sprawling ranch-style house.

Jon sat on his wraparound porch in a wicker rocking chair and waved as they approached.

Bryce took off toward the barn. "I'm going to see the horses." He ran to the fence, slipped in between the wooden slats, and approached a brown horse with a black mane and tail.

"Bryce. Wait a minute. Get back here!"

He stared into the horse's face enthralled, oblivious to her words, and gently petted the horse's muzzle.

Jessica ran after him and leaned on the fence. The slats were too narrow for her to squeeze through the way he had. "Bryce, come watch the horses from this side of the fence."

Jon jogged over and leaned beside her. "He's fine with Daisy. She's a good horse. All my horses are gentle."

"You're absolutely sure?"

Jon laughed. "Yes, mama bear. You know how much I love my horses. I only keep the sweetest ones."

"Bryce, Jon says you can stay there, but you better be careful. Don't go too close to the horse's feet. They kick."

"Okay, Mom."

Jon asked, "Do you remember the time when we went riding at Debbie's farm and it thundered? The horses got startled and mine bucked me off?"

"Wow, I do remember. That was a long time ago. I think I was ten. You broke your arm."

"I was mortified. You were a little girl, four years younger, and you held on, but I couldn't."

Jessica chuckled. "If I remember correctly, I was riding a pony Uncle Ted bought for the kids. Your horse bucked a lot harder than the pony. I thought you were brave for not crying."

"Really? I feel better then. Thanks."

"We were so young without a care in the world. We've both changed a lot since then, haven't we?" Tears flooded her eyes, blurring her vision.

Jon pulled her into his arms.

She melted into him and let out the loneliness, the fear, and the injustice of all the grief life had thrown at her. She hadn't experienced pure joy for longer than a fleeting moment in such a long time.

Jon whispered in her ear. "You've been through hell the past few days, but you're safe now. I'm here. So is Debbie. You aren't alone anymore."

She pulled away and wiped her tears with both hands in case Bryce happened to look her way. "I'll be on edge until that bastard is stopped. I'm sorry I broke down. I haven't had time to come to terms with all this, and I have to act normal for Bryce."

"It'll get easier with time."

"I don't think so. I'm terrified David will find us, and I'll be forced to run. Uproot our lives all over again."

He held her shoulders and gazed into her eyes with an intensity she'd never seen in him before. "That isn't happening. He's not getting near you and Bryce, and you aren't running and hiding anymore. If he has the nerve to show his face here, I'll take care of him."

She patted his hand, then turned and leaned against the fence to watch Bryce. "We aren't your responsibility. You've already done enough giving me a place to rent, and cheap, I might add."

"I trained to serve and protect. Besides, I think you're a good woman with a sweet son who deserves a happy life, free of looking over your shoulder." His brows furrowed. "Please, you have to let me protect you."

His wife. He's scared I'll die, too. "If anything seems off, or I think David may be around, you'll be my first stop."

He let go of her shoulders. "Bryce is obviously eager to ride. Let's get those steaks and potatoes on the grill. Want a beer or a glass of wine? I got Bryce chocolate milk."

"A beer would be great. Need any help?"

"No. I made salad earlier. Want to sit on the porch with me? We can watch Bryce while I grill the steaks."

"Sure, sounds great." She followed him onto the front porch.

He turned on the propane, then lit the barbecue. "Have a seat."

Jessica took the chair adjacent to the one he'd occupied earlier and alternated between watching Jon and Bryce. Jon shifted their steaks to give them perfect grill marks. Typical Jon. Every movement had a purpose. Bryce continued his one-sided discussion with Daisy.

She closed her eyes, savoring the deliciously warm sun on her face as the steaks sizzled under flickering flames. The scent of beef made her mouth water, and the sweet smell of hay carried in the light breeze.

She sensed Jon's gaze, opened her eyes, and smiled as their eyes locked. "This is really nice. Thanks for having us over."

"It's good seeing you so relaxed. Bryce seems happy too. I wonder what he's telling my horse. They're deep in conversation."

Jessica chuckled. "I bet he's still telling her all about his favorite tv show."

"He talked about it at dinner last night too, didn't he? He was listing off names and reciting catch phrases for Debbie."

Jessica said, "Yes, he was. She watched it with him last night."

"What are you doing tonight? You didn't get the cable and internet hooked up yet."

"No. They couldn't come out for a few days, and I forgot to pack my DVD player. I'll just read him a story."

"Watch his show here before you take him home to bed."

Jessica paused. *Should we stay?* From what Debbie had said, Jon had only recently come out of his shell. Maybe by staying she'd be doing him a favor, too. "Okay. Thank you."

"I can tell you've gotten to be an independent

woman who isn't used to having help. But, if ever you need anything, ask. I'm right around the bend."

"I don't like relying on anyone but myself."

Jon said, "I'm the same. I only trust one ranch hand to oversee everything when I'm not there. Chip took care of running this place after my father died while I was still in Washington."

"Sorry about your dad."

"Thanks." He pushed on each steak with one finger. "Still like your steak medium rare?"

He'd developed a new skill since she'd last seen him, the art of redirecting conversations on a whim. "Yes. You remembered after all these years?"

He looked into her eyes. "I haven't forgotten anything about you, Jess."

Her skin warmed, and her pulse sped as memories of being naked with Jon in the hayloft crept in. She could only imagine as a full-grown man what he must look like under those clothes now. "I haven't forgotten much either."

"So, what happened after you went home to school, and I moved to Washington?"

She picked at the label on her beer bottle. "I'll give you the quick version. I met Adam on campus and fell in love. After graduation, we got married, and moved into a tiny apartment together. We scrounged and saved every cent to buy our house. A little while later, I got pregnant with Bryce. A few weeks after he was born, Adam was killed."

She paused, waiting for the punch in the gut from uttering Adam's name out loud. "It's been nine years since that horrible night."

"That's rough. Sounds like you had some happy

years with Adam though."

"I did. He was a good man." She blinked away a new round of tears.

Jon's face fell, and the light in his eyes vanished. "I know what you're going through. You know I left for Washington to start work at the end of that summer."

"Yes, I remember."

"I met my wife Cynthia around the same time you met Adam. But I was really married to the FBI. Ambition moved me up the ranks and after a few years, they assigned me to undercover operations. I was away from home for over half the year. I'll never forgive myself for squandering my time on scumbags instead of Cynthia. Did your aunt tell you what happened?"

"Yes." The anguish in his eyes tugged at her heart. A man so good shouldn't have to suffer. "You can't beat yourself up. It would be like Adam blaming himself for getting shot. You were serving your country, and something awful happened. I'm sure you've saved a lot of people."

"I have saved lives, but I don't think I'll come to terms with not being there to save Cynthia."

Jessica didn't know what to say. No words would ever make something like that better.

Jon inhaled sharply. "Dinner is ready. Would you mind fetching Bryce?"

"Sure."

She ambled along the path to the barn to give Jon time to recover from their conversation. Jessica cupped her hands to her mouth. "Bryce!" He turned his head towards her. "Come. Dinner is ready. Jon said we'll go riding after we eat."

"I want to ride this one, Mom." Daisy nuzzled

Bryce's hand. He giggled. "I like her a lot. She looks at me when I talk to her."

"We'll ask Jon."

Jessica led Bryce back the way she came to the large ranch-style house. Fifteen years had passed since she'd last stepped foot inside. The main floor was spotless and inviting, remodeled in recent years, but still rustic, with dark exposed wooden beams, and warm, neutral decor.

Jessica led Bryce to the center of the long, antique, oak table where Jon had set a place for them. Years ago, Jessica had the privilege of sitting at that table for Sunday dinner in one of the twelve chairs now sitting empty.

She pulled out a chair. "Hop in, buddy."

Jon set a glass of chocolate milk in front of Bryce. "Dig in. Hope you like it."

Bryce asked, "Mom, how do you know Jon?"

Jessica took a swig of her beer and set the bottle down. "Me and Jon have known each other since I was your age."

Bryce gaped. "That's a really, really long time."

Jon smiled. "A really, really, really long time."

She chuckled. "Aunt Debbie and Jon's parents were best friends. When we were kids, I would come visit Aunt Debbie with your grandma and grandpa at least once a month, and for a few weeks every summer. Jon used to come over with his parents. We had bonfires, rode horses, and played games."

Jon said, "I used to love it when your mom came to visit. She was a lot of fun."

"Mom is still lots of fun."

Jon winked at her. "She sure is."

Dinner passed in a comfortable silence. Jessica savored every bite of her fresh, tender, juicy steak. Whatever they did with their cows on the Kent Ranch produced the most delectable beef around. She smiled, rested her fork on her empty plate, and held her full tummy. "That was delicious. Thanks so much for everything you've done today."

"It's been my pleasure. Are you ready to go riding, Bryce?"

Bryce asked, "Can I ride the brown horse?"

"Sure. You and Mom can ride her. Her name is Daisy. She's one of my favorites."

Jessica pushed her chair away from the table. "I haven't ridden in years. Hope I can still get on a horse."

"Don't worry, Mom. I'll help you."

She giggled. "Thanks, buddy. You're a real gentleman."

Jon led them out the back door to the stables. Jessica took in the familiar, comforting aroma of hay, manure, and leather while Jon saddled the horses.

"Daisy's ready for you. Hop on, Jess."

Jessica stepped in the stirrup, silently praying she'd make it onto the horse without doing anything embarrassing. She hoisted herself up and straddled Daisy without incident.

Jon petted Daisy's mane. "See? You haven't lost your touch."

"I might be sore by morning. Haven't used these muscles in a while."

He lifted Bryce onto Daisy in front of her. "Up you go. Hang on to the horn right here."

Jon climbed onto his horse. "Ready?"

Bryce shouted, "Yes."

Jessica wrapped her arms around Bryce and picked up the reins.

They rode side by side past fields of hay, and cows grazing on grass, to the trails winding along the edges of the Kent property. She gazed at the mountains in the distance. A gentle, sweet-smelling breeze caressed her face as she listened to the rhythmic pattern of hoofbeats. Soon, the sun descended, casting shadows over the mountains and turning them golden.

She glanced at Jon.

He turned to face her.

They smiled and locked eyes, communicating so much without words, the way they always had. The chemistry between them as palpable as it had been years ago. His pupils dilated, then her cheeks heated. To hide them, she faced forward and kissed Bryce's head.

Jon asked, "Getting sore? Ready to head back to the barn?"

"I'm not sore, but we should get back. I think Bryce is getting sleepy. He's being quiet."

Bryce yawned. "I'm not sleepy."

She bit her lip to suppress a laugh. "Okay, buddy."

Jessica followed Jon's lead and steered Daisy back to the stables.

"That was so much fun." Bryce asked, "Can we do it again?"

Jon lifted him off the horse. "Sure. If your mom is good with it."

Jessica swung her leg around and hopped off Daisy. "It's fine with me. I like riding too."

"It's a date then." Jon unbuckled Daisy's saddle. "Who wants apple pie and ice cream while they watch television?"

Bryce raised his arm. "Me! Me!"

"Apple pie is one of our favorites. Let me give you a hand this time."

"You can make coffee while I dish the pie and ice cream. I'll hang these saddles, then meet you inside."

"Sure." Jessica led Bryce into the kitchen to await Jon. He came in a few minutes later and brought out the coffee tin and mugs.

She brewed a pot while he sliced pie. "Still like your coffee black?"

"Yes, ma'am."

"That's easy."

They found Bryce sitting on the couch waiting patiently. He shoveled pie into his mouth while Jon found an episode of his favorite show.

Jon set his empty plate aside. "Now I understand why you like this show so much, Bryce."

Bryce's eyes fluttered and he lay his head in Jon's lap.

Jon smiled down at him and stroked his hair.

Jessica set her empty plate and fork on the coffee table. "We should head home. Looks like he's almost asleep."

"Too late. His breathing has already slowed. You can stay here tonight. It's no big deal. I can carry him to one of my guest rooms, and you can stay in another. Or I can carry him across the fields."

"I don't want to wake him. I'm amazed he's kept to a somewhat normal routine. Are you sure about us staying?"

Jon said, "Sure, why not?"

"Okay."

"I'll put him in my old room. You know the way."

Jessica's cheeks heated although they'd always behaved in his room. "All right."

Jon shifted Bryce to rest his head against his shoulder, then carried him down the hall. He cradled his head, then gently placed him in the center of the bed.

Jessica tucked him in and kissed his forehead.

They went into the hallway, and he gently shut the door.

"Jess, do you want another drink or snack before bed?"

"No, thanks. I'm fine."

"Guest room?"

"That would be nice. Thanks."

He gestured to the door across the hallway. "This is it. Some of my old shirts are in the closet if you want one to sleep in."

"Thanks again for today."

"It was my pleasure. Goodnight."

"Goodnight, Jon." She locked eyes with him, not ready to part ways.

He took a step forward, stopped for a few seconds, then closed the space between them.

She grasped his strong, sinewed forearm welcoming his advance.

He wrapped his arms around her, kissed her gently on the lips, then pulled back, and looked into her eyes.

A fire and a longing rekindled inside of her that had extinguished long ago. She pressed her lips to his again, deepening the kiss. She parted his lips and sought out his tongue. Her hands wandered along his back and shoulders, tracing the lines of his strong, labor-earned muscles. She ravaged his mouth, exploring every inch, pleased he devoured hers in return.

He pulled her into his body, untucked the hem of her shirt, then let go and backed away. "I can't. I'm sorry. Cynthia— it's too soon."

Poor, Jon. I pushed him too far.

She bit her lip. "Believe me, I understand," she said, breathless, putting a hand to her chest, waiting for her drumming heartbeat to slow. "I'm conflicted, too. Because of Adam."

"Thanks for understanding. Need anything else before bed?"

"No. I'm fine. Goodnight." She went into the guest room, shut the door, then leaned her back against it. *What was I thinking?*

****

Jon lay awake in bed. With his body overheated and throbbing, he tossed and turned. Jessica's presence down the hall only made his aroused state worse. He rolled onto his side and bunched his pillow under his head. The more time he spent with Jessica, the more the chemistry intensified, and the more his heart remembered years of being in love with her.

She'd penetrated the melancholy of his days since her arrival in Lewistown. He hated deceiving her and manipulating her into staying. She hated lies, and his lie by omission was sure to backfire in the morning.

At least Jessica would spend one more night believing she was safe. Spilling his guts and kissing her hadn't been part of the plan and boy did he regret it. She may feel safe, but he'd upset her at one of her lowest points. Never again. He needed to keep her at a distance for her own good.

After hours of struggling to fall sleep, a quiet

whimpering pierced the silence. He climbed out of bed and followed the sound to the guest room.

Jessica.

He opened then shut the door behind him and sat on the side of the bed. Jessica cried in her sleep.

Nightmares.

He rubbed her back. "Shhh, Jess. It's okay. I'm here. It's only a dream."

She opened her eyes, blinked a few times, then locked onto his gaze. "Oh, no. I woke you. I've been having these horrible nightmares."

"I understand. Go back to sleep."

He stood and headed for the door.

"Jon. Wait."

He turned back. "What?"

"This is incredibly selfish of me to ask with the way we left things, but I'm really shaken. Will you stay?"

"Sure."

She scooted over and faced the wall. He climbed in behind her and resisted the urge to wrap an arm around her, but he couldn't keep his hands to himself. He ran his hands through her silky, long hair, trying to coax her back to sleep. All the while he struggled to keep his breathing steady.

He understood recurring nightmares better than anyone having relived some horrible sights in his sleep. Usually, the broken bodies of the young victims he'd encountered. An instinctive need to protect Jessica and Bryce gripped him, along with an intense hatred for the man uprooting their lives and causing these nightmares.

Chapter Eight

Jon awoke to the first bit of morning light creeping in the guest room window with his hand still entwined in Jessica's hair. The swollen bags under her eyes had gone down since dinner at Debbie's. But she needed as much sleep as she could get before finding out David may have followed her.

He kept his footfalls light as he padded down the hall to his room. His ensuite bathroom was furthest away from his sleeping guests. He showered and then dressed in his usual denim and a long-sleeved red and blue plaid shirt. With guests to dote on for a change, his first stop, rather than chores, was the kitchen.

From his refrigerator, he grabbed cartons of eggs and milk, a pound of bacon, a loaf of bread, and a block of cheddar. He placed the bacon on a cookie sheet and put it in the oven to crisp while he layered bread in the bottom of a baking pan. After whisking the eggs and milk together, he poured the mixture on top of the bread, then added a dash of dry mustard, paprika, salt, and pepper. He placed the crispy bacon on the egg and milk-soaked bread and added a layer of grated cheddar. Then he popped the casserole in the oven for his special guests.

The rich fragrance of his Columbian brew drew him to the coffee maker. He poured a big mug to the rim, then texted Chip and put him in charge of the ranch for the day. Jessica and Bryce needed his full attention until the danger passed.

Jon picked up his newspaper and scanned the local headlines. The news never generated too much excitement in Lewistown. One of the town's many perks. The lead story featured an upcoming meeting about taxes and expenditures. Jon preferred to pay his bill without questions, so he skipped the article and moved on to the next featuring a truck stolen on the outskirts of town.

Jon's internal radar pinged. When teenagers got bored, these things happened, but the timing was questionable. The tracks he'd discovered on the dirt road behind his rental had been made by narrower car tires, but he'd be on the lookout for an old Ford truck. His instincts, while working undercover, saved his life on multiple occasions.

Slow footsteps padded on the hardwood. "Mom."

Jon found Bryce outside the guest room where Jessica slept and whispered, "Hi, Bryce. She's still sleeping. You fell asleep on my couch last night, so you guys slept over. Breakfast will be ready soon. Do you want to watch a show while you wait?"

"Okay."

Jon flipped the television on and handed Bryce the remote.

Bryce settled beside Jon and scrolled through channels. He picked a show, then sat quietly and watched it instead of getting up to mischief, unlike his nephews who found trouble around every turn. Jessica hit the jackpot. Bryce was an easy child to care for.

The timer beeped. Jon opened the oven, inhaling a burst of the most delicious breakfast smells. Bacon, cheddar, and eggs mingled together and permeated the kitchen. Once the cheese stopped bubbling, he dished two portions onto plates and carried them to the living room.

"I've got breakfast here for you."

Bryce looked at his plate then up at Jon. "What is it?"

"A casserole with eggs, cheese, and bacon."

"Bacon. Yummy. I'll try some."

Jon laughed. "I love bacon too, and we both love horses. We'll be best buds in no time."

Bryce picked a bite off a corner.

"So, what do you think?"

"Hmmm. It's good."

"I'm glad you approve. That's a big compliment coming from you."

Jessica surfaced in her rumpled clothes as they finished eating and sat between them on the couch. "Good morning. Why didn't you wake me?"

"Hi, Mom."

Jon said, "You needed sleep. We men had breakfast and hung out. I made a casserole. Want some food and coffee?"

"Sure, thanks. I can get it."

"Great. I'll run to the rental house to get clothes for you and Bryce while you eat."

"Are you sure? I could go."

"No, stay. I'll go." Jon hustled out the door before Jessica could change her mind.

The sun bathed him in a gentle warmth from a cloudless sky. Tipping his hat, he waved to Chip who drove an unwinder across the middle of the pasture to the delight of the cows who followed behind him munching hay.

As he crossed the field to Jessica's house, Jon sensed eyes on him. He searched for movement in the trees surrounding the property. Nothing. The hairs on the back of his neck prickled. Someone lurked, and after finding signs of an intruder yesterday, he didn't like it one bit.

Jon wanted nothing more than to put on camouflage, grab guns and knives, then hunt until he found the culprit, but he couldn't leave Bryce and Jessica vulnerable and unguarded.

So instead, he let himself into the rental house, threw some clothes and toiletries in a backpack, then left, locking the door behind him. He hustled past cows in the fields to his house, bolted the front door, then dropped the bags on the kitchen table.

Jessica was leaning her back against the counter, staring straight ahead as if she wasn't in the room.

He turned the deadbolt on the back door, rushed over to her, and held her shoulders. "Jess. What's wrong?"

She blinked and met his gaze. Tears filled her eyes and spilled down her cheeks. "I just got off the phone with Tim, Adam's former colleague at the RCMP. Some hikers found Sarah's body in Kananaskis County in a shallow grave after their German Shepherd wandered off the main path and started digging." She wiped her tears with her fingers. "I knew the odds were slim that she'd somehow survived. But to have it confirmed hurts. He murdered her."

Jon wrapped her in an embrace and rested his cheek against the top of her head in the crook of his shoulder. "I'm so sorry. The one positive is that it's much easier to get a conviction with a body and they may find evidence on her, linking him to the crime to go along with your testimony."

She put her hands on his chest and gently pushed him back, then glanced over his shoulder towards the living room. "I need to get it together. I don't want Bryce to see me like this."

He sighed. The discovery of the body confirmed his theory, and now he'd have to share the rest of his suspicions. He couldn't put it off any longer. "There's something I need to tell you."

"What?"

"I got the feeling I was being watched from the woods just now, and I found a few things yesterday after you left. Better safe than sorry."

"Yesterday?" She folded her arms across her chest. "What did you find?"

Reaching in his pocket, he pulled out the mower key. "I found this in the ignition when I went back to mow the lawn."

"I know the key wasn't there. What else? You said things as in plural."

"I found footprints near the rental house leading to a dirt road running along the edge of my property and fresh tire tracks."

She glared at him. "How could you have kept this from me?"

"I wasn't convinced it was David, and I didn't want to upset you. I watched your house from the woods to make sure you were safe yesterday afternoon. After you left with Bryce to come here, I ran home and sat on the porch seconds before you arrived. When you decided to stay the night, I figured there was no sense telling you until morning. I wanted you to feel safe for as long as possible. I see what this guy is doing to you."

"I understand your reasoning but promise you won't leave me in the dark again. You tell me everything, right away. I have a son to protect."

"I promise. I'll tell you everything from here on out. I know you're upset, but we need to focus on figuring this out. Okay?"

She paused before answering. "All right."

"Did David have access to your car?"

"Yes, at the grocery store. Why?"

"He may have put a tracking device on your car."

Her knees buckled and she grabbed onto the counter behind her. "What do I do now? Take the tracker off and leave?"

"You mean what do *we* do. You aren't alone. You hear?"

"Okay then, what should *we* do?"

"I have a friend in Colorado who specializes in surveillance and alarm systems among other things. He's a tech wiz."

She shut her eyes and pinched the bridge of her nose. "Whatever you think. I trust you."

He ached to wrap her in his arms. "I'll call him now. Bryce is content in the living room. Why don't you go freshen up?"

"All right." Her shoulders slumped. "I can't apologize enough for bringing all this trouble to your door."

"It isn't your fault. And I don't regret you wandering into my life again one bit."

The worry lines on her forehead and the sadness in her eyes, churned his gut. She needed comforting. He stared at her lips but resisted crossing the line again. Instead, he settled for resting his hand on her forearm. "You'll feel better after a shower."

She walked away with her head down. He didn't regret his decision not to tell her sooner one bit. She'd needed a mental reprieve from the fear.

After the bathroom door shut, he dialed his friend's number.

Thomas picked up after two rings. "Hey, Jon. I haven't heard from you in quite a while. What's up?"

"I need your help. I'll pay for the first flight here and your time." Jon told him about Jessica, Bryce, and the situation with David.

"Shoot. That's horrible. I'll pack my equipment and catch a plane to Great Falls. Picking me up?"

"Definitely. Text me your arrival time."

"Will do. Never mind paying me. If I get in trouble with the law, you can call in a favor and bail me out."

Jon chuckled. Thomas freelanced and occasionally took work from shady sources. "Deal."

After hanging up, Jon joined Bryce in the living room. Bryce knelt at the coffee table as he drew a detailed picture of a horse that resembled Daisy with some crayons and a sketch pad leftover from his nephews' last visit.

Well-behaved and talented. What a kid.

Jessica came into the living room, dressed, with her hair wrapped in a towel. She leaned over Bryce's shoulder and smiled. "Is that Daisy?"

Bryce beamed up at her. "Yes. The colors aren't quite right. I could do a better job with my pastels and textured paper."

Jessica said, "It looks just like her."

"Tell you what, buddy." Jon patted him on the shoulder. "I'll pay you to draw one with your pastels. I'd love to hang it on my wall."

Bryce handed him the one he'd just finished. "Sure. You can have this one for now."

Jon accepted the drawing, met Jessica's eyes, and inclined his head towards the kitchen. "Thanks."

Jessica followed Jon. "Did you get a hold of your friend?"

"Yes, Thomas is landing in Great Falls this afternoon. We'll have to pick him up. It's about an hour and a half away."

"What's the next step? Can we go back to the rental house after Thomas arrives?"

"This house is much safer." Jon stuck his head around the corner to make sure Bryce hadn't followed. "I have weapons locked up in the basement."

"I wanted to settle Bryce into one place, but safety first. Thanks for letting us bunk here."

"I know it's not ideal. Another thing on safety, do not start your car. Car bombs can be rudimentary and still have devastating consequences."

Her face blanched. "What will he do if I hole up here, and he can't get to me?"

"Pardon the old expression, but we'll cross that bridge when we come to it. Let's get on the road soon in case we hit traffic."

Chapter Nine

Jon unlocked the commercial padlock on his barn and ushered Jessica and Bryce inside. "Hop in."

Once they were buckled in, he pushed the ignition button on the dash of his Dodge Ram and pulled out of the barn. As he turned off the dirt road heading towards the highway, Jon spotted an old green Ford truck in his rearview mirror. His instincts had been spot on.

He motioned for Jessica to come closer.

She leaned into the middle of the front seat. "What?"

He whispered in her ear. "I think he's following us in a stolen truck. I read about one matching that description in the paper this morning. He's staying far back to be unobtrusive. We'll take a side trip into town to lose him."

She whispered in his ear. "I don't know what I'd be doing without you."

His skin tingled from her warm breath. *Focus.* "Fate led you back to me to protect you. And I will. I can handle this."

She swallowed. "I trust you."

Jon drove into the main area of town. He needed a populated area with buildings and more vehicles on the road to blend in with. The old Ford truck followed the whole way. Jon took a fast right turn followed by a fast left, leading them to an alley behind some shops facing

Main Street.

Killing the engine, he leaned towards Jessica and whispered, "I don't have a doubt the truck was following us. Since he lost our trail, he'll double back this way, then we'll get a look at the driver."

She looked at him with wide eyes. "Okay."

Bryce took the headphones out of his ears and looked up from his tablet. "Why did we stop?"

"I decided to take a different way to Great Falls is all. We'll get moving when traffic clears." Telling a partial truth to a child wasn't something Jon enjoyed, but he'd spared Jessica from having to do it.

Bryce nodded and put his headphones back in his ears and tapped on his tablet.

The old truck crawled by their hiding spot. The driver wore a ball cap. Short, dark brown hair poked out from underneath it, and his head almost touched the roof of the cab. Thankfully, the man's attention was on the vehicles in front of him as he passed them by.

Jessica put one hand over her mouth and reached for Jon's hand with the other.

Jon's hand throbbed in her grip, but he wouldn't let go. Instead, he said softly. "It's him, isn't it?"

Her whole body trembled. She turned to face him. "Yes."

Jon squeezed her hand gently and spoke into her ear. "Don't worry. He didn't see us. We'll wait a few minutes. Black Dodge Rams are common around here. I'm heading back the way we came. I'll merge onto the highway at the next town. He won't know the terrain as well as I do."

She loosened her grip. "All right."

Jon lifted her hand to his mouth, brushed her skin

with his lips, and whispered. "I promise, nothing is going to happen to you or Bryce."

He started the engine, crept out of the alley, then searched the street in both directions. The old truck was nowhere to be seen. He jammed his foot on the accelerator, headed out of town the opposite way they came, and down a dirt road leading to the next town over from Lewistown.

"See? No sign of him anywhere, Jess."

"I know. I've been watching. Thank God you know what you're doing."

****

Once they put distance between themselves and Lewistown, the lump in Jessica's throat went away. *If it wasn't for Jon.* She shuddered, unable to finish the thought.

Jon accelerated to pass an elderly couple driving an old, dark blue Ford Taurus.

Bryce giggled. "Do that again, Jon."

Jon glanced into the rearview mirror. "Next time we come across someone driving too slowly, I'll do it again."

Bryce smiled in the backseat. "Are we getting food soon? I'm hungry."

Jon said, "We still have a bit of a drive left before we get to Great Falls."

"Mom, can I have a granola bar?"

Jessica dug through her purse with both hands. "We didn't pack snacks. What's the matter with me? How could I forget? It's a wonder I remembered a water bottle."

"Don't beat yourself up. I should have remembered, too. We won't forget next time. He'll be fine."

"I'm his mother. It's my responsibility to take care of him. I never forget things like this." Her hand closed over something rectangular in foil packaging. She sighed. "Here Bryce, I found a cereal bar."

"Thanks, Mom."

Jon said, "See? It's fine. Try to relax."

"No." She snapped. "Nothing about this situation is fine. I appreciate you trying to make me feel better, but I have to get a better handle on myself."

Jon focused on the road again. "Whatever you think."

Jessica remained silent the rest of the way to Great Falls, lost inside herself. The past few days spun her head around like a top. Between David chasing her and seemingly wanting her dead, her friend's murder, and Jon kissing and then rejecting her, she didn't know what to do next or how to feel.

She glanced over her shoulder at Bryce. His brows were furrowed as he stared at something on his tablet screen. Then she shifted her gaze to Jon. The planes of his face were tight, and a frown sat upon his lips.

She'd offended him, but she couldn't let him continue to say things were fine when they weren't. His lie by omission also bothered her, but how could she criticize him?

Jon put himself in the line of fire for them. He was caring, gentle, loyal, brave, and troubled—very troubled. The connection between them was undeniable, even now with everything going to hell in a hand basket as Aunt Debbie would say. But was he protecting them because of what happened with Cynthia, or did he still have the same feelings Jessica hadn't come to terms with yet herself?

She touched the hand he rested on the gear shifter. "I apologize for being a bit clipped with you earlier. This whole situation is overwhelming."

He glanced her way and smiled. "I should stop insisting everything is fine when we had David following us earlier. But I hate seeing you so disturbed. I just want to do something to ease your worries."

"It might be better for everyone involved if I took Bryce and left town."

"Jessica…"

She held up a finger. "Listen. If you remove the tracker, I can drive off in a different direction. Find another middle of nowhere town. I'm scared. Scared for me, for Bryce, for you. How am I supposed to live with myself if you get hurt trying to protect us? What if we stay, and David manages to get to me anyway? Or worse, Bryce?"

"I've made my choice. We're going to survive this together. I spent years dealing with scumbags like David. Besides, we'll have help. Thomas is amazing. You'll see. Promise you'll stay? At least for now?"

She squeezed his hand. "I promise. I don't want to go."

Clamping her lips shut, she barely stopped herself from admitting out loud she didn't want to leave him. What was she thinking? Her heart was with Adam, and Jon's heart was with Cynthia. Physical attraction couldn't erase that.

The stereotypical damsel in distress persona suited her to a tee, and she vowed to break free. Falling for her protector and cowering in the face of danger wouldn't make things any better.

No more hand holding or kissing. Friend zone in effect.

****

After a trip through the drive-thru for lunch, they waited in the airport parking lot.

Jon's phone pinged. "Thomas is here." He started the truck and pulled up to the terminal. "That's him. The shorter guy with the dark hair, the glasses, and the big black cases. I'll help him."

"I'll climb in the back with Bryce. You two can catch up."

Jon hopped out of the truck, grabbed Thomas's cases, and loaded them in the tailgate. "This is quite the load. What did you bring?"

"Anything we might need. Hopefully it's a false alarm."

"Unfortunately, no. We spotted David on the way here. He found Jess."

"Darn. Any leads?"

"No. We'll talk more when we get back to my place. Bryce doesn't know what's happening. Also, I want to be cautious about getting you into my house without being seen. We don't want you on David's radar. I'll text Chip. He can leave an extra hat and chaps in the barn, so you'll blend in with the ranch hands."

****

After they got back to the house, Jessica sat between Thomas and Jon at the kitchen peninsula while Bryce played out of earshot in the living room. "So, what's going on?"

Jon sipped from his mug. "I filled Thomas in on our situation. We need a good resolution image of

92

David's face to run through databases. See if he's wanted anywhere else. His behavior and his avoidance of all social media, tell me he has something to hide. Possibly more dead bodies."

The hair on her arms stood on end. She shivered. "That's a morbid thought. How are we getting David's photo?"

Jon paused. "I'd bet he's hiding in the wooded area somewhere behind the rental house. Our best chance is to get him on one of Thomas's cameras. They're tiny. David won't see them."

Thomas wiped his glasses with a soft cloth and placed them on his nose. "If he is camping in those woods, I'm going to be hard pressed to set up cameras around the little house and get footage without him knowing."

"That does pose a problem, but I have an idea. Since David followed us once, he'll likely try again. We could go out somewhere long enough to give you time to set up." Jon asked, "How long do you think you'll need?"

"Twenty minutes at the most for a small one-story house. Of course, the longer you can give me, the better. If I have time, I'll grab anything Jessica and Bryce need from the house."

Jon sipped his coffee. "That's doable. I bet we could tie him up for at least half an hour. Maybe we can get ice cream after dinner. On a hot, sunny day the lines should be long."

Thomas stood. "Sounds like a plan. Can we shuffle things around in your office and make room for my video monitors? Probably the best spot for me to work unseen."

"Sure. We'll do that now."

****

Jessica followed on tiptoe as they left the kitchen. She leaned against the wall around the corner from where they'd stowed Thomas's equipment. She suspected they'd say more out of earshot. Sure enough, their conversation continued in hushed voices.

Thomas said, "What are you going to do if this doesn't work?"

"I'd be left with no choice but to hunt him on my own. I've loved Jess since we were kids. I can't let anything happen to her."

Jessica sidestepped away from the entrance and collapsed into a dining room chair. She flashed back to the morning of Adam's wake before guests arrived. Standing with Bryce cradled in her arms, she had stared down at her husband's lifeless body in his casket. Her mind conjured up an image of Jon laying in Adam's place. The notion of Jon initiating a one-on-one encounter with David sucked the air out of her lungs.

Don't let your mind go there. Get it together.

Having nothing to contribute to the investigation made her the third wheel. Determined to find a way to be useful, she glanced around Jon's oak wood kitchen. *I'll make them a nice home cooked meal.*

As Bryce worked on another sketch, she browned ground beef, boiled potatoes, and shucked fresh kernels of corn off a cob for Shepherd's Pie. The unique blend of spices she added to the beef came from Aunt Debbie's recipe.

At least Debbie isn't in the middle of this mess. Glad we didn't stay with her too long.

****

After dinner, Jon ruffled Bryce's hair. "Do you have room for ice cream after the amazing food your mom made?"

Bryce set his fork down, abandoning the rest of his dinner. "Anytime."

"I'll take that as a yes. Ready, Jess?"

She sighed. "As ready as I'll ever be. Go grab your shoes, buddy."

They climbed into the van, then Jon backed out of the barn.

Jessica clenched her hands together in her lap. Her body language screamed stress. She wouldn't be able to keep David a secret from Bryce much longer, but it was her decision if and when to tell him.

Jon kept his foot on the brake as they drove through the main gate onto the rural road, restraining his Ram from taking off, giving David plenty of time to see them leaving.

Sure enough, after he turned onto the road, an old car trailed behind them. He couldn't make out the driver at a distance, but whoever it was continued to follow. They came upon a traffic light as they neared the main part of town. Instead of driving through a yellow light, Jon braked jerking them forward in their seats.

The mystery driver stopped a full car length back, but not far enough away to conceal his identity.

A quick glance in the rearview mirror confirmed Jon's suspicions. "Send Thomas a text. He's driving a beat-up, old Buick this time, but it's him. That car could've made those tire tracks I found the other day."

Jessica turned her head.

He cupped her cheek directing her head forward.

"Don't look. We don't want him to know we're on to him."

"All right." Her hands shook as she typed the message and pressed send. "It's done. Now we need to do our part."

"We've got this."

Jon drove the speed limit and took the longest route possible to kill time. David stayed a few cars back. Jon took an obvious right turn into the drive thru line. Ten cars idled in front of them.

He smiled. "This is perfect. Thomas should have plenty of time to get everything done. David parked near the exit. He's waiting for us."

Jon faced forward and swept his eyes sideways to the mirrors every few seconds to keep an eye on David. The drive thru line crept forward at the rate of one car for every two to three minutes. They'd already given Thomas his allotted time. Their mission was a success.

Jessica moved into the middle of the bench seat and spoke into Jon's ear. "Something's bothering me about this whole situation."

Her smooth bare leg resting against his, the side of her breast pushing into his arm, and her warm breath in his ear, stirred his body to attention. *Mind out of the gutter. Focus!* He turned his head to whisper in her ear. "What?"

"Why would he risk making himself known by moving the lawnmower key and following us?"

"I've come across a few like him over the years." Jon sighed. "He gets a kick out of taunting you. He's circling you, like a predator would its prey, studying you and your routines, looking for an opening. He probably thinks he's too smart to get caught. No way he believes we're smart enough to know he followed us."

"Yikes. I wish I hadn't asked."

Jon glanced toward the entrance. "Text Thomas. David's leaving."

Chapter Ten

David slammed his hand on the dashboard of his stolen car. "What a waste of time!"

He'd followed, waiting for an opportunity to grab Jessica, but they'd gone to a drive thru. He pulled onto the main road to regroup. The fun of the chase dwindled by the day, but he'd get her sooner rather than later. Patience and persistence were of the utmost importance. Rash actions led to undesirable messes to clean.

Sarah was the perfect example of that.

The image of the perfect, doting husband had kept him above suspicion when tragedy befell his chosen victims in the past. But he'd majorly screwed things up for himself when he lost control and accidentally hit Sarah in the head too hard.

But if Jessica had minded her own business, instead of staring in other people's trucks and driveways in the dead of night, he would've gotten away with it. Selling the house would've seemed the reasonable thing to do, and he could've moved on.

Instead, he'd have to dodge the police and buy a new set of identification and reinvent himself after Jessica was dead. Until then, he'd hunt her and frighten her out of her wits. Once he got his hands on her, he'd make her beg for death. After all, on top of being a woman, she was also a witness, and witnesses could not be allowed to live.

David smiled. She must be so scared, leaving everything behind, running and hiding behind Jon Kent. Blood travelled south of his waistline. Nothing turned him on more than a petrified, overpowered woman.

On the way to Montana, he'd fantasized about finding her alone, covering her face with a rag soaked in chloroform, binding her limbs, and finding a nice, secluded place in the woods. A place so far away from people, no one would hear her scream or beg for mercy. Someplace where she'd die a slow, burning death in a barrel, and what little remained of her would never be found.

He'd planned on accomplishing this task within twenty-four hours of arriving to make his absence in Cochrane less obvious. Instead, she'd forced him to stay. She'd pay for that, too. But how?

Aunt Debbie.

David drove out of town towards Debbie's farm. What would he do to Aunt Debbie? He cringed at the thought of raping a woman in her sixties. *Gross.*

Fulfilling that need for control would have to wait until he captured Jessica. In the meantime, he wanted to inspire more fear in her. She needed to be made to feel less untouchable at the ranch with the glorified cop who couldn't save his own wife.

He covered his nose with his arm to smother a sneeze, preventing the spread of his DNA inside the vehicle. *Stupid FBI agent.* His nose was still full of dust from the previous night spent in the basement of the town hall.

No electronic records of the mystery man guarding Jessica existed anywhere. David had spent hours combing through old file boxes until he struck pay dirt. He'd found a copy of an old census form completed by a Sally Kent in 1987, living at the same address as his mystery man. A property she currently owned. She'd had two sons born four years apart. The other son, Jamie, was listed at a different address leaving Jon as the only remaining option.

A legal search pulled up old cases containing references to an FBI agent named Jon Kent. Fitting the pieces together proved to be child's play. Jon had abandoned his career to hide out on his family's ranch in Montana after his wife's disappearance. Now that was poetic justice. Losing his wife served him right for sticking his nose where it didn't belong.

David turned onto an old gravel path, forking off the road Debbie's farm stood on. He pulled over on the grassy shoulder, took his binoculars, and followed a path through the coniferous forest across from Debbie's property.

He hid behind a spruce tree, poked his head around the trunk, and lifted his binoculars to his face. No sign of anyone in the farmhouse windows or out in the fields, but Debbie's truck was parked beside her house.

The frigging old bat's always home.

He sprinted across the road, descended into a deep ditch, and kneeled.

She had a chicken coop and a barn fifty meters away from her house. As he suspected when he'd roamed in the dark on the night Jessica arrived at Debbie's house, both showed signs of age in their weathered, distressed wood. They'd go up like matchsticks. In a small town where nothing bad ever happened, fire and police were quick to assume no foul play.

Jon and Jessica would know he was responsible but wouldn't be able to prove it. Besides, what could a retired super cop do?

Burning Debbie's animals alive would be a nice demonstration of the misery he could cause, but would it make enough of a statement? Such a piddling fire wouldn't compare to the majestic ones he'd set in the past. Maybe killing the animals wasn't going far enough. Maybe Debbie should die.

He focused the binoculars on the house. The old, wooden back door leading to the deck had a simple deadbolt lock. If he waited until the middle of the night, he could pick the lock and arrange an accident.

His cheeks hurt from smiling as he considered his options. Household accidents happened all the time. Stoves left on, fires left burning in fireplaces, carbon monoxide poisoning, gas leaks — his pulse accelerated and his skin heated.

Oh, the glorious options.

The back door swung open, and Debbie stepped outside. She shielded her eyes from the sun with a hand and glanced around her property. Her sight travelled uncomfortably close to his hiding place, almost as if she sensed his presence.

He dropped onto his stomach. Debbie always made an appearance whenever he was around.

I'll have to be careful with this one. She's a hell of a lot more perceptive than her stupid niece.

The barn door creaked open and slammed shut.

He lifted his head and peered over the ditch.

Debbie was nowhere to be seen.

He sprinted across the road, slowing to a brisk

walk in the cover of the forest.

A raven cawed shrill notes, overpowering the delicate song of the other birds.

He tilted his head to the trees. "Shut up, dammit! I'm trying to think."

Wings fluttered, as he passed under a tree, and another burst of shrill cries rang through his ears. Warm, white liquid landed on his head, dripped down his ear, onto his right shoulder, and down the front of his black tee.

"Damn you!" He shook his fist at the raven as it flew away. "That's good luck you know!"

He took his shirt off and wiped the bird droppings from his head and ear. When he finished, he bundled the tee into a ball and launched it into a cluster of trees.

With the raven gone, he could concentrate on the decision at hand.

Arson or murder?

If she heard him fiddling in the lock, she'd only have herself to worry about. She might have time to call 911 or get her rifle. But if she found her barn on fire, her main priority would be to free her animals, distracting her, giving him plenty of time to escape.

His main priority was not to get caught. If the RCMP found Sarah's body, Jessica could ruin him, not Debbie. Jessica had to die.

He stepped out of the forest and onto the dirt road. The sun kissed his naked upper torso, yet another reminder of why losing his freedom wasn't an option.

He climbed in the Buick, used an old screwdriver to turn the ignition, then drove past Debbie's farm. The only neighbor lived miles away around a bend in the road. No way they would see or hear anything before

Debbie did.

A warning siren wailed on the car radio. A computerized voice described a severe thunderstorm warning for later that night.

What a happy coincidence.

Timed right, lightning would be determined as the cause of the fire. Perhaps if he got lucky, smoke inhalation would do Debbie in.

David took backroads to the abandoned, yet sturdy barn he'd discovered on a large acreage south of Lewistown. The old building suited his needs well. At least twenty acres of forest separated him from the property owners' newer house and barns. His own truck fit inside the barn with plenty of room to spare. He kept the two old pieces of junk he'd stolen behind the barn. He'd yet to encounter the landowners, but if they did happen to drive by, nothing would look out of place.

While he waited for the storm to arrive, he opened a gas can. He lowered his nose to the opening and closed his eyes as he inhaled the glorious fumes. A delicious odor he associated with victory. He wet cotton rags in a small amount of gasoline and wrung them out well. The cloth would burn quickly leaving little to no evidence. Whatever traces remained, would be eradicated by the wind and rain.

As he sat eating a cold dinner of trail mix and beef jerky, darkness descended, and the wind whistled through the cracks in the barn. He set his food aside and swung open the old wooden door.

The wind plastered his clothes to his skin as he lifted his eyes to the sky. Large black clouds sprawled from one end of the horizon to the other, billowing in from the west, and sagging with moisture. A long bolt of lightning forked in the distance.

David smiled. *Perfect. This storm is going to be a doozy.*

He grabbed his lighter and his bag of rags, then set out in the old Buick towards Debbie's farm. He parked in the same spot on the dirt path. Then taking cover under the trees across from Debbie's property, he waited for the storm to move overhead.

Thunder boomed, shaking the ground beneath his feet. The wind intensified, whipping the hood of his coat off his head. And branches and leaves danced around his face grazing his skin.

Ignoring the discomfort, he hurried across the dirt road, crept into the ditch, and waited for lightning to strike. The corners of his mouth lifted, visualizing the thrill of lighting his rags on fire. Then the clouds opened. Hail stones the size of quarters pelted his head and shoulders, stinging and numbing his skin.

Covering his head with his arms, he cursed under his breath. "Dammit. I hate women." *This is all her fault!*

Jessica had caused this by making him resort to these measures. He added this latest inconvenience to the list of offenses she needed to be punished for.

Lightning brightened the area around Debbie's barn. David inhaled its metallic odor as the static raised the hair on his arms, and he laughed. Adrenaline pumped through his veins, the pain of the hail all but forgotten.

He climbed out of the ditch and raced to the barn. The weathered, wooden door creaked as he opened it, but Debbie wouldn't hear the noise inside her house over the thunder and the hail. He placed his rags on a blanket of hay inside the door, cackling as he flicked the lighter and flames danced in his hand.

****

As the storm approached, Debbie rocked in her favorite, floral-patterned chair drinking tea, dressed in her pajamas and slippers.

The winds picked up, gaining strength by the second, vibrating the windows in their frames. A powerful crack of thunder shook the small house on its foundation, then an onslaught of hail pounded the roof.

Debbie jumped out of her chair. *My animals. Did I put them in their stalls?*

She shoved her arms into her jacket, jumped into her rubber boots, then flew out the back door under the cover of her awning to the deck railing. Upon finding her fields empty except for a coating of hail stones, she placed a hand on her heaving chest.

Thank heavens.

The stones slamming into the ground became smaller and smaller, turning into a heavy downpour. The wind carried the rain under the awning, soaking Debbie's cotton pajama pants, and chilling her to the bone.

She turned to go inside. The distinctive whiny creak of her barn door halted her steps. She peeked around the house. Lightning flashed in the sky, illuminating her field.

A man dressed all in black slithered into her barn.

Hell in a hand basket! David!

She clenched her fists and bared her teeth at the monster who hunted her niece. Debbie sprinted inside, flung open her coat closet, then grabbed and cocked her rifle. On her way out the door, she snatched her cell phone off the kitchen counter. She leaned over the deck railing and gazed through the sight post. Smoke poured out of the barn.

No! Not my animals! Where is the bastard?

She shifted towards the chicken coop a few feet to the right of the barn. The man in black approached her chickens. She had the right to protect her property and protect it she would.

Debbie wiped her wet trigger hand on the front of her pants. Aiming for his center mass, she pulled the trigger. Thunder boomed overhead, muffling the crack of the rifle. Wind carried the bullet to the right. The man flinched and went down on one knee.

Yes! Got you, you sick bastard.

Debbie maintained her watch hoping he'd collapse and lose consciousness, but he didn't.

He stood and took off at a limping run, disappearing into the ditch, then re-emerging on the other side.

She curled her finger around the trigger a second time, fired, and missed.

He was too far out of range. He disappeared into the woods.

Slinging her rifle over her shoulder, Debbie sprinted down the deck stairs into her yard. The fire fed by the wind, spread from the inside of the door to the roof, encapsulating the whole exterior structure.

My animals!

She covered her mouth with her pajama top and ran into the barn.

Her eyes burned from the smoke, and the flames licked at the edges of her cow's stall. She opened the door and Bonnie, her dairy cow, ran outside without prompting. Her horses were another matter. They neighed and glanced around frantically but refused to leave what they perceived as the safety of their stalls.

She grabbed each horse by their halter and tugged. "Come on, Sunny and Serge. You'll die in here."

She tugged with all her might. The horses stepped forward. "That's right, come with your mama."

Smoke filtered through the thin fabric of her pajama top. She coughed and coughed, her lungs craving oxygen, but she trudged forward pulling the weight of the two scared horses behind her. Her head swam.

Once outside, the horses stopped resisting and allowed her to lead them into a fenced area behind the house.

Falling on her knees, she gulped fresh air greedily into her lungs.

Wood crackled as the flames travelled from the front of the barn all the way to the back. The wind gusted, carrying sparks in the direction of the chicken coop.

Her heart lurched. *My chickens!*

Debbie stood, and the world tilted. She fought her balance, ran to the garden hose beside her deck, then turned the water on full blast. She drenched the area between the barn and the chicken coop, praying the fire wouldn't make the leap with the winds whipping through the air.

Getting a dozen chickens out of the coop with nowhere else to contain them would be impossible. She held the hose with one hand, dialed 911 with the other, and used her shoulder to hold her phone in place.

A male operator's voice penetrated the wind

whistling through the trees and the crackling of the fire. "What's your emergency?"

She smothered a cough. "My address is 5 Camden Road. A man set my barn on fire. The whole thing is in flames."

"What's your name?"

"Debbie Johnson."

"Ms. Johnson, help is on the way. I'm sending police, fire, and EMS. Keep a safe distance from the fire. The smoke coming from the barn may be toxic. Sit tight. They won't be long."

Debbie ended the call and shoved her phone in her pocket. Staying away from the fire wasn't an option, she had to keep the sparks from spreading to her chickens.

The rain intensified and the wind shifted directions, blowing at her back, sending the embers and smoke away from the house. The fresh air soothed her sore throat and burning lungs, and the world righted itself again. If she could keep the fire from spreading until help arrived, she wouldn't lose more than the barn.

Wet to the bone, she shivered from head to toe. To pass time, she counted the seconds between each flash of lightning and clap of thunder. When she got to thirty seconds, faint sirens wailed in the distance.

With numb fingers, she turned the tap off and coiled the hose around the reel. She shoved her hands in her pockets as a fire truck and a water truck drove onto her lawn.

The firefighters connected their hoses and doused the flames. The barn collapsed from the weight of the water, reduced to a pile of charred wood and debris. More sirens blared in the distance, getting closer by the second.

Tears threatened, but rather than give in to them, Debbie took shelter under the awning over her deck. Soon, she'd be bombarded with questions, but what bothered her most was the attack had nothing to do with her. Debbie's blood boiled.

David had wanted to send a message to Jessica and had forced Debbie to deliver it.

I hope that bullet hurt, you sick bastard.

Chapter Eleven

"Bryce is out for the count. I'm surprised he went down with the storm raging." Jessica sat next to Jon on the sofa. "Don't think I'm far behind. What an exhausting day." Her phone vibrated on the coffee table.

Jon said, "Let it go to voicemail. Tomorrow's a new day."

She picked up her phone and checked the caller ID. "Debbie wouldn't be calling at this time for nothing." She swiped her screen. "Hello, Aunt Debbie. How are you?"

"I've been better." Debbie's voice was scratchy and muffled. "I think David decided to pay me a visit. A man dressed in black lit my barn on fire. I got the animals out, but all that's left of the barn is a pile of embers."

Jessica turned to face Jon. "Oh my God. Are you okay?"

"Yes, don't worry. I'm fine."

Jon mouthed, "What's wrong?"

Jessica found her voice. "Barn fire. Are you sure you're all right?"

"The paramedics checked me over and gave me oxygen for the smoke inhalation. I'm fine now, bit of a sore throat. Hopefully, David isn't. I shot him."

Jessica sat up straight. "You did? Where?"

"Somewhere in the leg. He was running and it was windy, so I couldn't get a clean shot. He stopped and flinched. Too bad he was in good enough shape to get away."

Jon handed Jessica a tissue.

She dabbed her eyes. "I'm so relieved you're okay."

Jon patted Jessica's knee. "Let me talk to Debbie."

Jessica said, "Jon wants to talk to you."

"Sure."

Jon took the phone. "Hi, Debbie. Would you mind if I sent my friend Thomas over there to see if he can find David's DNA? He'll bring you back here to stay. You aren't safe there."

Debbie sighed. "Yes, please. Much appreciated. I hate asking you for anything after all you've done, but could my animals board at your ranch for now? I'll take care of them and pay rent until I can get my barn rebuilt."

"I would be happy to keep them, but I refuse to take payment from a dear family friend. I'll send Chip and Thomas for you and the animals."

"Thanks. Sheriff Hank wants to talk. I've got to go."

Jon hung up and wrapped his arms around Jessica. "Poor Debbie. Don't worry we'll take care of her."

Jessica rested her head on Jon's chest, closed her eyes, and inhaled his musky scent. She clung to the cotton fabric of his shirt and listened to his heartbeat. "Thanks for inviting Aunt Debbie to stay. I'd have been worried sick about her."

"She's like family to me, too. I hate to leave you, but I need to go tell Thomas what happened and take over surveillance detail while he goes to Debbie's."

Jessica lifted her head and met his eyes. "Go. Do what you need to do. I'll pull myself together. We have to put an end to this. I can't bear anyone else I care about getting hurt in the crossfire."

****

David drove from the scene of his crime using only his left leg. His right leg throbbed, and he scowled. *What sort of master criminal gets shot by an old lady?*

But he'd accomplished his mission. Jessica would be plagued with worries over whose house he'd torch next. Maybe Jon's with all of them inside.

David turned down an old gravel side road, then pulled over to assess the damage. He gritted his teeth as he widened the bullet hole in his black jeans. The wound bled but not at a life-threatening rate. The bullet had only grazed him, taking a chunk of flesh from the outside of his thigh. He'd require stitches and didn't have the luxury of being able to seek out a doctor.

Based on Debbie's statement, the police might check the local hospitals. If they believed her wild tale about a man wearing black in the dark out in the middle of nowhere. His only option to deal with his wounded leg was the emergency kit at his hideout.

He ripped a strip of fabric from the bottom of his shirt and dug a roll of duct tape out of the glove box. He pressed the fabric to his thigh to slow the bleeding. Breathing through red-hot, searing pain, he wrapped the duct tape around his leg to hold the fabric in place.

Blood dripped on the seat and the upholstery. Another inconvenience.

The car would have to be burned to destroy the DNA his blood left behind. Thankfully, the rain would wash away any blood that dripped from his leg on the way to the car. His DNA falling into the wrong hands before his business with Jessica concluded could spell disaster.

He pulled onto the road. The almost bald tires on the Buick struggled for traction, as heavy rain pelted the windshield. It took him double the time to get back to the abandoned barn.

David tightened the hood of his jacket, then climbed out of the Buick, wincing as he put his weight on his right leg. He limped at a run towards the barn, then shut the door behind him to keep out the rain, plunging him into total darkness.

He groped along the wall to where he'd parked his own truck. He opened the tailgate, felt around in the dark for his lantern, then flicked the on switch, bathing the area in dull light.

He pulled the medical kit and a bottle of scotch out of the backseat of his truck. Cursing Debbie to hell, he sat in a lawn chair and took off his pants. He took a large swig of scotch, poured some over dental floss and a sewing needle to disinfect them, and lastly over the wound.

He grimaced, clenched his teeth, and slammed his foot against the floor. "Dammit, that burns!"

His hand shook as he threaded the needle. He yanked his belt out of his black jeans and bit down on the leather to avoid biting his tongue. With immense willpower, he stuck the needle through his skin for the first time.

"Ahhhh!" Tears swam in his eyes and streamed down his cheeks, clouding his vision.

Throughout the twenty minutes it took to stitch his

wound, he managed the pain by drinking scotch and visualizing Jessica and all the ways he would torture her before ending her life. He'd yank out her finger nails one by one, shove painful instruments into her orifices, then he'd slice her to ribbons.

His hands fumbled with the dental floss. After three tries, he managed to tie it and snip off the excess length. He glanced at the bottle of scotch, and only half of the amber liquid remained.

The room spun and his body numbed, until the bottle dropped from his hand. All conscious thoughts faded, and everything went black.

****

David stood in a familiar little bedroom. His bedroom once upon a time, in the ramshackle house he lived in until age twelve, and the scene of his first masterpiece.

Gazing in the cracked mirror hanging above his rickety old desk, he studied his reflection and saw himself as an adult.

"How the hell is this possible?"

His mother slurred. "Bradley. It's dinner time. Come eat."

His heart raced in his chest.

This isn't right. How did I get here? How is she here?

His palms and armpits moistened as he left his room and turned the corner into the kitchen. His mother looked as awful as she always had—skinny and haggard, with dirty clothes and torn stockings, matted hair full of blood, and makeup smeared all over her face.

"Sit, Bradley. Mama's got your dinner here."

He sat at the filthy, gouged, wooden table without answering.

She staggered to the table with a bowl of processed mac and cheese, smelling as if she'd just climbed out of a man's bed. How she managed to stand, let alone make food was a testament to how often she went on benders.

David ran his hand along a scar on his hair line from a time he'd tried to climb onto the counter to reach boxes of food in higher cupboards. He remembered blood seeping into his eyes and crying. Needing help, he ran to the small house next door, and knocked.

An older couple had answered and ushered him inside. Mrs. DeGuire had held a cloth to his head to stop the bleeding, gently mopped the blood out of his hair, and wiped his face.

He remembered the delicious aroma of her spaghetti sauce wafting through the air and staring at the pot on the stove.

Mr. Deguire had followed his gaze and invited him to dinner. From that day on, they shared what little they had, even though they were as poor as he was.

Mrs. DeGuire was a saint in David's eyes. The one woman exempted from his scorn. David had repaid their generosity by sending them a money order for $500,000 with a letter of thanks. Half of the proceeds from his second masterpiece as a young adult.

His mother dropped the bowl of food in front of him and it teetered in a circle before settling.

He wrinkled his nose.

The pasta was full of clumps of powdered cheese and gave off a sour, rancid odor. The milk had gone bad days ago, and she'd been too drunk to notice.

"Bradley, why aren't you eating your dinner, you brat?"

His mother's words stirred memories of similar meals, and all the times he'd gone without food for days. His heartbeat thudded in his ears and what little control he had vanished.

He stood and threw his bowl across the small kitchen. The bowl shattered and lumpy, cheesy noodles slid down the wall, leaving an orange trail behind. "Shut up! You're a drunk and a shitty excuse for a mother!"

She staggered over to him, pulled her arm back, and swung.

He grabbed her arm and twisted it behind her back, smiling as her bones crackled and shattered.

She shrieked. "Stop! You're hurting me!"

I'm hurting her? Seriously? "No, you selfish bitch. I hate you! It's your fault the kids at school made fun of my dirty, too small clothes, and I had no friends. For years, I had to beg the neighbors for food."

He shoved her into a chair.

Tears, stained black from her overstated eye makeup, fell down her face. "Bradley don't hurt me! I'll sober up. I'll be a better mother."

He shook his head. "No. Knocking you out and burning you alive in this horrible shack was the best decision I ever made. At least in foster care people fed and clothed me, and I didn't have to worry about where my next meal was coming from. Sure, I endured beatings for rule breaking. But I got Christmas gifts for the first time at age twelve!"

"I'm sorry," she cried. "Please, just one more chance."

"Burn in Hell, Mother!"

He fisted his hands together and hammered them down on the top of her head.

She went limp in the chair and landed face first on the table in front of her. Blood trickled out of her nose onto the wood.

How is this all happening? He shrugged. *Who cares? I can enjoy killing her all over again.*

David turned the gas burner on high underneath the pot of rotten food, and the pasta blackened to a crisp. He draped a filthy dish towel over the stove near the burner, smiling as it caught fire. He covered his face with his shirt as a filter against the smoke, then sprinted to the bathroom.

To make sure she had no chance of escaping her fate, he poured a trail of nail polish remover from the top of the stove to her body. He placed the rest of the bottle near the hot stove, something a drunk woman might do.

The flames followed the trail of liquid to his mother's legs. He'd hit her so hard that she didn't wake. Before leaving through the back door, he took one last peek at the woman who had made his childhood hell.

He grinned as her clothes caught fire. The smoke in the air thickened, and the pungent odor of burnt flesh crept into his nostrils, turning his stomach.

He twisted and pulled on the knob, but the door didn't open.

What the hell? This door opened when I was twelve. Why won't it open now?

He threw his shoulder into the door. It still didn't budge.

The fire had engulfed his mother from head to toe.

Smoke so thick, he could barely see let alone breathe, enveloped the small house.

He slammed his whole body into the door. It flew open revealing black nothingness on the other side.

David tumbled forward, free-falling into the abyss. He groped around frantically, searching for something to hold onto to break his fall.

The blackness transformed into images of all thirteen women he'd killed, his mother included, then Jessica in the grocery store, pushing her cart toward him.

****

His lawn chair toppled over, and he landed hard on his right side. Sharp pains shot through his injured arm. He opened his eyes and found only darkness. Once they adjusted, he could make out the walls of the barn and his truck.

He shivered in his sweat-soaked clothes. Standing, he swayed on his feet. His head swam from all the liquor.

The world tilted as he took slow steps to his truck. Climbing in the front seat, he turned the key. The voices on the radio calmed his racing heart. He grabbed the woolen blanket from the back seat, covered up, and continued listening.

Damn scotch!

Why couldn't he tie one on without reliving memories of that witch?

He gritted his teeth. If Jessica hadn't taken off and fled to Lewistown, then he wouldn't have had to start that fire, and he wouldn't have gotten shot by Debbie, and he wouldn't have had to drink that scotch.

He fisted the blanket in his left hand.

It's time to get serious and stop dithering around.

Chapter Twelve

Debbie approached Jon's cattle truck pulling up as the sheriff and the fire chief drove away. Two men including Chip, climbed out, unlatched the back doors, and swung them open.

Chip tipped his hat. "Howdy, Debbie. I'll have your horses and cow loaded in a jiffy."

"Thank you," she called out to his retreating form.

The other man approached with latex gloves on, and a briefcase in his hands. "Hi, I'm Thomas. You must be Debbie. It would have been nice to meet you under better circumstances."

She forced a smile. "It's nice to meet you as well, Thomas. Thanks for coming to help."

"No problem. I noticed the police and fire chief leaving. Did they find any evidence?"

"Nothing. But I don't think they looked too closely. The fire chief ruled the fire an act of nature caused by lightning. Even after I told him and Sheriff Hank, I saw a man light the fire."

"Did you tell them about Jessica's situation?"

"Yes. Hank said he'd look for David, but I doubt he'll find him. I'm sure you and Jon already checked all the obvious places."

"Can you show me where David was when you shot him, and which way he ran?"

She led him to the area between the pile of debris

that used to be her barn and the chicken coop. "He was over here when I shot him. He ran around the left side of the coop. Follow me. I'll take the same path." She crossed the lawn and pointed into the ditch along the side of the road. "The last place I saw him was by this tree before he took off across the road."

Thomas followed the path she took with his high-powered flashlight trained to the ground. "Your memory serves you well. We have a trail of men's footprints in the wet ground. Let's follow them."

Debbie let Thomas take the lead. He emerged under the tree she'd indicated. The tree leaned left, sheltering the ground beneath.

Thomas's flashlight illuminated a splotch of red on the base of the trunk. "This looks like blood. Hopefully the rain hasn't spoiled our sample. I'll swab and ship it express to a friend of mine who works in a DNA lab in Colorado. I'll call the delivery service on the way to Jon's. We should know by tomorrow if we managed to get a DNA profile."

Debbie squatted for a better look. "I sure do hope this leads to something. This David is a loose cannon. What will he do next?"

****

Jessica wrapped her arms around Debbie after she came inside Jon's house and hung on tight. "Thank God you're all right. This is all my fault."

"Oh, Jess. Stop blaming yourself. It's David's fault, not yours."

Jon approached them with steaming mugs of tea. "Why don't we have a seat in the living room?"

Debbie sank into the couch and sighed with her mug cradled in her hands. "Thanks for all this, Jon, and for taking such good care of my niece and nephew. I'm surprised he didn't go after you at the little house, Jess."

"I slept here last night. Bryce fell asleep on Jon's lap, so we borrowed the guest rooms. I'll squeeze in with Bryce so you can have a room to yourself."

"What about Thomas?" Debbie asked.

"Thomas will be staying in my office," Jon said. "He's a night owl. He won't be leaving his camera feeds and equipment until someone takes over in the morning. I brought him a carafe of coffee and donuts earlier."

Debbie said, "Thomas seems to know what he's doing. He found the blood within five minutes, yet the locals found nothing in an hour."

Jon said, "I'm not surprised. Thomas used to work for the Bureau. He freelances now for whoever needs him."

Debbie sipped her tea. "Well, I'm sure glad he's a friend of yours. What else have you been up to?"

"We ran a bit of a sting earlier, Aunt Debbie," Jessica said. "We got David to follow us into town so Thomas could set up cameras and motion detectors across the street. He found a tracker on my car."

Debbie sat up straight and glanced around. "What about the ranch?"

Jon said, "Don't worry. We're wired up here, too."

Debbie sighed and leaned back into the couch. "Good. I feel a whole lot better knowing we're all together and safe."

Jon frowned. "I should have anticipated David would go after you."

Debbie tsked. "Stop apologizing, you two. The animals are fine. My insurance will cover the barn and they're quick to build."

Jessica swallowed around a huge lump. Her aunt put on a brave face, but she had to be rattled. "Is there anything else we can do to help?"

"I'm fine. The tea did wonders. I'm ready for bed if you wouldn't mind showing me to my room."

Jon stood. "Sure. Follow me."

After they left the room, Jessica frowned into her tea. She understood after multiple conversations with Adam that victims always blamed themselves, something he hated witnessing more than the violence. Despite this, guilt, all-consuming and heavy, weighed her down like a block of lead.

How could she live with herself if David succeeded in harming people she loved?

The couch sagged beside her. She jumped and turned to face Jon. The agony he'd endured since his wife's murder hit her full force. He had to live with himself knowing one of his enemies killed his wife. They shared a profound, dark understanding.

"I didn't mean to startle you."

"It's not your fault. My head wasn't here. I was thinking to myself, what would've happened if I hadn't gotten up to open my bedroom window four nights ago? David got away with murder regardless. All I did was put myself and other innocent people on his hit list."

"Don't think that way. By witnessing his crime, you may save countless other people from becoming his next victims. He did this tonight to get to you, but you can't let him. We have him off balance and so far, our defenses are sound. If he thought he had a chance of getting to you here, then he wouldn't have gone after

Debbie."

She stared deep into his eyes, willing him to accept her next words. "You understand why my mind is going there because yours does the same. Neither one of us is to blame. If you didn't know that on some level, then I don't think you'd be able to function."

"You're probably right. In this moment, I'm overwhelmed with the urge to protect you no matter the cost because I can't lose you. But I also feel like I can't let myself get too involved because my loyalty lies with Cynthia. At the same time, she'd hate it if I didn't move on, but whoever targeted her is still out there and could come after you."

She lifted a hand to reach for him, then stopped to reconsider. Whenever their skin touched, the pot stirred, making things harder for them both. She gritted her teeth at how the idea of him hunting her nemesis fed her nightmares.

The heck with it.

Jessica cupped his stubbly cheek. "I understand, but who's going to protect you? If the DNA doesn't turn up anything, you'll hunt David. Don't deny it, I overheard you with Thomas earlier."

He closed his eyes and leaned into her hand. "It could very well come to that."

Her voice hitched as she confessed. "I've lost too much in my life to lose you. I don't know how much more I can handle."

He brushed her lips with a feather light kiss, then touched his forehead to hers. "It'll be all right. We'll figure this out. When I say, this, I don't mean David."

"I know, Jon."

"There's something special between us. Even

though it's been fifteen years, my feelings for you haven't faded."

"But a lot has changed. We aren't the same people."

Jon said, "Definitely not. I'm damaged, and you're damaged. But we share the same pain."

"I know. I feel guilty moving on because my heart belongs to Adam like yours belongs to Cynthia. But I'm starting to think maybe we have room to love them and each other?"

"I think so."

She smiled. "One day at a time. No expectations."

"Yes, that's all I can manage, too."

Jessica yawned. "It's been quite a day."

"Why don't you sleep in my bed? I've got a body pillow I can put in the middle. I promise I won't try anything. You can't fit comfortably with Bryce in the single bed."

"I feel awful about last night. Waking you and asking you to stay."

Jon stood and offered a hand to help her stand. "I know. That's why I offered my bed. Maybe you'll be more at ease and the nightmares won't come.

Chapter Thirteen

Jon awoke to the first rays of daylight shining through the window into his eyes. He blinked, yawned, then glanced at the clock on his phone.

Ugh. Five AM. Time to get up and relieve Thomas.

He rolled over to face Jessica. Her eyes were shut, and her face was relaxed. With any luck, she'd sleep for a while after waking them twice with nightmares. He resisted the urge to move a strand of hair veiling her eyelid and climbed out of bed.

She couldn't withstand this torment for much longer. He needed to end her suffering.

He showered, shaved, and dressed in jeans and a tee, then headed to the basement.

Thomas studied something on his computer with his face an inch from the screen. An encouraging sign. "Good morning. How was the night shift?"

"Things got eventful about twenty minutes ago. I caught David on camera coming out of the woods and creeping around the rental house."

Way too close for comfort. "What was he up to?"

"He scouted out the electrical panel and looked in the windows. He was walking with a slight limp. Debbie must've missed an artery. I already suspected as much from what little blood I found at her farm."

"Did he touch anything with his hands?"

"He wore gloves, but I got a good shot of his face."

Thomas hit the enter key. "I put the image into the facial recognition system. FedEx should be by in a few hours to pick up the DNA sample."

"You've been a huge help. Do you want me to take over, so you can get some sleep? If you're hungry, you can help yourself to whatever's in the kitchen."

Thomas stood and stretched his arms over his head. "Sure, I'm starving. A nap is appealing, too. Wake me if we get a hit."

Jon settled in behind his desk and studied David's picture. Something about his face seemed familiar. He'd only gotten a brief glimpse of his side profile when he drove past in the stolen truck. David had dark brown eyes seething with malice. He wasn't a small man either.

No wonder Jess is terrified of him.

Jessica came in with steaming coffees. Her sleepy face looked good before the shower and makeup, despite the bags under her eyes. If only she'd slept longer.

She handed him a mug. "Good morning."

"Good morning. Thanks for the coffee."

She sat in the chair beside him. "I figured you'd need caffeine after I kept us up last night."

"It's no big deal. We'll work through your nightmares."

"Thanks for being so understanding." She sipped from her mug. "Thomas gave me an update in the kitchen. Have you found anything more since you took over?"

"Not yet, but I have a feeling I've come across David somewhere before. I've been staring at his face, racking my brain, but I'm coming up empty."

"Maybe if you start researching something else, it'll come to you."

"I'm waiting on the facial recognition before broadening the search. This system can be slow going, but it's worth the wait. I have a good feeling." Jon continued staring at the screen. "I wish we could find out more about him, but there isn't much out there. His name is an alias. David Hayes appeared a year ago in Alberta with no history."

"Do you want me to call Tim again? He said the RCMP wasn't giving up the investigation. Maybe he's found something."

"Sure. Give him a call."

Jessica pulled the burner phone out of her pocket and dialed Tim. She hit the speaker button. "Hi. Tim. It's Jessica."

"Jess. How are you?"

She sighed. "Not great. Things got a little crazy here last night." She proceeded to fill him in on the night's events.

"That's awful. How is your aunt?"

"She's fine. I'm hoping you can help us."

"I'll try. What can I do to help?"

"Has anyone figured out what David's motive may have been for killing his wife?"

"I'll call you back on this number in a few minutes."

"Sure." She hung up. "He must know something. Seems he's switching phones."

Jon pulled her into his lap. "You look like you could use a cuddle."

She wrapped her arms around him. "Thanks." Her phone rang and she answered. "Tim?"

128

"It's me. I needed privacy for this conversation."

"I understand. Can I put you on speaker?"

"Sure. Ready?"

She hit the speaker icon on her screen, "Yes. We're listening."

"The department wouldn't want me telling you this, but we have a motive. We found a million-dollar life insurance policy in Sarah's name. Because of you, he had to hide the body and won't be claiming that money."

"No wonder he hates me so much."

"The medical examiner informed us this morning that Sarah's primary cause of death was blunt force trauma to the head. We're waiting for forensic analysis to yield some DNA. But as you know, the results could be awhile. Then if we had enough, a warrant would be issued. The locals in Montana would be informed and could extradite him. But all that will take time."

Jon said, "Time we don't have."

"Thank you, Tim. Please keep us updated." Jessica hung up after bidding Tim farewell. "What do you think?"

Jon stared at David's picture. "I think he's done this successfully before. And it's no easy feat to use DNA to arrest a spouse when spouses are expected to carry each other's DNA. We can't count on the RCMP to nail him. You said he doesn't have a steady job?"

"No. He does cash repair jobs around town."

"How long was he married to Sarah?"

"Just under a year. They only moved in across the street six months ago." Jessica set her mug on the desk and brushed her hands up and down her arms. "Poor Sarah. I wish she hadn't met him. She was such a darling. So kind and easy going." Tears welled in her eyes.

"I'm sorry about your friend. We'll do everything we can to get her justice."

Jessica wiped her tears.

"I'll contact some old colleagues at the FBI. I need to place where I came across him before. Why don't you have a nice hot shower or bath? It'll help you feel better."

"I will after I bring you breakfast. Aunt Debbie is cooking up a storm in the kitchen. She kicked me out and told me to check on you."

He chuckled. "Debbie is a leader by nature. She's the type you say, 'yes ma'am' to."

"Yep. That's my aunt. And she's so charming and matter of fact, you don't even mind submitting to her will."

"Sums her up well." He stared at Jessica's back as she walked out the door.

Whether or not she was aware, she was a strong woman. Getting out of bed and facing the day rather than hiding under the covers was bravery.

****

Jessica returned to the kitchen after bringing Jon a plate of food.

Thomas sat in front of a half-empty plate, making appreciative noises.

Bryce wandered in yawning and stretching his arms over his head. "Hi, Auntie. How come you're here so early? What's for breakfast?"

Debbie smiled at him. "All stuff you like. Eggs, bacon, and pancakes. Sit down with him, Jess. Let me bring you breakfast."

Jessica admired the way Debbie skirted the reason for her visit so easily but worry niggled. How much longer could she keep the truth from Bryce? "All right but let me help clean up."

"Sure. You need to stay busy, too." Debbie joined Jessica and Bryce at the table as Thomas was finishing up.

Thomas put his plate in the sink and turned to Debbie. "Thank you very much for a delicious breakfast. I could help with the dishes."

Jessica shook her head. "You were up all night. Sleep. You've done enough."

Thomas smiled. "Thanks. I'll see you in a few hours."

"Mom, when are we going back to our new house?"

Jessica swallowed a bite of scrambled eggs around the sudden lump in her throat. *Crap, what do I say?*

The truth wasn't an option, and she had no idea how long they would be holed up in Jon's house. She didn't want to lie, but David left her no choice. *Bastard.*

"I really don't know, buddy. There are things that need to get fixed before we can live there. We're staying with Jon until the house is ready. Do you like it here?"

"I love Jon's big TV and Daisy. Jon is awesome."

Debbie laughed. "What about me? Am I awesome, Bryce?"

"Yes, Auntie. You make really good cookies, and you're a lot of fun."

"You know, he sounds like a typical man. TV and food. You're a fine young man, nephew. Will you show me the pastel you're working on for Jon?"

"Yes, Auntie." Bryce led Debbie into the living room where he'd set up his easel. Thankfully, Jon had remembered to tell Thomas to grab Bryce's art supplies while he was setting up his surveillance equipment.

Jessica finished her coffee, rinsed the breakfast dishes, and placed them in the dishwasher.

Bryce's laugh echoed across the main floor from the living room.

Her son was in good hands, and she could shower in peace. Life had taken such a drastic turn. After eight years of caring for her son mostly on her own, having two reliable adults eager to help was a welcome change.

She turned on the rainfall shower head and let the water warm. Jon was right. Something about the sound of water and all the steam soothed the soul. After folding her pajamas on the bathroom counter, she stood under the warm spray and let the heat unknot the muscles in her back. She closed her eyes and focused on the sensation of the water hitting her skin.

The water washed away the darkness dragging her down, leaving behind the light. Sure, David had driven her out of town, but he'd also pushed her closer to two people she'd missed, Aunt Debbie and Jon.

Having nothing left to wash, she begrudgingly turned off the tap and wrapped her body in an oversized towel. She unzipped the old duffle Thomas had packed her from beside the bed. The man was intelligent and efficient. He'd selected practical and comfortable items. She dug out a comfortable powder blue tee and jeans, then headed to the office to see if Jon had learned anything more.

She settled in the chair beside his. "Anything happen while I was gone?"

"Nothing new yet."

Thomas's computer pinged. The facial recognition program had finished running and displayed three driver's licenses from Washington, Oregon, and California issued in three different names.

Jessica grabbed onto the arms of the chair. "Oh my God. Different hair styles, facial hair, one has eyeglasses, but they're all David. Every single one of them. Who is this guy?"

"These are all fakes. His true identity remains a mystery. This is good though. It's a great starting point. Now we can pull public records on all these identities. It's a horrible thought, but I bet there's a dead woman for every single alias."

Thomas came into the room staring at his wristwatch.

Jon said, "I should have known you'd have a smart watch connected to these laptops for updates."

"I forgot to turn it off. I'm used to going solo on these missions. I got about half an hour of sleep anyways. What do we have here? Ooh, jackpot." Thomas concentrated on the computer screen. "This is good. I'll look into the Steve Williams alias in Washington, and I'll run the facial recognition through the database in Canada, if you check into Hank Tanner in Oregon and Charlie White in California."

Jon's brows furrowed as he typed on one of Thomas's laptops. "Deal."

Jessica studied the images. What Jon and Thomas perceived as progress was a new complication. The mystery surrounding David deepened. She wracked her brain for another instance in her adult life when she'd been so out of control. Nothing came to mind.

Even after Adam died and grief had consumed her, she'd remained in control of the funeral arrangements and had Bryce to care for. She'd had something to cling onto to keep pressing through each day, and she'd never been forced to depend on others for her family's survival.

Thomas asked, "Do you still have access to CODIS if we happen to get a DNA profile to link our sample to anything we may find surrounding these aliases?"

"No. I wish. I'll need one of my old colleagues to access CODIS for me." Jon shook his head. "If nothing else, the Canadian police should be able to generate a DNA profile on their end. But with how backed up police labs get, even with it being a homicide, it could be weeks. I think we have days, not weeks, before he comes after us again."

Jessica stood and let Thomas have her chair so he could get back to work. "Can I get you anything? I need to feel like I'm doing something to help."

Thomas said, "I would love coffee."

"A refill for me too please. Coffee helps." Jon said, "Desk work was always my least favorite part of the job."

In the tiny office, within ten seconds, both men forgot she stood there, each engrossed in the screen in front of them. They didn't mean to exclude her, but she was an outsider looking in, having to rely on others to save the day.

She slipped out of the office, and back upstairs to the kitchen. Coffee was the least she could do. After setting more coffee to brew, she leaned her elbows on the counter and rested her chin in her hands, watching the coffee drip into the carafe.

If only my thoughts would stop brewing.

She craved a distraction or better yet, a way to escape the cage David had locked her in. Making coffee wasn't cutting enough. She raided the freezer and pantry for ingredients to make a nice dinner.

Debbie hummed the theme song of Bryce's favorite show on her way into the kitchen.

Jessica laughed. "Got that song stuck in your head, eh? Happens to me sometimes."

Debbie stopped humming and joined in the laughter. "Yes. Unfortunately." She pulled a mug out of the cabinet. "Why don't we go for a walk or a ride around the ranch? The clouds are gone, and I reckon there are cameras everywhere."

"I don't know. Thomas spotted David across the street this morning."

"The ranch hands are all over the property with rifles plus all the cameras. I doubt David will try anything with so many sets of eyes. I'll even bring my rifle."

Jessica's gut churned, but Debbie's logic made sense. "Okay. Bryce must be going stir crazy, too. I'll double check with Jon before we go."

"What were you up to before I interrupted?"

"Figuring out dinner and dessert. I need to keep busy, so I don't go out of my mind. The guys are investigating some aliases belonging to David that came up on driver's license photos. I'm out of my element there. At least I can be useful here." Jessica continued sifting through pints of ice cream, frozen veggies, and packages of meat wrapped in brown paper in the freezer. "There's a large beef roast in here. That would do nicely, and we have enough potatoes and carrots too. I could make a nice apple pie or crumble. We'll have a feast."

"Sounds good. I'll make my famous Yorkshire pudding and the gravy."

Jessica set the roast in the kitchen sink and filled the basin with warm water. She hoped the meat would thaw enough for a nice spice rub and a quick marinade. "After I bring the coffee to the basement, I'm ready to go. I bet Bryce will want to ride Daisy again."

"I'll get him."

Jessica's hands trembled at the idea of leaving the house. *Maybe I'm developing agoraphobia.*

She held onto the railing as the tremors spread, wracking her head to toe as she made her way down the stairs to Jon's office.

She poured coffee from the carafe into their empty mugs, taking extra care not to spill with her shaky hands. Luckily, both men remained fixed on the screens in front of them.

I'm safe. I'm safe. Maybe if I think it enough times, I'll stop shaking. Focusing on her mantra, she willed her body to relax, then the tremors stopped.

She set the carafe down on a side table and rested her hand on Jon's shoulder. "Jon, Debbie, and I were thinking of taking Bryce horseback riding. Do you mind if we borrow Daisy? Think we'll be safe?"

He smiled at her over his shoulder. "Sounds fun. David was limping this morning. He'll probably take time to recover. You should be safe. I'll get Chip to meet you in the stables."

"Thank you."

With Jon's reassurances, she shoved away the nervous, apprehensive thoughts to the back of her mind.

She couldn't let David suck the joy out of every minute of every day.

Chapter Fourteen

Jessica met Bryce and Aunt Debbie at the back door. "Once I slip into my runners, I'll be ready to go."

"Hurry up, Mom."

Jessica laughed. "Hold your horses."

"But we're still inside. Not by horses."

Aunt Debbie chuckled and took his hand. "Hold your horses is an expression meaning be patient and wait."

Bryce nodded. "Oh. Now I get it."

When they got to the stables, they found Chip.

He tightened a strap on Daisy's saddle. "Howdy, folks. I hear you're wanting to ride."

Debbie tipped her hat. "Howdy, Chip. Yes, we are."

Chip slung his rifle over his shoulder. "I'll give you the grand tour."

Jessica hoisted herself onto Daisy and silently prayed nothing bad would happen.

Chip lifted Bryce onto the horse in front of her. "Up you go young fella."

Jessica held Bryce close as Debbie climbed onto Serge.

Chip climbed onto Reginald, the horse Jon rode when he took them riding only two short days ago. "Follow me, ladies and cowboy-in-training."

Bryce held onto the saddle horn. "Can we see the

cows?"

Chip grinned. "I reckon we can. There's no shortage of those around here."

Chip guided them along a different path than the one Jon had taken. They wove through grassy fields of grazing cows instead of riding the trails along the outskirts of the Kent property.

Jessica held onto the reins as the sun warmed her face, and the rhythm of Daisy's trot slowed her racing heart.

Bryce smiled.

She kissed the top of his head and committed this precious moment to memory. Childhood flew by. After a few good lessons, he'd be riding Daisy on his own.

Pop!

Bryce asked, "Mom, what was that? It sounded like fireworks but quieter."

Jessica searched her surroundings for the source of the noise. "No idea. Maybe someone splitting wood?"

Snap!

A long, thick branch landed on the ground in front of Jessica.

Daisy reared and neighed.

Jessica tightened her grip on the reins and Bryce. "Whoa, calm down, Daisy. It's only a branch. You'll be fine." The horse settled on command and Jessica guided her around the obstacle.

Debbie rode up beside Jessica and bellowed. "Faster! The branch exploded off the tree. Dig your heels in. A moving target is the hardest to hit."

A bullet! Don't panic and scare Bryce. Think. React.

Jessica dug her heels into Daisy. She plastered

Bryce to her body and hunched forward to shield him. "Let's have a little race to see who can get back to the barn first. Hang on."

"Go fast, Mom."

"We will. Hold on tight to that saddle horn." She dug her heels into Daisy again. "Faster Daisy. Come on girl."

The horse increased her tempo to a steady gallop, bouncing them around in the saddle.

Bryce giggled. "Whee."

A cow nearby bellowed a high-pitched moo.

Jessica looked over her shoulder.

Blood oozed out of a wound in the poor animal's round.

She leaned over Bryce again to block his view. The last thing he needed to see was an injured animal when he loved them so much.

She urged Daisy on, keeping a firm hold on Bryce as they bounced in the saddle. At long last, the stables came into view ahead.

Something brushed past her left leg, then whizzed in the air towards Chip riding Reginald in front of her.

No!

She screamed, "Chip, Steer right!"

Chip tugged his reins. The bullet landed in his chaps below the knee. "Dammit!" He glanced back at Jessica and Debbie. "I'm fine. Don't you dare slow down. We're almost there."

Jessica clenched her jaw. Another bullet whizzed past her right ear. She lowered her head and dug her heels into Daisy's side again. "Come on, girl. Faster."

Daisy accelerated past Reginald. In seconds, they reached the stables.

Jessica had to slow Daisy to navigate around the corner to the entrance.

Almost there.

The wooden siding splintered a few inches above Jessica's head as they turned the corner. Stopping to dismount before going inside would be awkward and slow with Bryce in tow, making them an easier target.

Jessica pushed Bryce's head down gently. "Duck and hug Daisy's neck, buddy." She leaned her head against Bryce's back. "I know, Daisy. It's weird. But go ahead inside."

Daisy trotted inside, stopping in front of her stall.

Jessica raised her head and patted the horse's shoulder. "Good girl, Daisy." She rubbed Bryce's back. "You can sit up now."

He lifted his head, turned to her, and smiled. "We won the race. We're first."

Jessica kissed his head and wrapped her arms around his middle. "We sure did." She leaned her head into Bryce, closed her eyes, and breathed him in, chastising herself for going outside and putting him at risk.

Her baby!

That monster shot at her while she held her precious boy in her arms. Tears threatened, but she wouldn't let David make her cry in front of her child.

Debbie led Serge and Reginald inside. "You all right there, Jess?"

"We're fine."

Chip limped in after Debbie, rifle in hand, and pulled the doors shut.

Debbie jogged over to him. "Where did you get hit? I don't see blood."

"My leg. I need to get these chaps off." Chip leaned his rifle against the wall, unbuckled his chaps, and pushed them down to his ankles. "That feels better." He twisted around and peered at his left leg. "The bullet didn't pierce my skin. Chaps saved me. Bet I'll have an awful bruise though."

Jessica closed her eyes and took a deep breath. She clutched Bryce to her chest. "I'm glad you're all right, Chip."

Bryce said, "Bullet? That wasn't a race, was it? It was David."

Jessica said, "Yes, probably. But we're safe now."

Chip walked towards her, stretched his arms out, and spoke quietly. "You can let go now, Jess. I'll take him so you can climb down."

She released her hold on Bryce and waited for Chip to lift him out of the saddle to dismount. Her legs wobbled as her feet hit the ground. She stumbled.

Her aunt steadied her and wrapped her arms around Jessica in a firm hug. "It's okay, Jess. We're fine."

Jessica whispered into Debbie's ear, "I bet his aim was so bad because you shot him. What a sick bastard. Did you see the poor cow he shot? I hope she'll recover."

"The bullet went in the fatty area of the cow's leg. A vet can patch her up."

Jon burst into the barn. He picked up Bryce, took Jessica from Debbie, and held them both close. "Thank God." He shifted his gaze to Chip without releasing his hold. "You, okay?"

"I'm fine. The bullet hit my chaps. I only ended up with a bruise. What are we gonna do about this, boss?"

"I'm going to have to call the sheriff. The ranch

hands will talk, and he'll find out about the gunfire. The sheriff will get men to search the woods anyhow. We'll be safer for a while."

Chip pulled out his phone. "I'll call a vet for the injured cow and move the staff indoors."

"Get the vet to save the bullet for the police." Jon put Bryce down and released his hold on Jessica. "Chip, why don't you come inside with us, and we'll get you a cold beer. The sheriff will want to talk to you when he gets here."

"Sure. I think I need a bourbon though. Beer ain't gonna cut it. I bet he thought I was you."

"Huh." Jon put his hands on his hips and paused for a moment. "You're right. We look alike at a distance. I am so sorry about this, Chip. We're making progress on getting him." Jon picked the chaps up off the ground, brushed away the hay, and examined the bullet lodged in the leather. "I'm no ballistics expert, but I think this bullet was fired by a Winchester M22."

Debbie leaned in for a closer look. "I agree. He had something long range with a homemade silencer. The shots were quieter, but we heard them. I couldn't see any sign of anyone, and the fields are mostly flat."

Jessica leaned into Jon's side, still unsteady on her feet. "Are we safe to go inside?"

"David's not going to stick around long enough for the police to arrive. He's gone by now." He wrapped an arm around her. "Let me check things out. Stay here."

Jessica squeezed his hand. "Be careful."

"Always."

Time stood still as Jon exited the barn and jogged towards the back door of the house. Jessica's stomach churned. What if David hadn't hightailed it out of there like Jon believed? Images of Jon unconscious and bleeding from a gunshot wound ran unbidden through her mind.

She glanced behind her. After a quick call to the vet, Chip was keeping Bryce occupied by letting him feed the horses apples while he whistled, and Debbie brushed her horse.

Jessica folded her arms across her chest. Why did fear climb up the back of her throat making her tremble when the others seemed fine? Why couldn't she muster that kind of bravery?

She peered out a window. Jon was nowhere to be seen. Where did he go?

The back door opened, and Jon strode outside toward the barn.

Of course. The cameras. She stood in the doorway and waited for him. "Can we go inside now?"

Jon nodded. "I think it's all clear. Let's move quickly."

****

Jessica stayed with Bryce in the living room while the others talked to the sheriff. He glanced up from his drawing to the television every so often as if nothing had happened. He got his resilience from Adam, and not from her. She couldn't focus on anything.

Debbie sat on the couch beside them. "I'll keep him company, Jess. Sheriff Hank needs to talk to you."

"All right." Jessica went into the kitchen and sat across from the sheriff.

He extended his hand. "You must be Debbie's niece, Jessica."

She took his proffered hand. "Yes."

"Can you tell me what happened from the

144

beginning in Cochrane?"

She told him almost everything, omitting what she assumed Jon wouldn't want to share, including Thomas's presence and their private investigation.

Jon leaned against the kitchen counter behind the sheriff and winked when she finished talking.

Sheriff Hank said, "Well, folks. I have everything I need. We've called in help from the neighboring counties. We'll search these woods with canines. No one got a positive identification, so of course, we can't say for certain this David Hayes is responsible."

Jon folded his arms across his chest. "Look, we've spotted him in town following us, and he's been on my property. I caught him on surveillance footage. What are the odds?"

"You've probably got a list of enemies a mile long from your FBI work. But I agree. It likely was David Hayes. I checked the hospitals and clinics after Debbie's fire last night. I couldn't find any trace of him."

Jessica aimed to diffuse the situation. Arguing wouldn't accomplish anything. "Thanks for trying, Sheriff. Hopefully the search turns up something."

Jon positioned himself behind Jessica's chair. "Yes, much appreciated."

"For you, Jon, I will do everything I can. You got a lot of scumbags off the streets, and you risked your life in the line of duty."

"You do the same, Sheriff."

Sheriff Hank paused. "I hear sirens. The cavalry is almost here. I want to get the search underway as soon as possible. I'll let you know what I find."

Jessica spun her wedding ring around her finger as

butterflies flitted in her stomach. While the property was surrounded by law enforcement, they'd be safe—for now.

Chapter Fifteen

Jon embraced Jessica in the kitchen by the window. Her head rested on his chest as the search got underway.

Police cars covered the gravel path leading to his house. Officers gathered around Sheriff Hank's cruiser in helmets and vests armed with rifles. A K-9 team stood off to the side.

A bunch of men trampling through the woods making all kinds of noise would never stand a chance of catching David. But maybe Jessica would get comfort from the presence of all those officers for a little while and relax.

She lifted her head off his shoulder and gazed into his eyes. "It's not even safe to go outside with cameras and people all over the place."

"I know. I cannot believe he was that brazen." *She could've been killed because I underestimated him.* "While you were out, we found victims associated to each identity."

She shivered in his arms. "What did he do to them?"

"Two of his wives died after a gas leak caught their homes on fire in the middle of the night. They didn't wake up to save themselves, having taken sleeping pills, and that bastard conveniently wasn't home. The third victim in Washington was found beaten, raped, and left naked in an alley which I'm guessing would have been Sarah's fate if you hadn't caught him moving the body."

"What a sick bastard. How could he get to know these women, live with them, make love to them, and then kill them?"

"Thomas is contacting the lead detectives to notify them of the link we've found. It'll take time for them to reopen those investigations."

"Wouldn't getting him into custody be a good start? He committed fraud with his false identities."

Jon sighed. "Using a fake identity doesn't rank up there with serious crimes. It may be months, or even a year, before they issue a warrant for him. We need a lot more on him if we want a quick resolution. Besides, if he isn't charged with something serious, he could get bail and disappear. Only to return whenever he sees fit to come at you again."

"Can you pull strings to get the FBI to take the case?"

"The FBI gets involved when they are called in by state police because there is an obvious pattern indicating a serial killer. We don't have that yet, but we're close. Only one death out of the three we uncovered was considered a homicide. Fire was ruled as the cause of death in the other two cases."

She hung her head. "Bet you're eager to get back to Thomas to keep searching for more."

"I am. Don't lose hope." He leaned his forehead on hers. "I know you don't want me hunting, but wouldn't you feel better if I just ended it?"

"No. I'm fine. I don't want you risking your life unless there's no other way."

"All we can do now is wait for someone to get back to me and watch the cameras. Unless..." He clenched and unclenched his fist. "He shot at you. And it's taking every ounce of control, and I mean every ounce, not to go out and bury him in the woods like he deserves. That's what I'd like to do."

"I agree. He deserves to die. But rotting in a cell in high security prison until he does would be punishment too."

"Then I should get back to the office and check my email again in case any of my colleagues replied. They may have a missing piece to connect the dots of where else I came across David before." He cupped the back of her head, pulled her close, and brushed her lips with a chaste kiss. "Glad you're all right. Thank God, the horses didn't spook and buck you off."

"You trained Daisy well. Get back to work. I'll make us all a nice dinner."

"Now you're kicking me out of my kitchen, too?"

She chuckled. "Seems I am."

The corners of his mouth lifted when her eyes lit up. "All right. You win, sweetheart."

Jon reluctantly let go and returned to his basement office. "Hey, Thomas. Find anything new?"

Thomas pointed to the monitor in front of him. "Facial recognition finished going through the Canadian Police Information Centre, and it pulled back two more identities. Two deceased women associated with them, both fires. Seems to be his modus operandi. So far none of these identities has a past. We've been through two countries worth of databases with that image. Normally by now, we would have come across a suspect's real identity. I think he was born in another country. I'm searching Interpol."

"There's another possibility. Plastic surgery. It would explain a lot."

Thomas spun around in his chair. "Maybe he had plastic surgery because he made a mistake. Another witness perhaps? That would explain his dogged determination to kill Jessica."

"You could be right. The problem lies in finding that mistake." Jon wracked his brain, searching for the piece that wouldn't click into place. "Bet you'll refuse, but I'll ask anyways. Do you want me to do the night shift tonight?"

"No, I'm a night owl. I'll take another nap after dinner, and I'll remember to leave my watch here this time. Besides, it seems like Jess needs you. I heard her scream last night. After getting shot at, that situation probably won't improve much."

Jon stared at the images of David, wishing he could jump through the computer screen, and wring his neck. "I'm glad Bryce is a heavy sleeper. I want to murder him for doing this to them."

"With what we now know he's capable of, this creep is giving me a case of the heebie jeebies. He's wounded. The ideal time for you to do your thing and take him out."

"I know, but Jess doesn't want me to."

"But he hasn't given up and he has balls of steel. What will he try next? He has all of us confined to one location. He could do any number of horrendous things. I don't want to sleep for any length of time for fear I'll die of smoke inhalation before I wake."

"I agree. Arsonists of his caliber are dangerous. We can't sit around waiting much longer." Jon logged into his email. He had a response from Sam, an old colleague at the bureau. Of all people, it had to be Sam's suspect. "Come look at this."

"What?" Thomas turned in his chair to see Jon's screen.

"Sam sent a sketch from an old unsolved case. He thought the eye spacing and facial structure were similar. I think the eyes are a dead ringer. The nose and the chin look altered, but I think it's him. I must have recognized him from this wanted sketch at the bureau."

Thomas spun back to his own laptop. "Can you forward me that email? I'll run it through a comparison program."

"Okay… done."

Jon peered over Thomas's shoulder as he brought up the two images side by side. The program analyzed them. A ninety percent probability message flashed on the screen.

"Ninety percent is very high for this program. I would say they're the same man. Now we might have help from the Feds."

Jon nodded, picked up his phone, and scrolled through his contacts. His finger hovered over Sam's name. Their last conversation had been tense, but surely their prior years of friendship counted for something. "This could be the break we need. Sam's resources would be invaluable right now." He touched his screen and listened to ringing on the other end.

A familiar gravelly voice answered, "Hello?"

"Sam. It's Jon. Our old friend, Thomas, just ran your sketch through a program of his. We're dealing with the same guy. Can you tell me more about your case?"

"My suspect set off an explosion in his apartment in a twelve-floor apartment building in Seattle. It killed his wife and three of their neighbors. Because of the slim possibility of terrorism, we were called in. A witness, Todd Collins, saw him set the blaze. He tried to hold him until the police got there, but the perpetrator stabbed him and escaped. Todd survived, and he managed to get skin underneath his fingernails. We got DNA, but no hits in the system."

Jon pumped his fist in the air. "We think we have DNA too, and the Canadian authorities may also soon have DNA evidence. Maybe you could make a call up North and press them to fast track their samples. Anyhow, Thomas managed to get a blood sample from our perp, and it's at a lab being analyzed now. The problem is it may be watered down."

"I'm catching the first flight to Montana. This is the most promising lead I've gotten so far."

The line went dead. "We may have our break and reinforcements. Sam's on his way here."

Chapter Sixteen

Jessica added butter and cream to a pot full of boiled potatoes. She'd always cherished the camaraderie that came along with cooking a big meal with her favorite aunt.

Jon's news only added to the good vibes. David was likely a serial killer and wanted by the FBI. If they could just catch him, this would all be over.

She picked up a mixer and pressed the potatoes down. "That's fantastic. How well do you know Sam Gardner?"

"Very well. He's an experienced agent."

Something flashed through Jon's eyes for an instant. Jessica paused. "Why do I get the feeling there's more to your relationship with him?"

"You know how it is with coworkers. Occasionally, you butt heads is all. Ancient history. Most of the time we got on well." Jon sniffed the air. "How long until this amazing dinner is ready?"

Jessica pressed the switch and the mixer whirred, pulling potato through the paddle. "About ten minutes."

Debbie said, "Why don't you take a break and spend time with Bryce? He seems unaffected by our ride earlier, but it wouldn't hurt to keep his mind busy."

Jon brushed his lips on Jessica's cheek. "I'll teach him a new card game."

Debbie grinned. Her eyes followed Jon's exit

153

before she spoke. "Things seem pretty cozy."

Jessica shrugged. "We agreed to take things one day at a time. Zero expectations."

"That's what I hoped would happen. You two always had a special connection."

"Don't get too excited. We both have a lot of baggage. And our baggage is intense. Neither one of us is sure if we're capable of a relationship."

Debbie placed a muffin tin in the oven for her Yorkshire puddings. "I'm glad to see you're at least giving yourselves a chance."

The scent of the beef drippings cooking in the puddings permeated the kitchen. Jessica's stomach rumbled. "This dinner smells amazing. Even better now that an FBI agent is on his way."

"Oh, I know. I hate being stuck here taking advantage of Jon's hospitality."

"I feel horrible about all this. I barged into Jon's life and dragged him into the trenches." Jessica rested her hand on her aunt's arm. "And I'm sorry that by helping me, you ended up in this position."

"Quit apologizing. You didn't do anything wrong. This David, or whatever his name is did, besides which, I'm glad to have you here."

"I'd have to say, even though the reason I ended up here is hellish, it's good to be here."

****

Jon held his stomach, stuffed after the most amazing roast beef dinner he'd had in a long time. "An excellent dinner, ladies. Thank you very much."

Jessica laughed. "I guess considering every morsel of food is gone."

Holding his own stomach, Thomas peered over his

laptop at Jon. "Exquisite. I feel a food coma coming on. Can you keep an eye on these camera feeds for me, so I can take a nap?"

Jon said, "Pass the computer over."

Thomas clambered from his chair. "A cop car is coming up the laneway." He ran down the hallway.

A hard knock sounded.

Jon gazed out the peephole. "It's Sheriff Hank. Jess, close the laptop, please."

She shut the lid.

Jon opened the door. "Hello, Sheriff. Would you like to come in?"

"No, that won't be necessary. I don't have much to report. We found a spot of flattened grass, shell casings, and gun powder residue. With the bullet from Chip's chaps and the one from the cow, ballistics will be able to match the gun if found. We tracked his movements to the old dirt road behind the wooded patch of land at the back of the property."

"It's what we expected. Thanks."

"I'll keep an eye out for our man around town. You have a good night now, Jon."

Jon shut the door and took the chair beside Jessica's.

She pushed the computer across the table to Jon. "Here's the laptop. I'll take care of these dishes."

Jon frowned. "You don't have to clean up. You're my guests."

"Stop fretting the domestic stuff. We need to keep busy."

Debbie stood and put her hands on her hips. "For heaven's sakes, Jon. You're feeding us and putting a roof over our heads. Let us be good houseguests."

Jon mock-saluted Debbie. "Yes, ma'am."

He headed to the basement eager to get back to work. About an hour later, new email flashed on Thomas's screen.

The lab report.

He brought the laptop monitoring the camera feeds upstairs to update the others. Debbie, Jessica, and Bryce were in the living room. He met Jessica's gaze, and they smiled at each other.

Bryce laid in her lap.

She rubbed his back, and his eyes fluttered as he struggled to stay awake.

Jon lifted Bryce into his arms, then Jessica ran ahead and turned down the blankets. After Jon laid him down, she bent to cover Bryce with a quilt and kissed his forehead. The peaceful, loving expression on her face stirred Jon's heart.

Despite the darkness of the past few days, her love continued to shine through. *Nothing like the love of a mother for her child.* And despite the persistent guilt coinciding with loving Jessica, he yearned to join her little family. Hopefully, she'd be willing to let him in.

Jessica turned, took Jon's hand, and led them to the hallway. She shut the door behind her. "What's going on?"

"I have to wake Thomas. Meet me in the living room."

Jon knocked on the guest room door gently.

Thomas swung the door open a moment later. "What's up? Did Sheriff Hank find something?"

"Come join us, so I can tell everyone at once."

Thomas followed Jon to the living room.

Jon took a seat beside Jessica on the couch and

three pairs of eyes bored into his. "Great news. The blood wasn't too watered down from the rain. Thomas's friend got a DNA profile. If Sam's sample matches, then it verifies without a doubt that David Hayes is a wanted serial killer and Sam can take him into federal custody."

Jessica patted her aunt on the shoulder. "Good aim, Aunt Debbie."

"Glad to help though I wish I'd gotten him in the heart or the head." Debbie glanced out the window. "Jon, a car's coming. Not a police car this time."

Gravel scattered as a black sedan came to a stop in front of the house. "That must be Sam. I have to let him into the barn."

Jon hurried to the door. If David was aware he'd been investigated by Sam years ago, he would recognize him.

He jogged out to the car, knocked on the driver's door, and waited for Sam to lower the window a crack. "That was fast. Did you get the feeling you were being followed?"

"No, I rented a car with tinted windows at the airport, and I was very careful. Is there somewhere you'd like to hide the car?"

"Yes, the old barn behind the house."

Jon jogged to the barn, unlocked the padlock, and opened the doors for Sam. After they stowed the car, Jon took Sam inside to the kitchen. "Sam, meet Jessica and Debbie."

Sam smiled. "Hello. It's nice to meet you both. Although it would have been better under different circumstances."

Jon asked, "Would you like to see the image we

captured of David Hayes? We can update you on what we've found."

Sam nodded. "Yes, please."

Thomas handed Sam the laptop with the image they'd captured zoomed in for comparison.

"That's him all right." Sam pointed to the image. "You can alter your chin and dye your hair, but you can't alter bone structure or eye spacing."

Jon said, "Yes, and we have a DNA profile for comparison."

Sam handed Thomas back his laptop, then opened his briefcase and retrieved a thumb drive. "My profile is on here."

Thomas slipped the drive into his computer and opened the file. He placed Sam's DNA profile alongside the profile they got from David's blood and ran them through a comparison program.

A circle spun on the screen for a few long minutes, then the results appeared on the screen.

Sam slapped Jon on the back. "You found a serial killer. Sam pulled out his phone. "I'll send out a BOLO and call in reinforcements. FBI people. No offense to the locals, but they aren't equipped to handle this guy. They'd botch it, and he'd get away. This one is way too slippery. You know the area. Do you have any idea where he's hiding?"

Jon said, "I thought he was camping in the woods behind my rental house. But the local police combed through the whole area and found no sign of him or his hideout."

Sam asked, "What about motels?"

Jon shook his head. "We checked. No sign of him there either."

Debbie said, "I reckon he's hiding on someone's property in the area. So many of us have old, abandoned buildings and huge acres."

"Makes sense." Jon said, "We know he's stolen at least two vehicles that haven't been located."

Sam asked, "How many farms are there around here and the surrounding area?"

Jon shrugged. "I'm not sure, but at least a hundred."

Sam undid the buttons of his suit jacket. "In the email, you said he followed Jessica here after she witnessed him murdering his wife and moving the body. So, he's fixated on killing the witness."

"Yes," Jon said. "So, what are you thinking for strategies on apprehending him? I've been running a few scenarios through my mind."

"I think we should camp out here and wait for him to strike next." Sam pointed to Jessica. "He's going to come back here for her. We'll be ready when he does."

Jon said, "I'm thinking of something more proactive. He checks on the rental house nightly looking for Jessica. We turn on some lights to lure him there."

Thomas shifted his gaze between Jon and Sam. "That isn't a bad plan, but he may not take the bait, or see through it and assume you're waiting for him. Sam, when you say wait and be ready. What are you proposing? How do you plan on getting a team out here without David noticing and taking off?"

"They could stay at a local motel. If David shows, and everything hits the fan, they would be a phone call away."

Jon ran his hands through his hair. "That isn't

going to help if he torches the house with us in it."

Jessica shook her head. "These plans won't work. He's as smart as he is crazy. We have to draw him out with something irresistible."

Jon struggled to keep his tone neutral. "You're *not* saying what I think you're saying."

Jessica said, "I'm willing to be the bait. I'll sit in the rental house at the table by the window until he sees me, then I'll lock myself in the bathroom, and wait for the cavalry."

Jon sat up straighter in his chair. *No way.* "You stopped me from hunting him because you didn't want to risk me. Now I'm supposed to let you sit alone in the house waiting for a psycho to break in?"

Jessica's pleading gaze bored into him. "You'll have time to get to me once you see him on camera. The bathroom door should hold him off for a while, even if he does get in before you get there."

Sam said, "Jon, she's right. If this plan works, then we are being proactive like you wanted. This won't be like last time. I promise."

Jon clenched and unclenched his fist as memories of working with Sam in the past flooded him. "That's a promise you can't make. He could muscle his way in and get to Jess before we get inside. I'll hide in the house while she's in the kitchen. That's the only way I'll agree."

Jessica put her hand on his arm. "If he's watching and sees you go to the house with me, he'll take off, and the plan fails."

Debbie said, "I'll go with her and bring my shotgun. It's risky, Jon. But she's right. This has to end."

Jon pulled his arm away. "This is way too dangerous."

Sam said, "I don't mean to be rude, but you're overruled. The majority are in favor."

Jon stabbed his index finger into Sam's chest. "If anything happens to Jess because we don't get there on time. I'm holding you personally responsible."

Sam held up his hands in surrender. "I understand, but he's evaded capture for so many years, and he will continue to go after Jessica if we don't get him. Not to mention all the other people he'll kill while he roams free."

Jon leaned back and folded his arms across his chest. "When are you planning to do this?"

"It'll take a day for me to get my men in place, so we can't proceed until tomorrow night. Things could change between now and then. He may attack here, and we may get him without using Jessica as bait."

Jon stood. "I need a stiff drink." He stormed off and headed for the stairs.

Chapter Seventeen

Jessica's heart plummeted as Jon ascended the staircase, leaving her behind. She hadn't meant to upset him, but she needed to do her part to capture the beast hunting her. Sam's mention of 'it won't be like last time' sounded ominous.

Debbie hugged Jessica. "I'm exhausted. A good night's sleep is in order. See you in the morning."

"Sleep well." Jessica stood at the bottom of the staircase and sighed. *Time to face the music.*

She trudged up the stairs to the dining room and stood in the archway, staring at Jon's back as he poured bourbon into a glass. His movements were stiff and precise.

He spoke without turning. "Do you want a drink?"

"A small bourbon, please. I'll never sleep."

He took a second glass out of the cabinet. "You don't have to do this. It's dangerous. We could wait for him to surface."

"I can't handle sitting and waiting any more than you can. I'd rather end the madness now." She approached him as he poured amber liquid into her glass. "Bryce asked when we're going home to the rental. I had to lie. I said the house needed repairs."

He faced her. The anger left his eyes as he handed her the bourbon and picked up his glass. "Come. Let's sit in the living room and talk."

She settled onto the sofa beside him, folded her legs underneath her, and waited for him to continue.

Jon set his drink on the coffee table and faced her. "You don't have to lie to Bryce. This can be your home. I love you both. When you were riding for your life to the barn, and I was helpless—" He rested his hand on her knee. "I want to hold you both close and never let go. Guilt be damned. What are we supposed to do? Be alone and guilt ridden for the rest of our lives?"

"Oh, Jon. I love you too, and I can see how attached Bryce is getting to you, but it's been years since we were in a relationship together. Plus, we've both been widowed under horrible circumstances. Bryce needs stability and what we have is too new and volatile."

"I don't think I'd describe this as either of those things. We've known each other a long time. Despite fifteen years and tragedy, the same chemistry is bringing us together. We both know from experience what true love is."

"I agree we have that strong connection, but I have to think about this. It's a major decision, and I don't want to make it lightly." She rested her hand on his knee. "Still angry with me?"

"I can never stay angry with you. I'm worried. For the same reason you're opposed to me hunting. Both plans are dangerous as hell."

She sipped her bourbon and a stinging warmth crept down her throat and into her stomach. "I know. Do you have any other ideas?"

"No. I see three options. One, we search Lewistown and the surrounding farmlands on a wild goose chase. Two we wait. Or three, lure him out the way we're planning too."

She downed the rest of her drink, cringing as the liquid burned her throat. "How are we supposed to sleep with all this going on? We're planning a dangerous takedown while David's still out there plotting his next move. How did you do this sort of thing for a living?"

He finished his drink. "I retired for a reason. The FBI robbed me of everything that mattered."

"I know. And I've stirred up memories by involving you in this."

"Not all the memories you've brought back are bad. There are a lot of good ones, too."

The times they'd spent in her aunt's hayloft came to mind. "Tons of good ones."

"Come, let's go to bed. We can lay beside each other awake all night if sleep won't come."

Her cheeks warmed. "Maybe we could do a bit more?"

"Maybe."

His crooked grin said maybe meant yes. They walked to his room hand in hand. She shut the door behind them. Once they crossed the line there would be no going back.

Am I doing the right thing?

Adam, Bryce, and Cynthia would always play a huge role in their undefined relationship. But Jon made a valid point. Living unattached in pain was no better. They deserved happiness.

"What's wrong, Jess? Change your mind?"

She shook her head and leapt into his arms. Worries be damned. Her need for him was the only thing that mattered. She explored his mouth, pressing her body closer to his, wanting nothing more than to lose herself in him for a little while. But her mind had other ideas.

Why can't we be a normal couple with normal issues? Instead, I'm bait.

Her body trembled; tears welled in her eyes.

He pulled back. "Are you okay? You're crying."

Not wanting the distance, she wrapped her arms around his neck. Desperation seeped into her words. "Yes, make love to me. I need you. Make me forget tomorrow. Please."

He tucked a stray hair behind her ear and gazed into her eyes. "Okay, sweetheart."

He followed the path of her tears with his lips down to her neck, lighting her skin on fire along the way.

She walked him back to the bed and shoved him backwards.

He fell onto the mattress with her on top of him cradled in his arms. He took his time peeling back layers of clothing, exploring every inch of her with his hands and mouth. Nothing else existed but him.

She relinquished control, gave herself to him completely. She ran her hand through his hair, soft and golden in the moonlight. The familiar arms enveloping her were strong and muscular, sun-kissed from all the time outdoors. She was cocooned and safe.

When he returned to her lips, she held his stubbly cheek, and gazed into his light blue eyes. The ones she'd lost herself in so many years ago, they still held the same adoration and passion after all the time that had passed.

How had she gotten so lucky? To have two men

love her this way in one lifetime, and to love them in return, a gift she vowed to cherish. Adam was gone, but Jon was here in her arms, real, solid, and unbelievably sexy. This love was worth crossing any obstacle standing in their path.

"I love you, Jon."

"I love you, too."

She crushed her mouth to his, pouring everything into the kiss, every emotion, and every ounce of passion rising inside of her from his touch.

Hands and lips roamed, tasted, explored, possessed until they finally came together, and rode the waves of their love together as one.

He panted, breathless from exertion, rolled off her, and pulled her into his arms.

He brushed golden strands of hair out of her face. "Better? Think you can sleep now?"

She wrapped her leg around his. "Much better. Cuddle me some more?"

He laughed. "All right, sweetheart."

Somehow, nestled in his arms, safety wrapped itself around her like a warm blanket. Her muscles felt lax, like jelly, and she shut her eyes.

Chapter Eighteen

Long after Jessica had gone to sleep, Jon lay awake in bed staring at the ceiling. He did his best to hide how many memories of Cynthia this situation dredged up for him. The idea of using Jessica as bait, and her being anywhere near David, sickened him. Especially with Sam Gardner in charge.

****

Two years earlier

Jon approached a scene unfolding in one of the most affluent neighborhoods in Washington. Tactical units had surrounded a large modern home with floor to ceiling windows, well-trimmed hedges, a tennis court, and a swimming pool. He walked into the mobile command center to find out why Sam had called, begging him to come.

His co-worker and friend stared straight ahead with a haunted look in his eyes.

"Sam, what's going on?"

Sam blinked and turned to face Jon. "This is a doozy. We showed up to arrest my suspect, and he answered the door with a gun to his daughter's temple. So, now we have a hostage situation." He handed Jon a picture.

The image depicted a happy, smiling family. Their suspect was a tall balding man with a pot belly and a cheerful expression. Based on his suspect's image, Sam had underestimated him. Shifting his gaze to the right, Jon took in a cute little girl with long red curls and freckles who strongly resembled the mother who held her hand.

Coward. Using his child.

Jon handed the photo back to Sam. "What can I do to help?"

Sam set the photo down on the table in front of him and ran his hands through his short, thinning brown hair. "I'm second-guessing myself. I want your opinion. We have snipers on the roof, but they're useless now. There are two heat signatures in the basement away from windows. The last thing I want is a dead child on my conscience."

"Did you ask for a hostage negotiator?"

"Yes. But I've been told she'll be a few hours."

"Have you tracked down his wife?"

Sam said, "Her name's Tammy Corson. She's on her way here. We haven't told her about the daughter yet. It's always a risk bringing spouses into the mix, but I don't know what else to try at this point. He won't answer our calls."

A hard rap on the trailer door interrupted their conversation.

Jon slid open the door. One of his subordinate officers stood with a woman in a cheerful, flowery sun dress and delicate, black leather sandals. She twisted the large diamond rings on her left finger. He recognized the red curls pinned up on her head from the photo. "Tammy Corson? Come in."

She raised her head and met Jon's eyes. "Yes. Officer?"

Jon stepped back to give her room to enter, noting

the southern accent, hoping she had nice family out of state to help her through this nightmare. "I'm Agent Kent." He showed her his badge and gestured towards Sam. "This is Agent Gardner."

Her eyes darted between them. "Why is my house under siege? Why did y'all call me at work?"

Sam took her arm. "Come sit down, Mrs. Corson."

She sat in the chair Sam offered, and Sam took the chair across from her.

Jon stood in the corner by the door doing his best to be unobtrusive so Tammy Corson wouldn't feel ganged up on.

Sam cleared his throat. "Mrs. Corson. Your husband has been laundering money and helping criminals evade taxes for the past ten years."

"Dangerous criminals?"

"Drug cartels and weapons dealers."

Her jaw dropped. She stayed silent for a minute before responding. "Mark wouldn't do that."

Sam sighed. "We have solid evidence. There's more."

"What?"

"When we knocked on your door, he answered with your daughter. He held a pistol at her temple and threatened to shoot if we tried to arrest him."

The color drained from her face, and she slumped into the back of her chair. Her face crumpled.

Jon noted she'd accepted the truth rather than continuing to argue. In such a volatile situation, a solid step in the right direction. Her cooperation could make the difference between life and death. If anyone could persuade their suspect, who was in obvious mental distress to surrender, it was the person closest to him.

She rested her elbows on the table and sobbed. "No! My baby! You have to get her outta there."

Sam handed her a tissue. "We're doing everything we can. But we need your help."

She dabbed her eyes, swallowed, and met Sam's gaze. "I'll do anything. Tell me what to do."

"Since he won't answer our calls, we want you to talk him into surrendering."

She fumbled with the zipper on her purse with shaky hands and pulled out a cell phone.

Sam said, "Wait a minute. I know you're upset, but you need to be calm. Don't antagonize him. No matter what he says, remain on an even keel."

She nodded.

Sam continued, "Try to convince him to do this for you and Hannah. Reason with him any way you can. You know him best. Follow your gut. Would you mind putting the phone on speaker?"

She took deep breaths and touched the screen.

Jon sat beside Sam and folded his arms on the table as the phone rang.

The ringing stopped, and a man's agitated voice answered, "Tammy?"

"Yes, sugar. How's Hannah?"

"Hannah's fine. Playing with her toys."

Tammy closed her eyes and placed her hand on her chest. "Mark, honey. You need to surrender. Please, I love you. I don't want to see you get hurt."

"No. I'm not going to prison. They'll kill me."

"Baby, we can get you some real good lawyers."

Mark's silence on the other end could mean he was considering what his wife asked. Jon wrote *deal* on a notepad.

Sam mouthed, "Good idea," before speaking. "Mr. Corson. This is Agent Gardner. If you can provide us with some credible information about your employers' illegal activities, we could broker a deal. But you must let Tammy take Hannah out of there."

"No. Hannah isn't going anywhere. If you want her, you'll email me a written deal offering immunity. And you'll put us in the witness protection program."

Jon scribbled on the notepad in front of him. *Agree. We can renege afterwards.*

Sam shook his head. "I can't unless you talk to me. Your crimes up until this morning haven't been violent. If your information is credible, I'm amenable to a deal involving witness protection."

Jon stopped himself from shaking his head. *Dammit Sam!*

Mark said, "No. It's my way or nothing. That information could get me and everyone I love killed."

Tammy sobbed. "Please, Mark. Talk to em." The screen on her phone showed the call had been disconnected. She grabbed onto Sam's sleeve. "Please, give him what he wants."

Sam shook his head. "We already have a lot of evidence against the people your husband worked for. His information would be useful, but not enough to warrant immunity."

Jon fisted his hand. The pencil he held snapped in half.

Why did he pull me into this if he didn't want to listen to me?

Tammy clenched her jaw, stood, and faced Sam. "I'm taking my daughter outta there."

Jon stood, unwilling to let Sam control the situation

any longer. "Please sit, Mrs. Corson. If you go in there and try to take Hannah, he may shoot you both. There's a hostage negotiator on her way here. Can you give us more time, please?"

She sat. "I'll give y'all five minutes. Then I'm getting my baby."

Jon took a deep breath. "Mrs. Corson, I understand your determination. But it isn't safe. If we wait him out, he'll have to go upstairs. The minute he's a floor away from Hannah, we can go in and get him."

"How will y'all know where he is inside the house?"

"We have special equipment that reads heat signatures through bricks and walls."

Sam said, "If he walks by a window, one of our snipers will take him out."

"What? No! Y'all can't shoot Mark. He never hurt anyone."

Jon narrowed his eyes at Sam, willing him to shut up. Sam used to have a heart. What the hell happened to him?

Sam raised his hands palm out, then folded his arms across his chest.

Jon said, "Shooting Mark will be a last resort. You have my word."

Tammy picked up her phone and tapped the screen. She held her chin high, lips pressed in a firm line.

Jon asked, "What did you do?"

"I told Mark I would be his hostage if he'd let Hannah go. If he agrees, I'm going in the house, and y'all can't stop me."

A feeling of unease churned in Jon's gut, but the intensity in her blue eyes said she wouldn't back down, and he couldn't blame her. He could, however, make the best of the situation. "Listen to me, please. Walk to the door, then the minute Hannah comes out, you grab her hand and leave. We'll get Mark out of there after you and Hannah are safe."

"But you won't shoot him?"

"Not unless he shoots at us."

Her phone buzzed. "He agreed. I'm going. I trust y'all will keep up your end of the bargain. Mark's a good man, a loving husband and father. He had to be coerced into doing what he did."

"Do you have family nearby? A place to go? You might not be able to get back in the house for a while."

"No, my people are in Mississippi. I'm taking Hannah there after this is over. I'd rather not stick around to be hounded by press and deal with the neighbors' gossip."

Jon handed her his business card. "If you need anything, call."

She strode away from Jon, out of the trailer, and across the street without a backward glance.

Jon followed. He stopped in the middle of the street as a brave woman approached a house with an armed man inside.

Hannah opened the front door and came outside. Her face lit up and she flew into her mother's arms. "Mom, you're home early."

Tammy stared at the front door of her home with tears streaming down her face, then turned with her daughter in her arms, and ran to a black Escalade parked down the street.

Sam touched Jon's shoulder. "She's safe. You handled that well."

Jon shoved his hand away. "That was all Mrs. Corson. What the hell is wrong with you? Why didn't you listen to me?" He paced in front of Sam. "Mark Corson isn't a violent criminal. All you had to do was agree and this whole thing would've been over. What she said is true. He could be the victim of blackmail, or they could've threatened to hurt his family if he didn't cooperate."

Sam stood an inch from Jon's face, voice raised. "I tried questioning him a few days ago and he wouldn't talk. I gave him every opportunity to help himself and his family. We arrested his clients this morning. He gets one last chance to surrender. He refuses, then we kick down the door and storm the house."

"When you corner people, they can surprise you. He already outsmarted you once. You thought he'd go with you easily, so you came to arrest him without backup. Am I right?"

Sam put his hands on his waist. "You can't blame this on me. He chose to be an idiot and use his daughter."

"At least wait until Tammy drives off before you traumatize them further."

Two muffled bangs rang through the air.

Seconds later, Sam's radio crackled. "Agent Gardner, shots were fired inside the target's home."

Jon drew his pistol and ran towards the door as Sam gave the order to move in.

Without waiting for assistance, Jon ran up the well-coiffured laneway and kicked the door in. "FBI, come out with your hands up."

Silence greeted him in response. His footsteps echoed across the marble floor, past the grand winding staircase.

Men flooded through the door behind him into the house making it impossible to listen for anyone. The main floor was open concept with no place to hide.

Jon opened a few doors along the right wall, finding a storage closet and a powder room before opening the third door revealing a descending staircase.

Light already illuminated a large, finished basement. The metallic odor of gun powder filled the air.

He raised his voice, "Down here." He continued down the stairs with men on his heels and made a grisly discovery.

Mark lay in a pool of blood with half of his head missing.

Jon placed two fingers on his carotid artery. No pulse as he suspected. He stood. "No one touch anything. Go back outside and secure the scene."

The men turned on their heels and headed back the way they came.

Jon followed them outside, numb and disgusted at the situation. A man took his life, for what? To avoid a few years in prison if his expensive lawyers didn't get him off? Some loving husband and father he'd turned out to be, and if Sam had agreed to offer immunity the man would still be alive.

Sam approached, shoulders hunched, and stopped in front of him. "I should've listened to you. You were right."

"I can't do this anymore. I'm out of here. Sorry, Sam."

"What? Wait."

Jon strode around him without responding. He got

in his car and drove straight home.

He opened the fridge and stared inside at the measly contents within. One egg, an old carton of milk, and a few tangerines. Emptiness and sorrow filled him not allowing room for hunger, thirst, or anything resembling happiness.

He went to his bedroom and into the adjacent walk-in closet. Running his hands along the soft fabrics of Cynthia's favorite cashmere sweaters, brought back memories of holding her in his arms. She'd been gone for over a year. Chances were he'd never hold her again.

Their home held so many good memories but remembering them brought nothing but pain. The job he'd dreamed of and excelled in no longer held any appeal.

Cynthia, I can't stay and wait anymore. This hurts too much. I need to go home.

He draped his clothes over his arms and loaded them into the backseat of his car along with his toiletries and Cynthia's black cashmere sweater. After emptying what little remained in the fridge and freezer into a black garbage bag, he locked the windows and doors. Jon couldn't bear the thought of selling the house on the slim chance Cynthia came home someday. But until such a day, he wouldn't return.

Chapter Nineteen

Jon rolled over in bed to face Jessica. *No way I'm letting you die. I won't fail you the way I failed Cynthia and Mark Corson.*

Jessica's forehead creased and she whimpered. Her thoughts as troubled as his, even in sleep.

He rubbed her back. "Shhh. You're safe."

She opened her eyes, locked onto his gaze, and held his hand. "Darn, I woke you, didn't I?"

He swept the stray hairs off her forehead and set them behind her ear. "It's fine. Go back to sleep."

She shut her eyes. Eventually her grip loosened, and her hand weighed heavily in his.

He, however, gave up on sleep and went to keep Thomas company. Adrenaline would carry him through their planned takedown later.

He showered and then went into the kitchen to make fresh coffee.

Sam's loud snores carried from the leather couch into the kitchen. Sam had always been able to sleep almost anywhere on command.

Jon had never acquired the ability, and he envied him. He took two mugs of coffee to the basement.

Thomas pecked away feverishly on his keyboard.

"Hi, Thomas. Anything eventful happen last night?"

Thomas jumped almost falling out of his chair. His

cheeks turned scarlet. "Christ, Jon. You scared me."

Jon held his breath, set his coffee down to avoid spillage, then gave into his laughter. He laughed so hard, he had to bend over and hold onto his knees for balance. A welcome relief from the gloomy memories of the previous night. "Sorry, Thomas. What did I interrupt?"

"If you must know, I was talking to a lady friend of mine."

Yeah, right. "Only a friend? Why are you blushing then?"

"Okay, okay. Friend with benefits. We were having a private conversation."

"Do you want privacy? I'll go upstairs and keep an eye on the cameras while I listen to Sam snore."

"No need now. The mood is spoiled. You might as well keep me company." Thomas pointed to the screen. "She can get some sleep for a change instead of helping me stay awake."

"I figured I'd keep you company or take over if you wanted sleep."

"If my calculations are correct, all sleep spaces are occupied. I would be stuck on the other couch with Sam snoring beside me. No point. I may as well wait a few hours until Debbie gets up at the crack of dawn."

"Can I run a few things by you? I'm not liking this plan. There are too many unknowns."

Thomas said, "Of course."

"David has the upper hand. We still don't know where he's hiding. Hell, we may never know. Did he surface on any of the cameras?"

Thomas shook his head. "No sign of him on either property. Could he have taken off after the shooting when the police swarmed the woods? He seems to know when to cut and run, considering no one has ever caught him."

"I doubt it. He shot from long range so he wouldn't be seen, and he didn't leave after the fire. Why would he cut and run now? Unless…maybe Sam wasn't careful enough, and he took off."

"Sam came alone in a black car at night. He's fairly competent." Thomas's forehead scrunched in concentration. "I'll sweep the house for bugs again."

"All right, I'll keep an eye on things."

Jon skimmed through the footage from the night before as he waited. A little while later, Thomas returned and sat in his chair. "I didn't find anything. He isn't listening in to our conversations."

"That's a relief. He hasn't had much success, so maybe he's letting his leg heal as he plans his next move. My gut says he's coming at us full force soon."

"Jessica is right about needing to shove things towards their conclusion. We're sitting ducks, giving David all kinds of time to plan. His past experiences probably give him advantages when plotting fires and breeching security systems."

"Yes, a scary thought. That's why I'm leery about Jess being bait. He could get in the house and kill her within the few minutes it takes me and Sam to get to her."

Thomas pushed his glasses farther up his nose. "Hide across the field in the woods. Worst case scenario, you're out there all night for nothing."

"Good idea. This creep will jump on the opportunity."

"You know I'll have both eyes on the cameras

while Jess is in the house with Debbie." Thomas grabbed the arms of his chair. "Wait, what about Bryce? Who is going to watch over him? If David got Bryce, then he'd have supreme leverage."

"We're pretty sure David mistook Chip for me the other day. Why else would he try to shoot him when Jess is his priority? I'm going to use that to our advantage."

"How?"

"We get Bryce to lay on the floor of my truck while Chip drives off the property. Then David will think I'm gone, making Jess seem even more vulnerable. Chip should be able to get away without being followed if Jess and Debbie cross the fields to the rental house at the same time to split David's attention."

Thomas grinned. "Brilliant. More dynamic and it'll swing probability towards him taking the bait."

Footsteps sounded overhead.

Jon stood. "I better see who is up and about. Do you need anything?"

"No, this fresh coffee was good for now unless there are anymore of Debbie's chocolate chip cookies kicking around."

"I'll check."

Jon discovered Debbie up and about getting coffee with uncharacteristic bags under her eyes. "I see you had a troubled sleep as well?"

"Yes. Tonight has me pretty shaken up."

"I've been fortifying our plan." He explained the new complexities to her.

"That's a relief. I'd feel much better knowing you're close by, and Bryce isn't. Do you want breakfast? If I don't keep busy, I'll lose my mind."

"It's funny you mentioned food. Thomas was asking if there are any of your cookies left."

"You tell him he can have a few after he eats his breakfast."

He chuckled. "I'll relay the message. He's a bottomless pit."

"I've noticed."

After Jessica woke, and everyone had been fed by Debbie, the adults convened around the table to talk over their plans.

Chip came into the house and pulled out a chair. "Hi, boss. You wanted to talk to me?"

"Yes, I need to ask a favor. Would you be willing to help us tonight? You'd be driving my truck away from here with Bryce hidden inside."

Chip said, "Sure. I'll take him back to my house in town until you call and give me the all clear. I'm sure my kids will love him. He could use some friends."

Jessica said, "Thanks so much, Chip. Bryce will love having children to play with."

Sam stood. "Now that we have the details ironed out, I'll make sure my men are in place. I'll assign two to watch Chip's house as a precaution. Are you good with that Chip?"

"Sure, that'll be fine." Chip gave Sam his address.

Sam said, "Jon, do you still have gear? I have an extra gun, but no vest."

"I have everything I need."

Sam asked. "What time should we start?"

Jon said, "At nine o'clock tonight. Once the sun is down, Chip and Jess should make their moves. We can sneak across to the woods right after Jess turns on the kitchen light. The light should distract him from our movements."

Sam said, "I'll make all the necessary arrangements. It'll be like old times."

Jon stood. "Old times is right, and I'm hoping tonight will be the last."

He wanted nothing more than to start a new chapter with the woman he grew up loving, and her son who needed a father. The family unit he'd dreamed of having all his adult life.

Chapter Twenty

In the storage area of his basement, Jon dressed in black from head to toe, tightening his jaw as he held his bulletproof vest. He kept the vest as a reminder of why he left the FBI behind and hadn't worn the thing since he walked off the job.

Sam, already dressed in full tactical gear, stood beside him. "You ready, Jon? It's been a few years. You might be rusty."

Jon unlocked his weapons cabinet and removed his pistol, handcuffs, pepper spray, and a knife. "I'm ready."

"I blame myself for Mark Corson's death and you quitting. Tammy and Hannah are doing well. They're living with Tammy's parents in Mississippi surrounded by aunts, uncles, and cousins."

Jon sighed and glanced into his friend's haunted eyes. "I'm glad they're with family." He checked each weapon before securing them in his belt as he spoke. "I didn't quit because of that case, but it was the final straw after Cynthia. I should've stayed long enough to help you close out the case, but I couldn't. I was in a bad place."

Sam patted his shoulder. "I understand. I was messed up then, too. Some cases wear on you more than others. You know the bureau would be happy to have you back anytime."

"They've contacted me. I have no interest in returning. I'm much happier on the ranch, especially with Jess back in town."

"So, think we can put the past behind us? Are we good again?"

Jon hadn't expected Sam to admit wrongdoing or apologize as he never had before. "Yes. Of course."

They climbed the stairs to the kitchen and joined the others. After closing every blind and curtain, Jon switched off the exterior lights, plunging his property into darkness.

Jessica knelt on the floor with Bryce enveloped in her arms. "You have fun at Chip's house."

Bryce touched his mother's cheek. "I will."

Chip took Bryce's hand and guided him towards the door. "Let's go have some fun."

Jessica whispered in Jon's ear. "I have a bad feeling about this."

Jon pulled her into his arms. "He'll be all right. You ready?"

"As ready as I'll ever be."

He brushed his lips against hers. "It isn't too late to change your mind. We can scrap this plan."

"Then what? You and Sam hunting around the woods trying to find David without being killed? That gives me bad vibes too. No. I'm not changing my mind."

Dammit, Jess. I wish you wouldn't do this.

Not wanting to sway her delicate confidence, he refrained from voicing his concerns. "All right. Want a weapon?"

She slipped her hand inside her jacket and pulled out a canister. "I've got my pepper spray."

He cradled her cheek and memorized every detail of her face, her grey-blue eyes, and the light spattering of freckles. He kissed the tip of her nose. "We're going to get into position. I'll be nearby the whole time. Keep your wits about you."

"I will."

Running footsteps pounded the basement stairs. Thomas flew into the kitchen red-faced, breathing hard, with a laptop in his arms. "David just hit Chip over the head, picked up Bryce, and ran. He's headed across the street."

****

Jessica sprinted out the kitchen door.

No. Not my baby! This can't be happening.

Jon and Sam were on her heels.

Sam spoke into his radio. "Agent Handcock, shutdown the perimeter. I want every road gravel and paved, blocked off. Our suspect kidnapped an eight-year-old boy on foot. He may have a vehicle nearby. I'm in pursuit."

The radio crackled. "Copy that, sir."

Jessica rounded the curve in the gravel laneway and charged through the gate. She spotted David running into the woods across the street with Bryce over his shoulder. "Bring me back my baby, you animal!"

Bryce kicked and pounded on David's back with his fists. "Put me down! Mom!" He outstretched his arms towards her. "Mom!"

Jessica grimaced, running through a stitch in her side. "We're coming, baby! Keep yelling so we can find you!"

David disappeared into the dense trees out of view.

Bryce screamed, "Mom!"

Jon clasped Jessica's hand as they neared the rental house while Sam picked up his pace. "I know you want to keep going, but you can't"

She pulled her hand out of his grasp and ran faster. She panted, "Bryce is my baby! Mine!"

Jon kept pace barely breathing from the exertion. He grabbed her arm and held her in place.

She wriggled in his grasp. "Let me go!"

Bryce screamed again. "Mom!"

"Sam, keep going. I'll catch up." Jon held onto Jessica. "Listen to me. David wants you. Bryce is a decoy. He could ambush you in the woods."

Jessica pushed against Jon's vest. "I don't care. Let me go. Now!"

"Bryce needs you alive. Sam's men are in position. David isn't escaping. Go back to the house. If David escapes, he'll call. He wants you, not Bryce. You must be there to take that call. To buy us time."

Jessica stopped struggling, chest heaving from exertion as she struggled to catch her breath. Her heart urged her to keep running, but Jon's logic made sense. "Go. You better get my son back."

Jon sped to catch up to Sam. Glancing over his shoulder he yelled, "I'll get him."

Jessica collapsed onto her knees in the dewy grass and wept as Bryce's screams faded into the distance. Tears spent; she wiped her eyes with her sleeve.

I can't lose Bryce. I can't.

She stood and ran back the way she came. She found Chip sitting at the kitchen table holding an ice pack on the back of his head. Debbie and Thomas sat on either side of him.

Chip stared into Jessica's eyes with a gaze full of sorrow. "I'm sorry. He must have been waiting in the barn. I never saw him. I opened the door of Jon's truck. Then something hit me in the back of the head and knocked me flat on my stomach. By the time I hoisted myself up, David had taken off with Bryce."

She couldn't form a response. Words wouldn't come. In a small part of her brain, she understood Chip wasn't to blame, but the overriding emotional portion condemned him all the same. She paced back and forth across the kitchen. "How am I supposed to stay here and wait?"

What could a little boy do to defend himself from a huge monster?

I should've run with Bryce while I had the chance. I was selfish thinking I could have Jon, too. What have I done?

Debbie placed her hands on Jessica's shoulders, forcing her to stop pacing. "Have faith in Jon. Trust me. He won't accept not saving Bryce."

"What do you mean he won't accept it? There's something else, isn't there?" Her voice rose involuntarily. "Please, I'm losing my mind here."

Debbie sighed. "Come sit on the couch with me." She steered Jessica out of the earshot of the two men. "You remember Sally, Jon's mother?"

"Of course."

"She confided in me awhile back about why Jon retired early, and it wasn't only because of Cynthia. He and Sam have a long history. It's Jon's story to tell, but under the circumstances, you should know." Debbie proceeded to tell her about the Corson family.

Jessica wiped away tears. *I haven't cried this much*

187

since Adam died. "Poor Jon. I wish he'd told me. How many other deaths is he carrying on his shoulders? No wonder there's tension between him and Sam."

Debbie squeezed Jessica's hand. "Jon was trying to shield you from an ugly event in his past. Honestly, I wouldn't have told you under different circumstances. I'm only telling you now to convince you Jon won't stop until he has Bryce."

"What if he fails? What if I lose them both? What if Sam makes a stupid decision? He's in charge."

Debbie's eyes filled with tears as she took her niece into her arms. "Come here, my girl. Jon is in charge this time. Didn't you notice?"

"You're right." Jessica rested her head on Debbie's shoulder, sobbing, and clinging to her for dear life.

****

Jon swerved through the trees with Sam on his heels, following Bryce's voice, each scream a little bit louder than the one before.

I'm closing in.

Jon and Sam came to a fork in the path.

Sam headed right. "Let's box him in. I'll circle around the other side."

"Right." Jon ran left, then rounded a bend. David ran with Bryce over his shoulder about thirty feet ahead. He dug deep and ran faster, ignoring branches scrapping his face and snagging in his clothes.

David diverted right and cut through trees out of sight. Jon followed the crackling of twigs, and the swaying branches. A door slammed.

No! The dirt road.

With a burst of speed, Jon broke through the trees.

Bryce peered out the back passenger door of the

old Ford, pounding on the window with tears streaming down his cheeks as David drove off.

Dammit!

Jon pulled his revolver, planted his feet, aimed for the back tires, and fired. His bullets fell short of their target as David drove out of range.

He grabbed the radio off his belt. "Suspect is heading east in an old, green, four-door Ford F-150, on the dirt road towards RR14. There's a kidnapped child in the backseat. Intercept. Do not shoot."

Sam's voice carried through the radio. "Copy that. You heard the man. Do not shoot. I repeat. Do not shoot. Box him in."

Chapter Twenty-One

David glanced over his shoulder at Bryce in the back seat and bellowed, "Stop crying. I can't drive with that racket."

Tears and snot rolled down Bryce's face as he gave up kneeling to look out the back window and sat in his seat. In a quiet voice he pleaded, "I want my mom. Please, David."

David met the little boy's eyes in the mirror. The child although distressed, had followed instructions. "If you listen and your mom loves you enough, you won't get hurt. Now be quiet. You hear?"

Bryce whimpered but held his head high. "Mom loves me enough."

As much as he despised Jessica, her love for the boy was evident. That led him to the snap decision to kidnap Bryce and set up an exchange after the FBI arrived on scene. With too many eyes searching for him around Kent's ranch, it made the most sense to take the boy to his hideout and initiate the trade, but first he had to get past the roadblocks.

He reached the end of the dirt road and needed to turn either right or left. Blue and red lights blinked on both sides, illuminating the night sky miles away in either direction.

Morons.

Rather than charging at his location, or at least

turning off the lights, they'd maintained their existing roadblocks. Instead of hanging a right or a left, David engaged the four-wheel drive and drove straight across the road into a field of tall hay stalks.

The truck bumped along the uneven ground and flattened hay for five miles until they encountered a flimsy wooden fence along the property line. David jammed his foot on the accelerator. The old metal bumper shattered the wood. He hung a left on the dirt road beyond the fence and wove his way through the property until he came to another hay field. This one wasn't fenced.

He crossed the field diagonally toward a rural road about seven miles on the other side. The FBI wouldn't have roadblocks so far out of range. A mile from the road, he turned off the headlights and relied on the moon and stars to light the way forward.

As his tires touched the paved, rural road, he glanced forwards and backwards. No red and blue lights lit up the sky. He'd gotten past the roadblocks. David turned his lights on and drove the speed limit along rural roads circling the outskirts of town, away from prying eyes and local cops. Ten minutes later, he parked behind the old barn and opened Bryce's door.

"Where are we going?" Bryce asked.

"Inside the barn."

"Why did you take me?"

"Because your mother did something bad to me and needs to be punished."

Bryce crossed his arms and sneered. "Liar. She saw you do something bad."

David slapped him across the face. "Don't you ever talk back to me again!"

Bryce clutched his red cheek and tears dripped down his face.

"I'm sorry, kid. You have a right to be angry."

Bryce looked at him through his tears and said nothing. The kid looked defeated. All the fight he'd displayed at the ranch and on the way to the car had petered out.

David took Bryce into his arms. As he carried him to the barn, he rubbed circles into the boy's back. He admired the child's bravery and defiance.

Maybe once everything settled, he'd keep the boy and raise him as his own. The irony wasn't lost on him that he'd accidentally murdered Sarah after she pressed the issue of wanting a child.

The single father angle might make it easier to find another wife when all this was over. He intended to keep fulfilling his deep-seeded need to control, punish, and kill women, and that was a lot easier to do with a wife and child to help him come across as the nice guy next door.

****

Jon drove a black, FBI-owned SUV with Sam in the passenger seat beside him. Since Cynthia's murder and Corson's suicide, anything having to do with him, and the FBI went to hell. Had he been cursed? The clock on the dash churned his gut. Too much time had passed since David got away with Bryce.

He glanced over at Sam. "How haven't we found them yet? I thought you said the area was locked down."

"It's secure. We've stopped every vehicle in the area. He must have stopped before the roadblocks and abandoned his vehicle. We'll find the truck, then get canines to track them."

"You better be right." Jon clutched the steering wheel. "I can't put off telling Jess about this much longer."

Jon spotted a flattened area of hay and slammed on the brakes. He jumped from the SUV and switched on his high-powered flashlight as he ran into the field. The glow illuminated a straight path of flattened and battered hay stalks wide enough for David's stolen truck.

He jogged back to the SUV. "Hang on, Sam. He went this way."

"Step on it. With our luck, we'll get stuck in the mud." Sam grabbed the radio. "I'll give them our location."

"I think I know where he went. There's an old rural road about fifteen miles northwest of here. Canines won't help since they aren't on foot."

"Shoot. That would have been outside our immediate perimeter. We didn't anticipate off-roading through hay fields. All routes leading out of town are secure, including the back ways you warned me about."

Dammit. How could he not have had a wider perimeter? I should've taken the lead.

Jon clamped his lips shut. Tearing a strip off Sam wouldn't bring them any closer to David and Bryce.

He reached the end of the field, and the SUV's headlights illuminated a busted fence. Jon steered through the existing hole and stopped on the dirt road beyond. He lowered his window and shone his flashlight on the road.

Sam did the same on his side. "There are fresh tracks in the mud over here."

Jon turned right and took his time. Going at a slow pace when David was getting farther and farther ahead damn near killed him, but they had to figure out where he'd gone.

"I see where he went," Sam said. "About twenty feet ahead to the left. He cut through another hay field."

Jon accelerated and hung a left, following the diagonal path of destruction through the crops. "This isn't good. We're headed directly for a rural road, and it's paved which means no tracks."

"Don't give up hope. He picked up quite a lot of mud and hay in his wheels. There may yet be tracks."

****

"We should've heard from Jon by now. It's been over an hour." Jessica stared at Jon's phone on the kitchen table, surrounded by Thomas, Chip, and Aunt Debbie. "So much for the FBI being superior to the locals."

"You've got a point, Jess." Aunt Debbie touched her arm. "We should call Sheriff Hank. He knows this area like the back of his hand." She looked to Thomas. "What do you think?"

"If the perimeter roadblocks failed, the ones set up on the ways out of town would at least, in theory, keep David confined to the area." Thomas removed his glasses, set them on the table, and rubbed the bridge of his nose. "The local authorities will know the area better and get word out to the public. Knowing Sam, there's no way he'll involve them."

Jessica pulled the burner phone out of her pocket not wanting to tie up the home phone. "Aunt Debbie, do you still have Sheriff Hank's card?"

"Here you go." Debbie dug the card out of her

pocket.

Jessica entered the number into her phone and waited. "Sheriff Hank? It's Jessica Miller. Something terrible has happened. I need your help."

She proceeded to fill him in on their plan, the FBI's presence, and worst of all, Bryce's kidnapping.

Sheriff Hank said, "I'll put out an amber alert immediately. With the FBI having roadblocks in place, my units are free to search all the backroads and acreages around town."

"Thank you. But hold off on the alert until I hear from Jon. Jon and Sam might be in the middle of something, and Sam was adamant about no alerts and not involving you."

"You made the right decision calling me, Ms. Miller. But I disagree about the alert. The more people we get looking the better."

Jessica paused to consider. After learning of the mistakes in Sam's past, should she really trust Sam's lead? "You have a point. What do you guys think about an amber alert? Yes, or no? David must have noticed the FBI presence by now."

Debbie said, "Yes. What do you say, Thomas?"

Thomas didn't hesitate. "Yes. Chip, what's your vote?"

Chip said, "If it was my child, I would."

Jessica closed her eyes and prayed they were making the right decision. "Go ahead and issue the alert, Sheriff."

"Good decision."

"I'm grateful. Please let me know if you hear anything." Jessica hung up and said, "That was the right thing to do. I wish Jon would give us something."

Jon's house phone rang.

Jessica picked up the receiver. "Maybe that's him." She paused with her finger over the accept button. Whoever was on the other end and whatever information they had to impart couldn't be erased. But Bryce needed her to be strong.

She pushed the button and held the phone to her ear. "Hello?"

"Your son's asleep, and you didn't get to tuck him in. What a pity."

David's menacing tone held an air of smugness. Jessica's heart pounded in her throat. Jon had guessed right. His warning had given her some time to prepare.

Thomas had coached her on what to do in case this happened, and the phone line was bugged.

She couldn't let David get to her. If she said the wrong thing and angered the monster, he could take it out on Bryce. She also had to focus on every single word and background noise in case David gave away some clue about their location.

Jessica held up one finger in a universal gesture of silence. The others nodded their understanding. Jessica pushed the speaker button wanting the others to hear so not a single word would be forgotten. She set the phone on the table.

David said, "Are you there? I seem to have made you catatonic. Maybe I should hang up."

Jessica said, "No! Let Bryce go. I'll recant my statement and tell the RCMP I was dreaming."

"It's too late. You stuck your nose where it didn't belong, and the FBI is breathing down my neck."

"I'll do anything if you let my son go. What do you want?"

"You. Dead. If you want your son to remain sleeping peacefully rather than permanently, you're going to do exactly as I say."

Debbie paled and clasped Jessica's hand.

"My life in return for Bryce unharmed?"

"Yes."

"Where do I go?"

"You'll find a burner phone inside your boyfriend's truck. I'll tell you where to go when I see fit. If you bring anyone with you, alert either the FBI, or the local idiots, I put a bullet in your son's brain. Got it?"

"Yes. But—"

The line went dead. The dial tone echoed through the kitchen.

"That means—" Jessica's voice broke. "Jon and Sam lost him. David got away with Bryce. And the amber alert is going out, and he said no alerts."

"Don't lose hope, Jess." Thomas pressed the disconnect button. "Chip, would you retrieve the burner phone, please? I'll get to work tracing the call David just made to the house. I might get David's exact location or narrow it down with how long Jessica managed to keep him on the line."

Jessica's breathing accelerated, and she gasped for air. Her worst nightmare was coming true.

Chapter Twenty-Two

Inside the old barn, Bryce kept his eyes shut in the backseat of David's truck as he listened to the conversation between David and Mom. He'd only been pretending to sleep because he didn't want to deal with David anymore.

Bryce could barely make out his mother's muffled words coming through the phone.

She said, "What do you want?"

David said, "You, dead."

No! Mom can't die!

Bryce wanted to cry, but if he cried, David would know he was awake. He mustn't make a sound. David told Mom to come when he called her, and Bryce needed to stop him. Staying still and not moving wasn't easy, but if he managed to lay there and stay awake, then maybe David would leave or fall asleep. Then he'd take the phone. If David couldn't call Mom, she wouldn't come, and Jon would keep her safe.

The songs and voices on the radio helped to pass the time. Bryce's mind wanted to shut down and give in to sleep, but he had to stay awake for Mom.

David hadn't made any noise in a while.

Bryce opened his eyes.

David's head rested against the window, but his face was hidden.

Hanging onto the passenger seat, Bryce leaned

forward.

David's eyes were shut, and his mouth hung open. The phone was in the cup holder beside him.

Bryce reached between the seats and closed his hand around the phone.

David moaned and shifted his head.

Bryce shoved the phone in between the cushions of the backseat. He lay down and squeezed his eyes shut. But what would David do when he noticed the phone was missing? He'd probably get crazy mad.

Song after song played on the radio and nothing happened. Bryce chanced another look.

David's head leaned against the seat. Maybe he was still sleeping.

Bryce leaned forward.

David's eyes were closed.

Bryce pulled the phone out of the seat.

If he tried to call for help, David would hear him. Bryce touched his cheek. It still stung from when David hit him. If David woke and noticed his missing phone, he would hit him again.

Maybe I can run away!

Bryce put his hand on the handle and debated opening the door. But it might make too much noise. He glanced around the truck. Behind him, a small, open window led to the truck bed.

He stuffed the phone in the pocket of his shorts and wiggled through the window. Perching on the bed on the other side, he peered inside the truck.

David hadn't moved.

Bryce crawled to the tailgate. He lifted one leg over and used the tire as a foothold, then lifted the other leg over and dropped. The hard packed dirt on the ground smothered the sound of his landing. Next, he needed to get out of the barn.

The door they came in was padlocked shut. Maybe there was another way out, like the back window of the truck. A pile of wooden crates sat in one corner.

Should I hide?

He crawled between the crates and came upon a hole in the wall. Sticking his head through, he discovered forest on the other side.

A way out!

This hole was smaller than the truck window, but he had to get through. He stuck his head and arms through the opening. The sides of the barn dug into his shoulders, trapping him in place. He pressed his hands on the ground outside and wiggled and wiggled. With each wiggle his shoulders moved a little farther forward, then the pressure released as they came through. His shoulders ached, but he crawled forward on his hands, pulling the rest of his body through.

The fresh night air tasted good, but he didn't know which way to go. The dirt road wove around the forest in both directions. One way would lead to the last paved road they were on and the other would have to lead someplace. Maybe a house?

Bryce couldn't stay where he was, so he turned right and ran along the dirt road. He turned his head, and the barn was no longer in view. Now he'd be far enough away to call for help. He didn't know where he was, but couldn't they trace locations from phones?

He reached in his pocket for the phone, but it wasn't there.

Oh no. I dropped it.

Turning around, he considered going back. What if

David woke up?

Roads always led somewhere. Whenever he'd come across a barn before, there had always been a house nearby. If he kept going forward, he'd find one.

****

Jon and Sam continued following bits of hay and mud that David had left behind. Luckily, the debris had led them along relatively unused backroads that hadn't been obscured by traffic, but the trail had thinned over the past few miles.

Sam said, "We may end up having to backtrack to pick up his trail again."

"I know. I'm trying to stay positive. Time is not on our side."

"David can't hide in the woods forever."

Jon's cell rang and his home phone number appeared on the screen. He couldn't put off updating the others any longer.

He set the phone on speaker. "Hello."

"David called about an hour ago." Jessica's anguished voice knifed Jon in the gut. "Why didn't you tell us David got away with Bryce? Didn't you think I deserved to hear it from you?"

Jon sighed. Sugar coating things wouldn't help. She needed facts. "We picked up David's trail through farmers' fields and onto backroads. He hasn't gone past any of the roadblocks. I didn't want to call until I had news."

Sam asked, "What did David have to say?"

"He wants me to trade myself for Bryce. He left a burner in the barn that he'll call when he sees fit."

"Jess, you can't. Once he has you, then you're both dead." Jon pleaded. "Promise me you won't go."

"I'm hoping I won't need to. Thomas traced David's call to a five-mile area. He's texting you and Sam the coordinates."

Sam smiled. "That's fantastic news. We'll find him, Jessica."

"There's something else you should know. While you two were incommunicado, I called the sheriff. An amber alert is going out anytime. I haven't given him the five-mile area, but I'm sorely tempted."

Jon slammed on the brakes and pulled over to the side of the road. "You have to stop that alert. David will move if he thinks we're too close, and the location Thomas traced will be useless. Call the sheriff now."

Jessica's voice raised, "If I tell Sheriff Hank you've got the location narrowed, and you're handling it, then you two mess up again, I'll never forgive you."

Jon swallowed around the lump in his throat. *Angry is good. Means she's not falling apart.* "I'm not coming home without Bryce."

Jessica's tone mellowed. "I know this is David's fault and not yours, but I'm losing my mind here."

"I'll call the minute I have Bryce in my arms. I love you, Jess. Stay strong for Bryce."

"I will. Goodbye, Jon."

Sam tapped his screen and zoomed in on the map Thomas had sent. "We need to head south of town. Do you know this area?"

"Yes, there are some large properties and dense forests around there."

"If you hadn't brought Thomas into this, we'd be out of luck."

Jon rammed his foot on the accelerator. "I know. We still might be. It's already been over an hour. David could be on the move."

"I don't think so. It makes more sense to stay in one place if you've got a good hiding spot rather than risk being seen."

"God, I hope so. I'm parking outside the perimeter, and we're moving in on foot. We *cannot* risk him figuring out we're onto him."

"Right, but we'll start in the middle, then fan out. We have the radios. If we split up, we can cover more ground."

"Sam, whoever finds David and Bryce first, radios the other person and calls for backup before doing anything else. Deal?"

"Count on it. We aren't letting David slip away with Bryce again."

Chapter Twenty-Three

David opened his eyes and stretched his arms over his head as his vision adjusted to the darkness. He'd slept two hours, longer than he'd intended. The boy had been quieter than he'd expected him to be. He glanced over his shoulder. The backseat was empty.

Where did he go?

The padlock secured the door, and the windows were too high for a little boy to reach. He had to be in the barn somewhere.

David climbed out of the truck with his flashlight and walked around expecting to see the boy, but he was nowhere to be found. Maybe Bryce had gotten scared and decided to hide.

"Come out. I won't hurt you."

David stood still and tuned his ears to his surroundings. No rapid breathing, nor footsteps, or noise of any kind. "Fine, have it your way. We'll play hide and seek."

Bryce could only be hiding in two places, behind drywall sheets leaning against one wall, or in one of the old wooden crates in the corner.

"Come out, come out wherever you are." David tilted the drywall sheets forward. No Bryce.

"Come on, kid. I don't have time for this crap. I know you're in those crates." He paused and waited in front of them. "This is your last chance. If I have to look for you in those dirty things, you're getting another licking."

He expected Bryce to give up and come out, but nothing happened. "Damn you, kid."

David kicked the nearest crate into the rest of the pile. The crates scattered under his force, revealing a hole in the wall behind them. A hole big enough for a little boy to squeeze through.

"Shit!" *Wait until I get my hands on you. You're going to pay for this.*

David stuck his flashlight in his mouth, pulled his keys out of his pocket, and unlocked the padlock. He circled the building and kneeled beside the hole in the back of the barn. Small footprints in the dirt led away from the hole. He shone his flashlight ahead and followed Bryce's tracks to the dirt road.

David smiled. Instead of heading towards the main road nearby, Bryce had gone down the dirt road in the opposite direction farther into the woods. The nearest inhabited house was a good ten miles away. The kid had at most an hour and forty-five-minute head start with the time it took him to find his way out of the barn. Being a kid and scared of his own shadow, he'd stick to the road instead of trekking through the woods.

David jogged back to the old Ford parked behind the barn.

****

Bryce trudged down the dirt road. The house couldn't be much farther. He alternated between running and walking when he needed to catch his breath. His legs were heavy like bricks and his throat dry like sandpaper, but he pushed ahead. Whenever he stopped to catch his breath, he remembered David's mean voice telling his mom he wanted her dead. He needed to find help.

Wheels crunched through the dirt and scattered rocks in the distance behind him. A car. Maybe the person who owned the barn was on their way home. Bryce turned to wait for the car to come closer then reconsidered. People didn't come home in the middle of the night. They slept in their beds at home.

What if David had woken up?

Fueled by a new burst of energy, Bryce fled into the woods, and kneeled behind a tree. His body trembled as the rumbling came closer and closer. Headlights pierced the darkness as an old truck came around a bend in the road.

David.

Bryce's chest rose and fell quickly. He pulled his head behind the tree, wishing he could disappear into its bark, and waited until the truck passed to start walking again. The road wouldn't be safe anymore. He'd have to stay in the woods where David couldn't see him.

The farther he moved into the forest, the harder it became to make out his hands in front of his face with the trees blocking out the moon and stars. The leaves rustled in a tree over his head and an owl hooted.

Bears live in the woods too.

He searched the dark shadows all around him as he walked. He stumbled over a branch, then grabbed onto a nearby tree trunk to stop himself from falling.

The branch.

He picked up the branch to use as a walking stick, or maybe a weapon if an animal or David came after him. Bryce pushed on, guessing at the direction from the last curve in the road he'd glimpsed before fleeing into the woods.

As he trudged uphill over uneven ground, his legs grew heavier and harder to lift. How much farther away was this house? A tear trickled down his cheek. If only he hadn't lost the phone.

Branches rustled and something trampled the ground off to the left. Bryce froze and turned his head. A large shadow crept toward him.

He turned and fled in the opposite direction. Glancing over his shoulder as he ran, he expected whatever made that shadow would follow, but nothing did. He stopped, rested his hands on his knees, and gobbled big breaths of air. After catching his breath, he moved again. A little way in, the trees ahead of him thinned, allowing moonlight into the forest. On the other side of those trees stood a small, log cabin.

Finally. I'm saved.

He pounded on the door. No one came. Standing on his tiptoes, he peered through a window near the door. Two empty armchairs sat across from an old television with antennas sticking out of the top. The small kitchen was also unoccupied but had a sink and a fridge.

Bryce licked his dry lips as his tummy rumbled. Surely whoever lived here wouldn't mind if a kid who needed help went inside, had a drink of water, and borrowed the phone. He tried the knob. Locked. Maybe they hid an extra key like his grandparents did. He lifted the dirty welcome mat under his feet.

Yes. A key!

He opened the door, flipped the light switches on, then locked the door behind him. "Hello. Is anyone here?"

No one answered. His shoulders sagged. If ever he'd needed an adult, it was now. Bryce opened cabinets in the small kitchen. He stood on tiptoe to reach a plain, white mug and filled it with cold tap water. He drank half before setting the cup aside to find the phone.

The small kitchen adjoined the sparse living/dining area. Besides the two chairs and the television, a small table was pushed up against a wall. No phone.

Down a short hallway, Bryce discovered a small bathroom across the hall from the only bedroom. Surely the phone must be in the bedroom. He walked around the double bed and checked both side tables. No phone.

He sat on the bed and contemplated what to do next. Once again, he had no way to call for help. Maybe wait and hope someone comes home? His stomach rumbled again.

Maybe there's food.

Bryce slid one of the dining chairs across the kitchen to the front of the stove. The upper cabinets were the only ones he hadn't searched. He swung them open and discovered metal cans and boxes of crackers and cereal. Cereal would be easier than trying to find a can opener.

He set the box on the counter and opened the fridge. There were bottles of beer, condiments, orange juice, and a carton of milk. The milk wasn't expired. He gasped and bounced on his toes.

Someone lives here.

****

Jon hiked through the forest as fast as the uneven, hilly terrain allowed. Even with his headlamp, the blackness of the night swallowed him up with the tall trees blocking out the moon and stars. He'd already trekked through six different properties and searched dilapidated structures and barns to no avail.

According to his calculations, he was near the center of Thomas' five-mile radius. Sam was four and a half miles through his search area as well approaching from the opposite side. Ahead, Jon's headlamp illuminated a narrow, dirt road. He bent to examine fresh tire tracks.

I might be on to something here.

He turned off his headlamp in case David was within range, moved inside the tree line, and followed the dirt path. Ahead in a clearing, stood a large, old barn in good condition with high windows and a sturdy door. An ideal hiding spot.

Jon crept into the shadows of the trees around the barn. If he could find a good vantage point, then he'd climb a tree and look in one of the windows. Around the back of the building sat the burnt-out shell of a larger vehicle.

David had followed them in an old Buick the shape of this one the night they'd lured him out for Thomas to setup his cameras. Burning the interior made sense to erase evidence he'd left inside. Did he clean up before he moved on?

Please let me not be too late.

Jon backtracked into the woods far enough to ensure he wouldn't be heard, then radioed Sam. "Sam, you there? I think I found David's hideout." His words echoed back to him from nearby. Jon spun around.

Sam answered, "Yep, and I'm approaching."

Jon clipped the radio on his belt then flashed his headlamp on and off to get Sam's attention.

Sam jogged through the trees and extinguished his headlamp as he approached. "What did you find?"

"An old barn and a stolen Buick that David followed us in the other day. It's a shell now. He incinerated it." Jon turned and headed back the way he came. "Come. I'll show you."

Sam followed. "Is Bryce there?"

"We're about to find out. I waited for you before making a move."

"How do you want to do this?"

"I was considering climbing a tree and looking in a window." Jon stopped and pointed. "There are the Buick and the barn."

Sam put binoculars to his eyes "How many ways in?"

"One door."

"Maybe there's another way. I see a hole in the building on the other side of the Buick."

Jon looked through his binoculars. "I see it. No way we're fitting. We might be able to peek inside, get Bryce's attention, and have him come through."

"That's what I was thinking. You want to go have a look? I'll watch your back."

Jon sprinted to the hole. He dove onto his stomach and positioned his head in front of the opening. A newer Ford 150 matching the description of David's truck was parked inside the barn. He couldn't see into the truck, but no feet stood on the floor of the barn anywhere. They'd have to go inside to be sure, but Jon had an awful feeling in the pit of his stomach no one was in the barn.

He waved Sam over and took his pistol out of the holster. "The only place they could be that wasn't visible, is in David's truck inside the barn."

"Lead the way."

They moved around the front of the barn to the door. Jon made eye contact with Sam and held up three fingers. He lowered one finger, then the second, followed by the third. In unison, they kicked the door in and stormed inside. They approached the truck from either side with their guns pointed at the windows.

Empty. Jon's heart sank. "Damn it."

"You sure this is David's?"

"Alberta plates. Right color and year."

"Right. Let's search this thing. I'll radio for canines. His scent will be here, and they could be on foot nearby."

"You're forgetting something, Sam. The old Ford he kidnapped Bryce in. It isn't here."

Jon walked around to the tailgate and kicked something with his foot. He spotted a phone on the ground. "Wait a sec. What do we have here? A cheap burner."

"Recognize any of the outgoing calls?"

"Sure do. The last call was to my number."

"Why would David leave his burner?"

"David would've kept a close eye on the phone. He meant to call Jess to arrange a meeting." Jon's jaw dropped. "Children tend to lose things a lot more than adults. Maybe Bryce got away with the phone and dropped it. Get those canines here ASAP."

"We need them to be stealthy. Two handlers and two dogs. I'll have them dropped off. We'll keep men parked farther down the road."

"Let's move. If I'm right, then we need to find Bryce before David does."

Jon shut the door behind them leaving the barn as they found it in case David returned. If David figured out they were close, he'd take off again.

Chapter Twenty-Four

David drove five miles on the dirt road finding no sign of the kid. Bryce couldn't have made it any farther on foot in the time he'd been gone. He'd likely headed into the woods somewhere along the way, but David had to be sure the owners of the abandoned barn hadn't wandered onto their older parcel of land and found Bryce.

The vein in David's neck bulged as he clenched then unclenched his hands on the steering wheel. All his plans were unravelling. If he couldn't get things back on track, and fast, he'd have to skip town leaving another living witness behind him.

No, I can't. Unacceptable.

He drove another seven miles along the dirt road to where it ended at the newer homestead. The owners lived there in a sprawling ranch-style house with a greenhouse and barn on either side surrounded by woods. A gravel road connected them to a main road giving them no reason to use the dirt road at all.

David had selected their abandoned barn as a hideout for that reason.

Their vehicles sat in their usual spaces along the side of the house under a carport, and the windows were dark. He glanced at the toolbox in the backseat, then the glove compartment.

Should I take them out of the equation?

This was a question he'd been asking himself for the past three days. David slammed his palm on the steering wheel.

Jessica should've been on her way to the middle of nowhere by now while Bryce waited at the hideout, handcuffed.

To make matters more complicated, time wasn't on his side. Lewistown was a small town made even smaller by the FBI agents crawling all over, looking for him. He'd chosen a good remote place to hide, but they'd find him if he stayed too long. The more immediate danger was Bryce loose and discovering this house.

If he eliminated the husband and wife, Bryce could wander all he wanted. Without help, he wouldn't last long. In fact, David's timeline would get back on track if he abandoned the boy.

Serves him right for taking off.

David pulled on leather gloves, then retrieved his Smith & Wesson pistol from the glove compartment. He kept the gun loaded and ready to go, complete with a silencer. He circled the house and peered in the windows. The young couple who inherited this property from their grandparents, slept side by side in their bed.

Child's play.

The unlocked, sliding glass door leading into the dining room slid open soundlessly. David shook his head. Being in the middle of nowhere gave them a false sense of security. He slid out of his shoes and padded down the hallway in his socks to the master bedroom.

The husband slept on his back snoring so loudly, he could drown out a rocket launch. His wife lay on her side facing away from him. If she could sleep through that racket, then the small burst of noise the silencer didn't suppress shouldn't wake her.

David approached the husband, aimed for his forehead, and pulled the trigger. The man's snores stopped as blood poured out of the center of his forehead into his dark curls, then spread into his wife's long blond braid trailing behind her. David put the gun to the back of her head and pulled the trigger.

He laughed as her blood and brains mixed with her husband's. *Til death do us part.* Well, death did them part all right. Best of all, Bryce had no one to help him now. After disposing of his mother, perhaps he'd come back for him if there was time.

David collected the cell phones off the side tables and left the way he came leaving the screen door open. He set the phones on the ground beside his truck, then smashed them with a hammer from his toolbox. The boy wouldn't be using them to call for help anytime soon.

Time to call the bitch.

He peeled off his sweaty leather gloves, then reached in his pockets. The burner wasn't there.

Damn it! The phone's in my truck inside the barn.

He jumped in the old Ford, drove back the way he came, then parked behind the barn. David grabbed his gun and toolbox from the Ford and launched them in the backseat of his own truck. He swung both barn doors open wide, then drove outside.

The old Ford had served him well, but the evidence within needed to be destroyed. David stopped beside the old truck, launched a lit Molotov cocktail through the open window, then jammed his foot on the accelerator to get ahead of the explosion.

When he arrived at the rural road, he looked left, then right. A black SUV, possibly an FBI vehicle, approached from the left. Rather than turning right, he turned towards it. Driving away from them would arouse more suspicion. He faced forward and drove the speed limit as he passed.

In his rearview mirror, the SUV disappeared in the distance. He slammed his foot on the accelerator, then reached in the cup holder where the phone had been and touched only air. Good thing he had a spare burner in the glove box. Since there were no other vehicles around, he pulled over. He broke open the packaging and dialed the number for the burner he'd left for Jessica in Jon's truck.

Jessica answered in a clear, but agitated voice. "Hello?"

Her distress pleased him. "Ready to turn yourself in to save your son?"

"What other choice do I have?"

"Take Jon's truck and start driving. I'll text you a location once you're far enough away from your friends at the ranch. Don't bring anyone else with you, alert the authorities, or arm yourself. If you do, I'll know, and your son will die. Got it?"

Her voice trembled. "Yes. But what about Bryce?"

"We'll drop him off with your burner. If you behave, then maybe I'll let you say goodbye to him."

"Can I talk to him?"

"No. Hurry up before I change my mind and kill him, too."

"Okay," she cried. "I'm leaving now."

****

Jon shone his flashlight on the small footprints in

the dirt leading away from the hole in the barn. "Bryce escaped. I was right."

Sam patted him on the shoulder. "Let's follow those tracks. The canine units will radio when they arrive, and we can tell them where we are."

Jon followed the tracks to the dirt road. His heart dropped into his stomach. "He went away from the main road. Away from help, and if we found his tracks this quickly, then David would've, too. That would explain the fresh tire tracks."

"We'll have to be careful not to get ambushed. David could be close by with him. If we spook him, he might hurt the kid."

"Sam, the old Ford he used to kidnap Bryce isn't here. If he found Bryce they're gone. We move fast. David can't hit moving targets. Remember the horseback riding incident? Jess would be dead if he could. We run."

"You're right. Lead the way."

Jon resisted the urge to sprint and instead, using his headlamp and flashlight, followed Bryce's small footprints at a fast jog. If they landed in a confrontation, they needed enough air to be able to fight. They stopped when the tracks veered off the road into the woods.

Sam asked, "Why would he go off the road here?"

"My guess is David noticed he was missing and followed in his truck forcing Bryce to head into the woods for cover. How far off are those canines?"

"They can't be far. I have our GPS location. We keep going."

Jon cupped his hands to his mouth. "Bryce! It's Jon. If you're out there come out now. You're safe."

Sam grabbed his arm. "Jesus! What are you doing? You announced our position to the world."

Jon pointed at the ground. "There are only our tracks and Bryce's. David has huge feet and hiking boots. I've seen his footprints."

"Maybe he skipped town after Bryce got away."

Jon followed the tracks behind a tree. "Maybe. Look, Bryce must've heard him coming and hid here to watch for him to pass." He moved his flashlight around the ground. "Yes, and then he wandered farther in."

"He can't be far. Keep going. I bet he had to move slow without a flashlight."

Jon zigzagged around trees and bushes farther and farther into the woods. A rumble pierced the quiet hoots of the owls in the trees around them. "Hear that, Sam?"

"It's probably the canines."

"But the noise is coming from the opposite direction."

Sam spoke into his radio. "What's the ETA on those canines?"

A reply crackled. "We're turning in now, sir."

"Told you it was them. I'll give them our coordinates."

Jon shrugged. If David was headed in the opposite direction, Sam's team would come across him anyway. "Wait here for them. I'll keep going."

Keeping his head down, Jon followed Bryce's tracks. What a brave boy Jessica had, making it this far all by himself in the dark.

I'm coming, buddy.

Jon stopped to take a closer look at the tracks as they lengthened, and their trajectory changed. Bryce had stopped, turned, and then ran in a different direction.

Oh no! What was chasing him?

Jon followed Bryce's footprints another fifty yards. Ahead, the trees thinned. Bryce was close, he could sense him. Jon pushed through the last stand of trees, finding a small wooden cabin. Best of all, only one set of small footprints led to the door.

Jon twisted the knob. Locked. He pounded his fists on the door. "Bryce! You in there? It's Jon."

The door swung open, and Bryce barreled out and jumped into his arms. "You found me before David. You rescued me. You're a hero like my police dog. No. You're human. Maybe you're more like Captain Commando."

Jon laughed and held Bryce close. "I don't think I'm quite that special."

"Where's Mom?"

"She's at my house, buddy. Safe. We'll call her right now." Jon spoke into his radio. "I found him, Sam. He's fine. Get someone to notify your team and the locals. We only need to find David now."

Sam said, "You were right about the vehicle coming from the other direction."

"Do we have David?"

"No. The canine unit passed him on the way here. He was wearing an old ball cap, driving the speed limit, the vehicle description didn't match, and there was no child on board. They assumed he was a local."

Jon shook his head in disgust. "We missed him by a hair."

****

Jessica met her Aunt Debbie's gaze across the table. "We're out of time. I have to go."

Aunt Debbie frowned and took Jessica's hand. "Are you sure?"

"We talked about this. David has to be stopped or he's going to keep coming after me. This way there's a chance I can get Bryce away from him. Jon and Sam must be close, and they'll get a precise location on David while I'm with him."

Chip shook his head. "Jon would blow a gasket if he knew you were doing this."

Jessica stood and shoved her chair in. She bit her tongue to keep from blurting out her first thought—*rich coming from the man that lost Bryce in the first place.* "I'm a grown woman. I make my own decisions."

"It'll be fine. I removed the listening device from Jon's truck but left the tracker so David would know where you were. If I disabled both it would've been too fishy. Little does he know, I also cloned the burner he gave you. Using the burner, we'll hear and see everything you do along with your exact location."

Debbie pulled Jessica in for a tight hug. "You take care of yourself my brave girl."

"I will."

Bryce. I'm coming, baby.

Jessica bolted out the door and climbed into Jon's truck before anyone could stop her. David would start to think something was fishy if she didn't hurry.

****

Debbie' stomach clenched as her niece drove off headed to meet a monster. She sat at the kitchen table with Thomas and Chip. An uneasy silence hung over them. The phone rang. Debbie jumped and glanced at the others. No one made any motion towards picking up the phone, so she answered it herself. "Hello?"

"Auntie, it's me. Jon rescued me."

"It's Bryce." Debbie laughed as tears streamed down her face. "Baby! Are you okay?"

"Yes, Auntie. I'm fine. When David fell asleep, I stole his phone and crawled out a hole in the barn. Then I hid in a cabin in the woods."

"Wow! You did? That's amazing."

"Where's Mom?"

Debbie clenched her eyes shut and swallowed around a lump in her throat. "She isn't here, buddy."

"Jon wants to talk to you."

"All right. I love you, Bryce."

"Love you, Auntie."

Jon said, "Debbie, where's Jess?"

"She left to meet David. Thomas is tracking her movements. He can put you on her tail."

"What? No. She's walking into his trap. Put Thomas on the phone."

Debbie pressed the speaker icon. "We can all hear you, now."

Thomas said, "He's calling her with specific instructions once she's away from the house. She's headed towards town now. I have the phone cloned. If he calls or texts, we'll see it."

"And I'm nowhere near there. I'm at least twenty minutes behind her. I'll have an agent bring Bryce home, and I'll go after Jessica with the rest of the cavalry."

Thomas said, "I don't want to call that burner phone on the off-chance David calls at the same time, but I can send her text messages letting her know we have Bryce."

"Do it. I'm driving, so send updates to Sam on

Jess's location."

Debbie's heart raced, and her chest hurt. She closed her eyes and focused on slowing her breathing.

I never should've let Jess leave. What was I thinking?

Chapter Twenty-Five

David monitored Jessica's progress on his laptop. She did as she was told so far, but the listening device he planted inside Jon's truck wasn't working. The ranch hand had surprised him by coming into the barn and giving him the opportunity to kidnap the boy before he'd had time to test the audio.

This put him at a slight disadvantage. He couldn't be sure she wouldn't share their meeting spot with anyone else. He'd planned for every scenario in the event she pulled something. If everything went awry, a bullet to her brain would be less satisfying but would accomplish his goal. Then he'd have to disappear.

After he'd snatched Bryce, Jon and Jessica hadn't been the only ones in pursuit. David had glimpsed Agent Sam Gardner over his shoulder which could one mean one thing. The FBI had made the connection between his current identity and his old one. They were coming after him for the murders in Seattle.

The dot representing Jessica on his screen crawled through town.

Why would she assume I'd want her anywhere near people?

He chalked her behavior up to stupidity. Time to text the detestable witch for the last time. The last message she would ever get.

He sent her directions to an abandoned cabin off a

network of dirt roads in the Judith Peak area. With numerous ghost towns, mines, dirt roads, trails, and forests, this location offered many places to hide and avenues of escape.

****

The burner phone in Jessica's pocket buzzed, she glanced at the screen. A text from David listed a series of instructions.

It's about time.

Those instructions gave her a reason to stop the truck long enough to put her plan into action. She signaled right and pulled over to the curb.

Sheriff Hank pulled up behind her, parked, then climbed in the backseat behind her.

"Thanks so much for doing this, Sheriff."

"Well, I couldn't exactly refuse, could I? This is crazy! You shouldn't be doing this."

She handed him the burner, then pulled onto the road. "Can you figure out where this leads?"

"Sure." Sheriff Hank said, "Hold up a second. You got some other messages from someone named Thomas. Jon found Bryce. He's unharmed and on his way back to the ranch. Jon is coming after you."

Jessica clutched the steering wheel and blinked back tears. "Thank God. Bryce at least is safe. For now."

Sheriff Hank handed her his phone. "I dialed Jon and put it on speaker."

Jon's voice projected through his truck. "Sheriff Hank, what's going on?"

Jessica said, "He's with me, Jon. I got him to jump in with me on the way to meet David."

"Where are you?"

"I'm still driving. Sheriff Hank is figuring out where David's instructions lead."

Sheriff Hank said, "Looks like we're headed to one of the dirt roads on the way up to the Judith Peak. I'll send a picture of the instructions to you from my phone, Jon."

Jon said, "Never mind that. Turn around and come home. We'll figure out another way to capture David. Or you could stop, jump out, and let Sheriff Hank continue. As long as the tracker is progressing towards the right destination, he'll wait there long enough for the FBI and the local PD to get there."

Sheriff Hank met her gaze in the rearview mirror. "Wise advice, Ms. Miller. I'd take it if I were you."

Jessica's resolve wavered. Should she pull over and send the sheriff in her place? She flashed back to her run in with David in the grocery store. With his massive body pinning her in place and the metal shelf biting into her skin, she'd been so powerless and alone. But this time she wasn't alone. All hands were on deck.

She gripped the steering wheel tighter. "He wants me. If he doesn't see me, he'll bolt, and all is lost. Guaranteed he's planned an escape. You need to let me drive up first before storming in."

Jon's sigh carried through the phone. "Fine. We'll do this your way. It's similar to the first plan, but please, I'm begging you, be careful. Watch out for anything unusual on or along the road. Drive slowly so the rest of us can catch up."

"I will. Next time we talk, this will be over." Jessica hung up and gave Sheriff Hank his phone.

The sky lightened as a new day began. Whether it was the light driving out the dark shadows, or the idea that good held supremacy during the day, it bolstered her spirits.

****

Jon slammed on the accelerator leading a parade of black SUVs towards Jessica. The drivers of the few cars they passed on the backroads craned their necks to stare as they whizzed by.

They had to catch up before Jessica got too close to David.

Slippery bastard.

If only they had waited a few minutes longer to walk into the forest after Bryce. David would have driven right past them. This whole thing could've been over by now.

The only thing keeping him sane was the discussion taking place over the CB radio. Coordinating played to Sam's strength. The locals under Sheriff Hank's direction had joined their frequency and helped to identify possible escape routes from the area. But the location was problematic. They'd need a lot of manpower to cover that kind of territory chalked full of dirt roads and hiding places. David had chosen well.

If he gets his hands on Jess and drags her off, it'll be like looking for a needle in a haystack.

Jon took a deep, cleansing breath. Bryce had foiled David. He had to believe Jessica could, too.

A familiar truck ahead of them, drove the speed limit on the nose. As he closed the distance, he could make out the sheriff's police hat and Jessica's long, blond ponytail.

I'm here, sweetheart.

Jessica held her left hand out the window and gave him a thumbs up, then waved backwards, signaling him to keep his distance. He groaned and then lifted his foot off the accelerator until she moved farther up the road.

Sam touched his arm. "I can't imagine what you're going through, but we aren't going to let anything happen to her. And remember, Jessica may think rotting in prison is good enough punishment for this scum, but it's not. Shoot first and ask questions later. And trust me, no one will ever ask questions."

"I know and I agree wholeheartedly."

Chapter Twenty-Six

Jessica's hand shook as she distanced herself from Jon and the line of black SUVs behind her. "How much farther, Sheriff?"

"Not much. Once we make this next left up ahead, followed by a fast right, we'll begin our climb up the mountain."

"I sort of figured."

"You're doing a really brave thing." Sheriff Hank handed her the burner phone with the instructions. "I'm lying on the floor under the blanket. David could be watching from farther up the mountains."

This is real. I'm actually doing this. Driving to meet a sick serial killer.

After taking the left turn, she followed the instructions and took the next right leading down a narrow, bumpy dirt road. She let off the accelerator as the truck ascended twists and turns while scanning left to right for nasty surprises. The trees moved ahead of her. A bighorn sheep strolled out of the forest and into the road in front of her, followed by another, then another.

"Oh, no!" She slammed on the brakes. The truck stopped within inches of a sheep's nose. The animal paused and aimed an indignant stare in her direction before continuing across the road.

"Shoot. That was way too close."

His muffled voice from under the blanket asked, "What happened?"

"There's a bunch of bighorn sheep crossing the road."

"Are we getting close?"

"Unfortunately. Once we come to the fork in the road, the next stop is the clearing."

The burner phone pinged in her hand with a text message.

—*Why aren't you moving?*—

She snapped a picture of the stream of sheep crossing the road in front of her and sent it to David. Hopefully, that would reassure him, and he wouldn't get spooked.

The prospect of facing him was awful, but not seeing him could be much worse. Deep in her bones lay a certainty he'd come back for her another day when she least expected him and wasn't prepared.

Once the whole flock of sheep had crossed the road, she took her foot off the brake and coasted. After almost hitting the sheep, the beauty of her surroundings took on a sinister quality.

Ageless mountains reaching all the way to the sky, so beautiful during the day, cast eerie shadows in the night. Those tall rocks witnessed more than any human ever would in their lifetime. They provided shelter and sustenance, but one wrong move could mean plummeting to your death.

Jessica shuddered and then slowed as she came to the fork in the road. Swallowing around a lump in her throat, she steered left down the narrow, overgrown, rocky trail. This patch of land hadn't been used in a while and nature was in the process of taking it back.

Branches scrapped the side of Jon's truck. She cringed imagining the damage to Jon's paint.

The burner phone beeped in her hand and displayed a no service message. No one could track her now. David had made sure they couldn't. But little did he know Sheriff Hank had his CB radio on silent in the backseat.

She crested a hill, arriving in a clearing. The land sloped upwards towards an old, weathered cabin still standing by sheer force of will. Half of the roof had caved in, and the door hung crookedly on only one hinge. Behind it lay a drop. How deep she couldn't tell at a distance.

The old Ford truck that David had followed them in was parked there.

David's massive, unmistakable form emerged from the door with a rifle, probably the one he'd used to shoot at them the other day. He pointed the gun at her as she approached.

She turned the truck away from him, hiding her face, to get one last message to Sheriff Hank. "He's got a rifle pointed at me already."

Jessica shifted Jon's truck into park, left the windows down so the sheriff wouldn't overheat, and killed the engine. She leaned her head back against the seat, inhaled deeply, and caught a faint whiff of Jon's natural scent and aftershave. If things went wrong, she'd have that last reminder of him, and the other man she loved, Adam, would be waiting for her on the other side.

Holding onto that small comfort, she climbed out of the truck to draw David's attention away from Sheriff Hank.

David approached with his rifle trained on her. "Stay where you are. Hands in the air."

Her heart pounded against her ribcage. She stopped walking and raised her arms.

Please let the cavalry arrive fast.

David stopped next to the truck and peered inside the driver's window. She needed to distract him. The last thing she wanted was Sheriff Hank's blood on her hands.

She blurted out, "I did as you asked. Where's Bryce?"

David turned away from the truck and focused his attention on her. "Flip your pockets inside out."

She dropped the burner on the ground in front of her. Suspecting David would search her, she hadn't brought anything else. She pulled the pockets of her jeans and her zip-up hoodie inside out, then repeated her question to keep up David's charade. "Please tell me where my son is."

"He's inside the cabin. Come. You go first." He kept the rifle pointed at her.

Despite his lie, Jessica followed instructions. She kept her steps slow to buy time for Jon to find her. The sheriff would be able to use his CB radio to let the others know where they were, then she prayed he'd come after her.

Along with the crunch of her sneakers crushing the overgrowth, engines rumbled far away in the distance. Not wanting to let on anything was up, she kept walking.

The closer she got to the cabin, the harder her pulse pounded in her eardrums. Horrible things had to be waiting inside. And with each step she took, the drop behind the cabin revealed itself to be deeper and deeper.

Bet he wants to throw me over the edge. Should I really be heading in that direction and giving him the opportunity? Where's Sheriff Hank?

Three rotted steps led to what was left of the door. She placed her right foot on the first step and pressed gently to test her weight.

A gunshot went off behind her, then another.

Her ears rang, blotting out all other sound. She covered her ears and pivoted as the scent of burnt metal filled the air.

David yelled at her. "Stay here, or I shoot you, and your son is dead." He ran away from her towards Jon's truck.

His body jolted as he returned fire. Two bullets had left holes in the back of his shirt but no blood.

Dammit! He's wearing a bulletproof vest!

The jig was up. David now knew she hadn't followed his instructions.

She needed to hide. If he killed the sheriff, the next bullet would be aimed square at her. The problem was she didn't have many options. If she ran out of the clearing either left or right towards the forest, he'd see her running and shoot.

She scurried up the cabin stairs, glanced inside the door, and froze.

Oh, this is not good. This is not good at all.

A chair sat in the middle of the only room. Zip ties, a toolbox, a big jug of gasoline, and plastic were lined up next to each other on the floor. He meant to tie her up in the chair and torture her. And if help didn't arrive soon, that may still be her fate.

Her breathing accelerated and the room tilted. She

forced her breaths to slow and her feet to start moving. She couldn't hide in the cabin. The front door was the only way in and out, a trap, and the huge drop behind the cabin, certain death. Gunfire continued to erupt. She spun.

David and Sheriff Hank were on opposite sides of Jon's truck in a standoff.

A red stain spread on Sheriff Hank's chest, and he fell to the ground.

Her gorge rose. She covered her mouth and swallowed down the sick taste in her throat.

I'm on my own. Hurry up, Jon!

She sprinted behind the cabin while David still faced the sheriff, then peeked around the corner.

A black SUV emerged in the clearing, braking hard behind Jon's truck.

Finally!

Jon and Sam stormed out of the first SUV, and using their car doors for cover, unleashed a string of bullets. She should've known Jon wouldn't let the FBI team go in ahead of him. He'd be the next one with a bullet in him.

What have I done? Why didn't I listen?

David fired a string of bullets as he retreated towards the forest to the right of the cabin near the drop.

Jon and Sam returned fire from behind Jon's truck to no avail.

David ran into a dense grove of spruce trees.

Six more black SUVs arrived and fanned out in the clearing. Around twenty men emerged from them in tactical gear. Surely, with so many agents on scene they'd subdue David fast.

From Jessica's vantage point, David was visible behind a thick spruce tree, but could the others see him? And if she could see him—she clung to the side of the house, her knees buckled— he could see her. She dropped onto her stomach in the tall grass and peeked through the blades at David.

The FBI team advanced. Five men holding shields led the way, and the others followed with rifles on their shoulders. They surrounded the cluster of trees. David couldn't escape. The only ways out were through the trees towards the FBI agents, or off the drop behind him.

Sam yelled. "It's over. Come out with your hands up."

David's head turned Jessica's way, and he raised his gun in her direction.

He'd seen her after all. Tears welled in her eyes. If he was going down, then he wanted to take her with him. She had no time to run. Staying low to the ground, making herself a harder target was her best option.

She covered her head with her arms, curled into a fetal position, and waited for the pain to come.

A shot exploded in the air from behind her. She peeked through her fingers.

David staggered backwards holding his neck. Blood poured through his fingers. His left foot collided with a rock and his legs went out from under him. He groped behind him for something to grab onto, finding nothing but air.

David tumbled headfirst off the drop.

Jessica stood, ears stinging and ringing, and walked towards the edge. She held onto a tree, peered over the edge, and her head spun. It wasn't just a drop. David had fallen off the side of a mountain so tall, she couldn't see to the bottom.

He's dead. It's over.

Strong arms wrapped around her waist and pulled her away from the edge. She spun in Jon's arms and met his gaze. He smiled from ear to ear, but his eyes were troubled. She connected the dots. He'd gotten to her first because he'd been the closest to her.

She cradled his cheek. "You fired the shot?"

"I did."

"You saved my life." Tears spilled down her cheeks. "But you had to take another life to do it."

"Hey, don't feel bad for a minute. With him dead, other potential victims get to live, and his past victims got the ultimate justice."

"But your eyes. I know you. Something's wrong."

"Do you realize how close I came to losing you?" He pressed his forehead against hers. "When he ran into the patch of trees, I knew he was headed there to get a clear shot at you. I sprinted behind the SUVs to the back of the cabin. Luckily, the first shot connected."

"It's all over. And thanks to you, we're both in one piece. Did anyone else get shot?"

"No. Sheriff Hank will recover. He's conscious and lucid. The bullet was closer to his shoulder than his heart."

"Oh, thank God." Jessica asked, "When can we go back to the ranch? I need to see Bryce."

"The FBI witnessed the whole thing. I'll send Sam our statements later and borrow one of the SUVs. My truck is part of the crime scene with the gazillion bullet holes."

"Sorry about your truck."

"That's what insurance is for."

"I just have to do one more thing." Jessica let go of Jon and wandered to the ledge again, then looked down. As horrible as the sight would be, she wanted—no needed—to see David's dead and mangled corpse. "Do you see his body anywhere? I don't."

Jon held onto a tree beside her. "No. With where he fell between those mountains, there's no chance of recovering it. He'll be ruled dead."

"Could he possibly be alive, Jon?"

"No. No one could survive that."

"He meant that to be my fate after he was finished with me. I'm certain."

Chapter Twenty-Seven

When they got back to the ranch, Jessica went in search of Aunt Debbie and Bryce while Jon took off his gear and put his weapons away in the basement. She found her aunt in the kitchen filling the kettle with water.

"I'm so glad this is over and you're safe." Aunt Debbie set the kettle aside and wrapped her arms around Jessica. "Bryce went right to sleep after Jon dropped him off."

"How did he seem to you?"

"Surprisingly calm and normal. Kids are resilient. He said he was tired but to wake him when you came home."

"I will. You should sleep."

She had to see Bryce with her own eyes. Only then could she begin to move past the whole horrid episode with David. Jessica went to Jon's old room where Bryce slept and opened the door. A blast of cold air brushed past her and caressed her cheek.

She whispered, "Adam, is that you?

A shadowy figure about six feet tall with Bryce's hair and eyes materialized beside the bed, disappearing as quickly as it appeared. She reached her hand into that spot and an electrical charge made the hairs on her arm stand up.

"It is you. I love and miss you so much. Come visit

more often."

A sense of calm permeated the air around her. She smiled. Adam only materialized maybe once or twice a year for a few precious seconds. If he could've managed more, without a doubt, he'd manifest longer. Normally his visits brought a few seconds of joy before a wave of despair, but this time the intense sadness didn't come. Her sorrow was sweeter because although Adam's loss haunted her, she had Jon to warm her heart. She wasn't lonely anymore. Although most people would think her crazy, she got the impression Adam approved.

Jon came in the room, stopped beside her, and whispered. "It's awfully cold, but only in here."

Jessica considered explaining but decided against it. Not everyone believed in ghosts and Adam's special visits were something she preferred to keep to herself, close to her heart.

She sat on the edge of Bryce's bed and kissed his cheek. "I'm back, buddy."

Bryce opened his eyes and then wrapped his arms around her. Glancing over her shoulder at Jon, he asked, "Did you catch David?"

Jon smiled. "Something like that. He won't be hurting anyone ever again."

Jessica covered Bryce to his chin with his favorite blanket and covered his face with more kisses. "Go back to sleep."

Bryce giggled. "I will. I'm really tired still." He rolled over and closed his eyes.

Jessica followed Jon into the hallway and closed the door. "Hold me?"

Jon wrapped his arms around her and kissed the top

of her head, enveloping her in much needed warmth. "Always."

The calm and quiet she'd craved for days soothed as she melted into his arms. But as much as she wanted to shut off her mind and live in the moment, she couldn't. A major decision loomed. With David's reign of terror over, she'd have to figure out what the future held for her and Bryce.

****

Jessica opened her eyes to sun shining through Jon's window. For the first time since sleeping in his bed, she woke before him. His light snores brought a smile to her lips.

What would it be like to wake up beside him every day?

She crawled out of bed and padded down the hallway to check on Bryce. She twisted the knob, pushed the door open an inch, and peered inside.

Bryce slept in the same spot she'd left him in, covered up to his chin.

Jessica wandered into the kitchen, following her nose to the pot of coffee. Aunt Debbie must have awoken earlier. She poured a mug and sat at the kitchen table to consider her dilemma of where to live.

With David dead, she could return to Cochrane with Bryce, and they could go back to the way things were before. All their friends were there and her parents, but would things ever be the same? She'd be forced to look at the house next door where her nightmare had begun.

And could they live without Jon in their lives? Bryce and Jon had already formed an attachment, likely a much stronger one after Jon found him the previous night. Besides, her own attachment to Jon was one she couldn't live without anymore. She had two choices, the first, stay at the rental house and see how things played out, or the second, move in with Jon as he'd asked.

Debbie came in the kitchen door and took off her work boots. "Good morning, Jess dear. Is Jon awake?"

"No. Not yet. I think he's worn out. We had quite the night."

"One we'll never have to repeat. Chip has the ranch under control."

Jon hurried into the kitchen in jeans and a plain white t-shirt with his hair mussed. "I slept in, ladies. I'll join you after I feed the cows."

Jessica patted the chair beside hers. "No need. Chip made sure it was done." She stood and poured him a mug of coffee. "I'll make you a late breakfast. Eggs over easy and toast? You're out of bacon."

He gave her hand a squeeze. "Thanks. Sounds great."

"Aunt Debbie, can I get you some brunch?"

"No thanks. I ate earlier." She glanced between them and smiled. "I'm getting my stuff and heading home. Thanks for your hospitality, Jon."

"It was my pleasure. I'll drive you. We'll borrow someone's vehicle."

"No hurry." Debbie headed down the hallway to the guest room.

Jessica put butter in a heated skillet and cracked two eggs into the pan.

Jon sipped his coffee. "I need groceries. You must too. Want to go together after we drop off Debbie?"

Jessica's cheeks heated. *This is awkward. I need to*

make up my mind. "Sure. Until you get your truck back, we can use my car."

"First, we'll run Thomas's scanner, and I'll look the car over again."

She piled his eggs on top of his toast the way he liked them and sat his plate in front of him. "I haven't made up my mind about living together yet."

He gave her one of the signature lop-sided grins she adored. "It's fine. Take your time. I love you either way."

"Ahh. I love you too."

****

Jon held Jessica's hand as they crossed the fields to the rental house, like they had so many years ago in a different time. It felt right having her at his side once again. "Make sure you stay away from the car."

Jessica narrowed her eyes. "What has you so spooked?"

"David was in my barn, and we didn't know it. Who knows how long he was on the property? He must've spotted the cameras and worked around them."

"Are you sure this is safe?"

Jon said, "The scanner won't trigger anything."

"Be careful."

"Relax. I'll take care of this."

She sat on the porch steps.

Jon swept the scanner over every inch of the car. "It's not picking up anything."

Jessica stood. "Well, that's a relief."

Jon stuck his palm out. "Wait. Stay there. There are other ways to sabotage a vehicle. Cutting brake lines or a gas line."

Her face blanched. "All right. Do what you need to

do." She plopped down on the step again.

He checked the exhaust pipe. Clear. Then popped the trunk. He shone his light inside and underneath the lid. Nothing. He lifted the hood and examined the fuel and brake lines, the engine block, and fluids. So far so good.

He swept the light farther down. "A few spark plugs have been disconnected. He wanted to ensure you couldn't start this thing. I reconnected them."

"Jon, be careful. David's smart."

"I can handle it, sweetheart."

"It's not worth the risk. Why don't we call in a specialist?"

"I'll be fine. I know what I'm doing." He lay back on the gravel and wedged himself underneath the car with his flashlight. A small black box was attached to the under carriage by the driver's side. He scuttled sideways to get a closer look.

Tick, tick, tick.

"Jessica! Run! Back of the house! There's a bomb!"

Chapter Twenty-Eight

Jessica sprinted to the side of the house and peered around the corner. "Over here!" Why was it any man she loved ended up in deadly situations?

He pulled himself from underneath the car and ran towards her. "Stay there. No matter what."

"Oh God! Hurry, Jon. Hurry." Bright light flashed, then stars bloomed in her vision.

Boom. The ground shook under her feet. She stumbled forward, fell to her knees, and clung to the corner of the house. Her ears rang.

"Jon, no!"

Metal screeched. Jon dove, landing on his stomach a few feet away from her, covering his head with his hands.

No, he's still exposed!

The car rose a foot in the air, then came apart. Pieces of metal and plastic scattered in various directions. One of her car doors slammed into Jon's back, covering his body from the waist up.

"No! This can't be happening!"

The shell of her car burst into flames, blasting her with waves of heat.

Despite his orders to the contrary, she ran to Jon, and yanked the door off his upper body. His head and neck shouldn't be moved, but she needed to get him to safety. Grabbing him under the armpits, she tugged his motionless body towards the side of the house, staggering backwards from his weight.

Footsteps pounded on the gravel laneway.

Thomas asked, "Are you hurt, Jessica?"

"I'm fine. Jon got hit in the head with a car door. Help me!"

Thomas took an armpit from Jessica. "I called 911."

With their combined efforts, they managed to pull Jon to cover.

Thomas peered around the corner of the house. "I think we're safe. Any secondary explosions should've happened by now. I'll run to the gate to watch for the ambulance. Debbie is watching Bryce."

"I'll take care of Jon." She put two fingers on his sweaty neck. "Jon? Can you hear me?"

He didn't move or respond.

"Thank God your pulse is strong. Hang on for me. Help is on the way."

An ugly gash on the right side of his forehead oozed blood. She shook off her cotton button up shirt and tied it around his head. She wiped dirt, grass, and sweat from his pale face through the blur of her own sweat and tears. Her head swam from the fumes and smoke.

She wiped sweat off her forehead with the bottom of her tank top, then held Jon's scrapped hand and glanced at the empty road. "Jon? If you can hear me, I have news. If you hang in there, and come back to me, I'll move in with you. You hear? We'll be lucky if this house doesn't catch fire anyhow."

Her eyes darted from his face to the road. She peered at her flaming car for a fleeting moment before shifting to Jon's face. "Please squeeze my hand, blink, shift your head, anything!"

Jon remained unresponsive. Seconds seemed like hours and minutes like days. *What is taking so bloody long? Hold on, is that?* She cocked her head to the side. *Yes, sirens!*

An ambulance with blinking lights rounded the corner, followed by a fire truck.

Thomas ran into the dirt road and waved his arms.

The ambulance stopped and two paramedics, one male and one female, ran over to her and Jon. Four firemen surrounded the blazing inferno that had been her car. The medics wrapped a brace around Jon's neck, strapped him onto a gurney, and loaded him into the ambulance.

The female paramedic turned to Jessica. "Ma'am. You'd best come with us. We should check you over, too."

Jessica climbed in beside the gurney and held Jon's limp hand in her trembling grasp. "Hang on, Jon Kent. Don't you dare leave me now. You hear?"

She shifted her gaze to the female paramedic sitting on the bench beside her, monitoring Jon's vitals. "Why isn't he waking up?"

"At the very least, he has a concussion. Head injuries are a serious matter, but his vitals are strong." The paramedic angled her body towards Jessica. "Where are you hurt?"

"Me? Please, take care of Jon. I can't lose him. I just can't."

"He's stable. Close your eyes and listen to the monitor."

Jessica shut her eyes.

Jon's heartbeat thumped a steady rhythm, reminding her of the ultrasounds she had while pregnant for Bryce—the sound of life. She opened her eyes. "Thanks. I needed that."

"Now will you let me help you? Do you hurt anywhere?"

Jessica stopped to consider the question. She'd been so focused on Jon. "Well, you sound like you're talking from the other end of a tunnel, and my ears won't stop ringing."

The paramedic looked in Jessica's ears. "Your drums are intact. The ringing should subside in a while." She wrapped a blood pressure cuff around Jessica's arm. "Anything else?"

"Nothing major. I think I pulled a few muscles hauling the car door off Jon and pulling him to safety. I got off easy compared to him."

"Your blood pressure is a bit high. Normal considering. I'll have a listen to your lungs. The car was smoking pretty good when we arrived." She pressed a stethoscope to Jessica's chest and then her back. "Your breathing is fine. You check out."

"Thanks." She gazed into Jon's expressionless face as the ambulance flew down the backroads, sirens wailing. The driver slowed and leaned on the horn as they neared town, and still, Jon didn't wake.

Please be okay.

After what seemed like an eternity, the ambulance halted in front of the rectangular brick façade with a triangular archway above the main doors of the Central Montana Medical Center. People in scrubs rushed to the back doors of the ambulance and whisked Jon away.

Jessica climbed out of the van and followed the

signs to the waiting area, struggling to process the past twenty-four hours. David's death and Bryce's safe return, and a precious night in Jon's embrace believing the nightmare was over, then the explosion.

A nurse approached and handed her a pair of blue scrubs.

Jessica glanced down at her clothes. Her jeans were filthy and torn as was the white tank she'd worn under the blouse wrapped around Jon's head. Jessica thanked the nurse and wandered into the restroom.

She scrubbed her hands with soap and hot water, used damp paper towels to wipe off as much of the soot and dirt off her face, neck, and arms as she could, then put on the scrubs.

Eager for news on Jon's condition, she returned to the nurses' station. Unfortunately, they had no updates and suggested she take a seat in the waiting area. She sat in the closest row to the nurses' desk.

Twirling her rings, she tried but failed to shut out the image of Jon laying on the ground bleeding. The corner of the diamond nicked her finger. She gazed at the ring, a symbol of her love for Adam.

Aunt Debbie is right. He'd want me to be happy.

She slid the ring off her left ring finger and placed it on the other hand instead. Her love for Adam would endure forever, but she had room for Jon as well. If he survived.

Life couldn't be that cruel to me twice. He'll be okay. He has to be okay.

A hand rested on her shoulder.

She turned and gazed into the kind face of Sheriff Hank. His arm hung in a sling to support his injured shoulder, but besides that he seemed no worse for the wear. She prayed Jon would be up and about soon, too.

"How's the shoulder? I feel awful for getting you involved."

"Don't worry about me. It's part of the job. Any updates on Jon?"

"No. Nothing yet. We only arrived a few minutes ago."

"I got word from my deputies the fire is out. We've sealed off the area until the county sends in some experts to make sure it's safe." He paused. "You're pale, probably shock. I'll get us some coffee from the cafeteria, then you can tell me the rest."

She didn't want anything in her knotted stomach, but she sat and waited for Sheriff Hank to return. A few minutes later, he held out a tray with two steaming Styrofoam cups.

She cradled the coffee in her hands for warmth. "Thank you."

"Can you tell me what happened?"

"Jon decided to go over my car before we went grocery shopping. I told him we should get an expert, but he wouldn't listen." She proceeded to tell him about Thomas and his various gadgets, leading to Jon connecting the spark plugs before the explosion.

"Wow. David was a piece of work. The world is a better place without him."

A woman Debbie's age with well-groomed spiky auburn hair and a pretty face rushed into the waiting area straight to the nurses' station. "Sheriff, is that Jon's mother? I haven't seen her in about fifteen years."

"Yes, I'll go tell her what we know, then I'll let you two catch up."

"Thanks again for everything, Sheriff."

Jessica hung her head. Sally would hate her for bringing this trouble into her son's life and getting him hurt. She could only imagine how she would feel if the shoe was on the other foot. In no way prepared to face Jon's mother, she buried her face in both hands. Tears fell and she made no move to wipe them away.

A tissue appeared between her fingers. She accepted the tissue from a well-manicured hand in stark contrast to her dirt-embedded nails. The floral scent of Sally's perfume mingled with the ever-present smell of bleach found in hospitals.

"How are you, Jess?"

She dabbed her cheeks, then gazed into Sally's eyes. "I'm fine. Thank you."

Sally sat in the chair beside Jessica and patted her knee. "You're welcome. I heard from Debbie you've had quite the rough go of things lately."

"It's been horrible, but Jon has been a Godsend. He saved me and my little boy, and now he's hurt because of it. I'm so very sorry, Mrs. Kent."

"Please, call me Sally. Don't apologize, dear. Jon's tough, and he knew what he was getting into when he rented you the house. He's always been very fond of you. I'm sure he'll be fine."

Jessica took a deep breath. Sally had forgiven her, but she couldn't forgive herself so easily. "I rode here with him. His vitals were strong. His heartbeat kept me sane on the way."

"Speaking of hearts, I hear you two have reconnected in a big way. Debbie told me he's asked you to move in with him. That's not the type of thing Jon does on a whim. He's only ever lived with Cynthia. He's always loved you."

"I know. I love him, too."

A doctor, small in stature with thinning grey hair and bifocals approached. "Good day, Mrs. Kent. I have news about your son."

Sally took Jessica's hands in hers. "Is he going to be, okay?"

"He sustained a severe concussion. I expect he'll wake in the next few hours or so. There's a good chance he'll experience some side effects such as dizziness, headaches, muscle aches. I'll get one of the nurses to talk them over with you, and what to do if they occur."

Jessica asked, "Are you sure he'll be all right? There are no other signs of brain trauma?"

"Considering the circumstances surrounding his injury, he got lucky. You can see him now. He's in room four around the corner."

Sally said, "Thank you so much, doctor."

Jessica sighed as the weight of the world lifted from her shoulders. She texted Thomas so he could tell Debbie and Chip the news. Her eyes filled with tears again. She wasn't sure why this time, relief maybe?

Sally hugged her with tears in her own eyes. "Told you he'd be fine. Let's go see him together."

Jessica wandered down the hallway to Jon's room. She pushed open the door with Sally behind her, then covered her mouth to suppress a gasp.

Jon lay so still in the hospital bed. With his head bandaged and equipment hooked up to him, he appeared vulnerable in stark contrast to the man who'd saved her life a short while ago.

Jessica kissed his hand. "I'm here, Jon. I'm not going anywhere. You hear me? You heal and come back to me so we can have our happily ever after."

Sally took his other hand. "You hear my boy? She's a fine woman, and your mother approves so you better come back to us."

Jon remained unconscious in the bed.

Jessica sat across from Sally in a comfortable silence and shut her eyes. Hours passed until the sky darkened in the windows of the hospital room.

Jessica shifted her gaze from her phone to Jon's face. She pointed, "Look Sally, his eyes, they're moving."

"Are you coming back to us, son?"

His eyes fluttered open. He covered them and croaked, "Ouch. The lights."

Sally scrambled out of her chair. "Shut your eyes. I'll turn them off."

Jessica poured a glass of water and held a straw to his lips. "Drink. You sound like a frog."

He sipped the water and then pushed the cup aside. "Thanks."

Sally touched his arm. "I'll go tell someone you're awake. Sounds like you could use some pain meds."

"Thanks, Mom." He took Jessica's hand. "I'm in the hospital, right? The car bomb?"

"Yes, my car door hit you in the head. You have a severe concussion."

"It was the strangest thing. I couldn't move or open my eyes, but I heard what was happening around me. Did you call my name a few times?"

"Yes, I wanted you to wake up so badly."

"You made me a promise."

She kissed his hand. "I did. And I'll make good on it. They say home is where the heart is, and my heart is with you. I'm never leaving your side. Not after coming close to losing you. Life is too short to waste any time we're given."

He smiled in the dim light cast by the beeping machines. "The past few days have been a wakeup call. In the spirit of making the most of every minute, let's have a baby."

She was speechless as she processed his words. "Did you just say you want a baby?"

"Do you?"

"I always planned on having at least two."

The corner of his mouth lifted. "Well then. When my head feels better, we'll have to get on that."

"Whoa. Slow down cowboy. We reconnected a week ago after fifteen years apart, we're moving in together, and you want to make a baby. Don't you think we're jumping the gun a bit?"

"We've had a special connection since we were kids. We love each other. What we have is real, and that's all we need to worry about."

"But I'm still reeling. I need some normal time, and Bryce needs a chance to adjust to us being together."

"Makes sense. We'll revisit it when you're ready." His eyes fluttered. "I need sleep."

Jessica kissed his forehead. "You do. Sleep and recover. I'll be here. I don't plan on leaving you ever again."

Chapter Twenty-Nine

On a sunny morning two days later, Jon was released from the hospital. Jessica sat at the kitchen table across from him with a steaming mug of coffee. A fresh cool breeze carried the voices of songbirds through the open window into the blissfully empty house. Thomas and Debbie had both left earlier that morning to return to their own lives.

Jessica sipped her coffee. "This is so peaceful. I could get used to this."

The right corner of Jon's mouth lifted into his signature crooked grin. "I sure hope you do. When do you want to tell Bryce about our living situation?"

"I think we should tell him together when he wakes." Footsteps squeaked on the hardwood floor, and a door creaked open. She smiled. "Here he comes."

Bryce wandered into the kitchen rubbing his eyes. "Jon. You're home." He ran over to the table and gave him a fist bump. "Are you better now?"

"Yes. Good as new. Thanks for the card you made me."

"You're welcome." Bryce climbed in the chair next to Jon. "Mom, can you make eggs and bacon?"

Jessica stood and ruffled his hair. "Sure, buddy."

"Do you want help, Jess?"

"No. You sit there with Bryce. Do you want another breakfast, too?"

Jon patted his tummy. "Sure. I've got room."

Bryce asked, "When are we going home?"

Jon asked, "What do you think of this place?"

Bryce scrunched his forehead. "Well, it's bigger than our house and you have Daisy."

Jon asked, "Would you like to live here from now on?"

"Yes. Does that mean you and Mom are getting married? Are you going to be my dad?"

Jon's eyes widened like a deer in headlights.

Jessica smiled and bit her lip to stifle a laugh. She shifted the pans off the heat and went over to the table to rescue Jon. "You know your dad died and went to heaven when you were a baby. Jon can't take his place, but he can be your friend until you get to know him better. When you decide you love him as much as you love me, then you can call him dad. If he agrees. We will be a family from now on."

Jon put his hand on Bryce's shoulder. "I'm good with being friends until you're ready to call me dad. I hope you'll love me that much someday. I'll be there for you, and I'll teach you all kinds of fun stuff. The more time you spend with someone the closer you become. Let's get to know each other better, sound like a plan?"

"Okay," Bryce said.

Jessica smiled and returned to the stove, convinced in her heart the happy memory they'd just made together would be one of many more to come.

****

A few weeks later, Jessica met Sally at the nail salon. Jessica hated the fumes and having to wait for her nails to dry, but Sally asked, and she wouldn't refuse and risk offending her so early on into their budding friendship. Jessica parked her rented Mustang and went inside.

Sally flipped through a magazine in the little waiting area.

Jessica pecked Sally on the cheek and sat in the chair next to hers. "Hi, Sally. Nice to see you again. Thanks for inviting me."

"It's nice to see you again too, Jess. I got us a package for a full French mani and pedi. I thought it would give us a chance to enjoy some girl time."

"Thanks. Sounds great. It'll be nice to spend time with you under much better circumstances."

Jessica enjoyed Sally's company, but a manicure *and* a pedicure? She almost cringed. At least by the time it was over she'd have beautiful nails. She sat in a massaging chair and set her feet in the foot spa.

Ah. Maybe this won't be so bad after all.

Her body went limp in a way she wouldn't have believed possible.

****

Back at the house, Jon and Bryce tidied to get the house extra clean before Jessica returned.

"Did you get all those toys picked up, buddy?"

"Yeah."

"Good man. Time to go to Aunt Debbie's. Are you still fine with spending the night? She promised there would be lots of cookies and popcorn."

"Yeah, it's going to be fun. I bet she'll let me watch movies and stay up late."

Jon grabbed Bryce's backpack off the counter. "All right. Let's hop in the truck and go. Thank you for not telling Mom about her surprise."

"I couldn't. You said it was top secret."

Jon laughed. "Totally top secret."

After dropping Bryce off at Debbie's, Jon hurried home. He aimed to woo Jessica with his culinary skills. Cynthia used to love his cooking. He'd chosen her favorite dish, pasta primavera, to cook for Jessica.

He set water to boil, then combined melted butter and white wine in a pan for his beurre blanc sauce. The simpler the sauce, the less chance there was of messing it up, and the flavor of the fresh pasta he'd snagged at the grocery store would sing through.

The roaring engine of the Mustang approached as he finished chopping broccoli into florets. He dropped the broccoli in a pan alongside snap peas and a red pepper, then dropped his pasta in the boiling water.

Jessica opened the door and came in like she belonged rather than knocking. "Hi. What's that amazing smell?"

"Come on in here and give me a kiss, sweetheart. It's homemade pasta primavera."

"Yum." She stood on her tiptoes, kissed his cheek, then glanced around the main floor. "It's really quiet in here. Where's Bryce?"

"He's sleeping over at Debbie's."

She put her hands on her hips and smiled. "Oh, really? Was your mother involved in all this?"

"She promised to keep you busy. She was very happy to get you all to herself."

She pressed her chest to his back, wrapped her arms around his middle, and gave him a quick squeeze. "Sneaky, but I appreciate the gesture. It'll be nice to have the house to ourselves tonight."

He added the al dente pasta to the sauce. "We haven't really been alone since you got here. I figured it was about time."

She stood on her tiptoes and peered over his shoulder at the food on the stove. "I'm very impressed. Fresh pasta? I can never get the consistency of the dough right."

"Why, thank you. I was hoping to impress. I want to demonstrate all my best qualities, so you know what you're getting. But seriously, I bought the fresh pasta at the grocery store."

She laughed. "You've been doing a good job of showing me your many skills. Can I help?"

"Nope, I have it all under control."

He took the bottle of champagne out of the fridge, popped the cork, and poured some into two flutes he'd set out on the counter earlier.

She picked up the glasses and walked to the table. "Wow, champagne too. You pulled out all the stops."

The corner of his mouth lifted. "Dinner is ready."

He twirled the pasta into perfect mounds, added vegetables, then spooned on some extra sauce. After garnishing with fresh parsley, he set their plates on the table, then lit the candles and turned off the lights.

She lifted a forkful of saucy noodles and vegetables to her mouth. "This is delicious. I'm one lucky lady. Where did you learn to cook like this?"

"I learned a lot from my mother, Cynthia, cooking shows, the internet. You know. Here and there. I bet you'll teach me some new tricks."

"I'd be happy to. I have a feeling you could show me a few things as well. The fun part will be teaching Bryce and someday our future little one to cook."

"That's the main reason I did all this tonight."

"Really?"

Butterflies flitted around his stomach in anticipation of his next move. "You're the most amazing woman I've ever met in my life. I don't want to let you slip away like I did fifteen years ago. We're going to be living together and raising a family, and I want it to be forever."

He had planned to wait, but the conversation had taken the perfect turn. He kneeled beside Jessica's chair, reached into his shirt pocket, and pulled out the ring he'd picked up earlier.

"Jessica Miller, will you marry me and make me the happiest man in the world?"

Her jaw dropped, and her eyes widened. Seconds ticked past with no response, making him wonder if he'd jumped the gun and pushed her too far. He wished he could crawl inside that beautiful head of hers to know what she was thinking.

****

Jessica's mind went blank, eyes locked on the solitary diamond in front of her. After recovering from the shock, she flashed back to a similar moment years earlier. One of her most treasured and precious memories.

Adam had kneeled in front of her on top of a mountain pass with an equally simple, yet perfect ring. The clean breeze had rustled the colorful fall leaves, raining them down upon her as the most handsome, amazingly sweet man she'd ever known declared his love and proposed marriage.

Adam would approve of Jon. Getting engaged seemed no crazier than anything else they had done in the past few weeks.

She looked into Jon's eyes so full of kindness and

love. "Yes, Jon. I'll marry you. But not until at least six months from now so we can be sure we're still good together."

He smiled and slipped the ring on her well-manicured finger. "That's definitely a deal. I thought you would make me wait longer. We'll have a special Christmas this year."

"You're right. Christmas is in six months. Sounds amazing. A Christmas wedding."

She slipped out of her chair, kneeled in front of him, and pulled him into her arms. *What a blessing. Two chances at true love in one lifetime.* She held him close as happy tears dripped from her eyes onto his shoulder.

He had tears in his eyes, too. He grinned. "Should we finish dinner or reheat our food later?"

"The pasta is probably already getting cold. I think we both have other ideas."

"Yes, I think we do." He scooped her up and carried her down the hallway to their bedroom.

Chapter Thirty

As summer faded into fall, they prepared for their Christmas Eve wedding, an intimate affair with only their family and closest friends. Jessica found a cozy venue at Grand Union Hotel in nearby Fort Benton for their wedding and reception. The hotel agreed to provide the food, decorations, and photographer saving her from having to hire multiple people.

On the morning of the big day, while Jon tended his animals in the wee hours of the morning, Jessica stuck a bow on a special gift for Jon. She put the present on the table in front of his usual spot with coffee, then sat with her mug to wait for him. She chuckled. Boy, would he be surprised. Their wedding day would be even more memorable for years to come.

So far, things were going off without a hitch. Her mother had phoned from the hotel while Jessica brewed coffee to assure her the venue was picture perfect. Each table was adorned with real pine garlands, white twinkle lights, candles, and red and white poinsettias. And a ten-foot real, decorated blue spruce stood beside the archway woven with coordinating flowers under which they would exchange vows.

Jon came in the back door and took his boots off. He kissed Jessica then sat down in front of his coffee and the gift. "Where did this come from?"

She had to stop herself from bouncing in her chair.

"Me, of course, open it."

Jon unwrapped the paper and opened a small box. He unfolded the little bundle of tissue and held up a onesie that read, 'My Daddy's Number #1'.

Laughter erupted from his belly and tears dripped down his cheeks at the same time. "Oh my God, sweetheart. What a dream come true."

She pushed her chair back and went to him. He pulled her into his lap, and they held onto each other. The past six months had been the best of her life, made sweeter by the hardships they endured along the way to get to where they were now. Insomnia and nightmares had been replaced with falling asleep each night satiated in the arms of a man she loved.

After a few minutes intertwined in each other's arms, Jon wiped his tears and gazed into her eyes. "How long have you known?"

"I took a home test two weeks ago. That's why I went to see the doctor. So, I could be sure before I said anything."

"Does anyone else know?"

"No. I've kept the pregnancy to myself. It's best not to tell anyone until we're past the twelve-week mark, including Bryce. We still have four weeks to go."

"It'll kill me keeping the secret. I'm glad you told me on a day when I have an excuse to be this happy. We'll make sure the staff at the hotel know to bring you non-alcoholic sparkling wine and be discreet. A shotgun wedding. I swear, I'm the happiest man alive."

She laughed and wrapped her arms around his neck. "And I'm the happiest woman."

Bryce wandered into the kitchen rubbing his eyes. "Good morning, Mom. Good morning, Dad."

Jessica climbed out of Jon's lap, and hugged Bryce. Since David kidnapped him, she couldn't get enough hugs. "Hi, buddy. Ready for the big day?"

"Yeah. I swear I won't lose the rings."

Jon held out his hand for a high-five. "Good man. Let's get you fed so we can get this show on the road."

****

Jessica struggled to contain tears as Jon pulled into the hotel parking lot. They would officially be a family, an even bigger one when their new little one came on the scene in another eight months or so. Her cheeks ached from the permanent smile she wore as they walked into the hotel. Their first stop, the venue where the ceremony would take place.

Her hand drifted to her mouth. The room was like a Christmas scene out of a magazine, picture perfect and festive, exactly as her mother described. A tear escaped despite her best efforts not to cry. "It's absolutely beautiful. Can you believe this is happening?"

Jon chuckled and glanced her way, Christmas lights twinkling in his eyes. "It's a miracle we finally made it here after all these years." He kissed her cheek and wrapped his arm around her. "You probably need to start getting ready, sweetheart. We'll give you a few minutes to take this all in." He squeezed Bryce's shoulder. "Tux time."

Jessica kissed her men. "I'll see you two at the altar."

Jon winked and smiled. "We'll be there."

****

Jessica stood gazing at her reflection in the floor-length mirror after the stylist left. A decade older and wiser, she hadn't expected to feel as beautiful on her second wedding day.

Her hair was curled, half up and half down, full of volume and shine. Her makeup was subtle but accentuated her blue-grey eyes and her high cheekbones. She zipped up her wedding dress and adjusted the neckline. The simple boatneck A-line hung right above her toes dipping onto the floor with a simple train.

A quiet yet persistent knock demanded her attention. She opened the door and found nothing but a white envelope on the carpet, addressed to her in first name only written in elegant, distinctive cursive. The calligraphy was exquisite. If she'd seen it before, she would've recognized it. She tore open the envelope and unfolded a single sheet of paper.

Dear Jessica,

I wish you and Jon all the happiness in the world. You both deserve nothing less, but beware. There are those out there who wish to make Jon miserable. His double-life will always come back to haunt him and those he loves most. I know this better than anyone. This is your last chance to walk away. Once you become his wife, you and Bryce will have targets on your backs.

Jessica reread the unsigned letter. Who would've left this at her door on her wedding day? Jon's double-life? They spent every waking minute together. It could only refer to his time in the FBI, and he retired with no intentions of ever returning. Maybe a scorned colleague sent it?

Another knock sounded on her door this time accompanied by a voice. "It's Mom and Sally. Can we come in?"

Jessica looked at the letter and the envelope one last time, then threw them in the fireplace. Marrying Jon was no riskier than being a cop's wife. As the ashes from the paper disintegrated into the flames, she said, "Come in."

The door opened and her mother, Virginia, and Sally came into her room.

Virginia dabbed her eyes with a tissue. "Spin around and let me see your dress."

Jessica spun in a slow circle.

Sally said, "Oh my gosh! You are the most beautiful bride I've ever seen."

Virginia sniffled. "Is she ever."

Jessica waved her hand in front of her eyes and laughed. "Please don't cry. You'll get me crying, and I really want to make it to the altar with my makeup intact."

Virginia took Jessica's hand. "Oh, baby. I can't help it. You look so beautiful. I'll do my best to stop for now."

Sally took her other hand. "Jessica, my son is a very lucky man. I can't wait to see his face when he sees you."

"I'm the lucky one. We get along so well, and Bryce loves him so much. He's filling a huge hole in my heart I thought I would have to live with for the rest of my life. I never expected to get this lucky, twice."

Virginia said, "It's about time for the big show. The officiant is here and so are the guests. Let's find your father so he can get himself together to walk you down the aisle."

"I'm ready, Mom. I've never been readier for anything in my life."

As Jessica followed her mother and Sally out the door, she reread the letter in her mind. One line from the burnt letter stood out from the rest. *I know this better than anyone.* Only one person would be able to make that claim. *Cynthia.* But that didn't make sense. If she was able to send a letter, she'd reach out to Jon. Maybe one of her relatives? Either way, it didn't matter. Jon wasn't returning to the FBI, and David was dead. Nothing stood in the way of their happily ever after.

Jessica's father, Henry, waited outside the tall, wooden doors concealing the ceremony room from view. His eyes travelled over his daughter from head to toe, and tears welled in his eyes.

Jessica laughed. "Oh no, not you too, Dad. I'm doing my best to keep myself together here."

Virginia kissed Jessica's cheek. "We'll go on in and get things started." She took Sally's arm, and they went inside, closing the doors behind them.

Henry pulled Jessica into his arms. "You look amazing. You have a special glow about you, too. Are you pregnant again?"

She pulled back and circled around to make sure no one else had heard him. "Quiet, Dad. I can't believe you figured it out. It's early. Don't tell anyone."

"I don't know how your mother didn't notice the glow. Your skin shines when you're pregnant. I promise my lips are sealed, but I've got to say, I'm excited. Maybe you'll have that elusive granddaughter to go with the four grandsons you and your sister have given me."

She chuckled. "We'll see. I hope so. I love you so much."

"I love you too, Princess. Let's get you married." He took her arm. "Jon is a very fine man. I approve. You sure know how to pick them."

"Thanks, Dad. That really means a lot."

Henry nodded to the ushers manning the double wooden doors, and they pulled them open.

Jessica stood inside the entrance on her father's arm, waiting for the music to begin. The pianist played the traditional bridal march, and she walked in step with her father.

The room was full of loved ones watching them walk down the aisle, but her focus centered on Jon in his tuxedo, white shirt, and black tie, standing at the altar beside Bryce.

****

Jon's breathing hitched as Jessica walked towards him, towards everything he dreamed they'd do together in the future. Everyone else in the room faded into the background.

He did his best to keep his composure as the woman he loved walked towards him to become his wife. He couldn't help but remember Cynthia walking down the aisle. The memory stung, but she'd want him to move on and be happy with Jessica.

Henry offered Jessica's hand to Jon. "You take good care of her now."

Jon smiled and took her hand. "I most certainly will, sir."

The minister started the ceremony. Jon fended off tears as Jessica cried while promising herself to him. But his tears flowed freely when he pledged his love to her in return.

On cue, Bryce handed each of his parents a ring.

Then came the moment Jon looked forward to the most. The officiant pronounced them husband and wife, and he finally got to lift Jessica's veil over her head.

He wrapped his arms around her waist and tasted salt on her lips to a loud round of applause.

"You're all mine now, Mrs. Kent."

She laughed through her tears that wouldn't stop falling and leaned her mouth close to his ear. "Not yet Mr. Kent. First, we have to put our son to bed and read him, 'The Night Before Christmas'. Then I'll be all yours. I can't wait. I wish we could leave now. You look pretty darn sexy in a tuxedo."

He breathed into her ear. "What do you think you're doing to me looking this beautiful? I'm one lucky man. We'll sneak off after we cut the cake."

She laughed and recited his favorite line. "Deal."

****

David reclined in bed at a fancy medical resort with bandages wrapped around his face after his final surgery. In a few more weeks, the bandages would be coming off, and he'd get to see his new face for the first time. Vanity wasn't becoming, but he wanted to look interesting enough to draw in more victims.

After the FBI made the connection between the face he was born with and his surgically altered one, he'd taken extra care to find a better surgeon. The one he chose guaranteed he wouldn't be recognizable. Unfortunately, once his face healed, it would take many months of physical therapy to get back into shape after his partial trip down the mountain.

His most reckless escape of all time had come at a high cost. An expensive and painful setback to say the least. Falling with a neck spurting blood from a bullet graze and trying to stop his momentum with a rock pick had resulted in multiple injuries.

With one leg and one arm incapacitated, he'd been stranded in a cavern on the side of the mountain and forced to call for help. Satellite phones were the best invention. Without his, he would've perished.

When you needed to be rescued and smuggled out of the country, you needed someone powerful to help you. Usually, money wasn't a big enough incentive for someone to take that kind of risk, but information sure was.

During the previous week, David had shopped word around the criminal underworld that he had information on the whereabouts of the elusive Jon Kent. He found an interested party in one Hugh Jones, king pin of the Kansas City mob.

As he sat in the cavern shaded from the sun with his shirt pressed against his neck wound, he called the home phone number he'd been given.

An older gentleman, likely a staff member, answered the phone. "Hello, Jones's residence."

David followed the script he'd been instructed to use. "I'd like to speak to a Mr. Hugh Jones about a special quote he requested for a gift for his niece's upcoming graduation."

"Yes, sir. He's expecting your call. I'll fetch him promptly."

David shifted his position trying to relieve the pressure on his sore shoulder. Pain shot through the nerves of his arms. He gritted his teeth and suppressed a groan. It wouldn't do to let on how desperate his situation was during negotiations. If he didn't present a confident, self-assured front, then Jones wouldn't respect him.

An authoritative voice, much less polite than the first gentleman blasted out of the phone. "I don't normally take direct calls. Trust that if what you told my associate turns out to be false, you'll incur my wrath."

David grimaced. Powerful men were normally disagreeable, and this Mr. Jones seemed as surly as any other. "It's nice to make your acquaintance as well, Mr. Jones."

"Let's dispense with the brown-nosing and get to the heart of the matter, shall we? You claim to know where ex-FBI agent Jon Kent is living. Have you told anyone else, and what do you want? Money?"

Given David's deteriorating condition, cutting the crap was a refreshing approach. "I haven't told anyone, and as I'm sure you've discovered, I've made it impossible for anyone to trace me. If you agree to my terms, then you will be the only one with the information other than me."

"What do you want?"

David needed more than safe passage. He'd likely have to do more than give up Jon's location. "First, I want Jon Kent and Jessica Miller, his new squeeze, dead, but you need to wait six months before sending anyone in. No one can make the connection between me and their death, and considering my failed assassination attempts, you need to let the heat die down anyhow. Second, I want transport and safe passage to South America. Then I'll tell you where I am which isn't far from Jon Kent."

"No money?"

"No. I have plenty of my own."

"Who the hell are you?"

"Right now, I'm David Hayes, but I work alone and change identities often."

"Your terms are reasonable, Mr. Hayes. However, there's something else I want from you."

"Name it."

"You claim to be an assassin? How many have you killed?"

"Fourteen. And I've never seen the inside of a jail cell. I'm in hot water now, I give you that, but I had no idea Jessica Miller knew Jon Kent. And I did manage the situation. The FBI thinks I'm dead."

A long pause on the other end of the line was the response.

Just make up your mind! I'm wasting precious battery here!

David was about to give up and move on to the next name on his list when he got a reply. "What I want in return is for you to stay in touch and on my payroll for when I have a particularly delicate target."

"We have a deal, Mr. Jones. I'll need time, probably a lot of it to recuperate. I'm in medical distress, and I plan on having facial reconstruction done."

"I can live with these terms, Mr. Hayes. Where should I send my team to collect you?"

David cringed. The last thing he wanted to give up, more so than the pleasure of killing Jon and Jessica himself, was his freedom of movement. In his current condition, Jones would have no problem tailing him and keeping tabs. But he didn't have a choice, for now. If Mr. Jones demanded too much of him, then he'd send him to meet his maker.

"I'm in a cavern on the side of a mountain near Judith Peak in Lewistown, Montana."

A word about the author...

Growing up as an only child in a small town, I dreamed of becoming an author. My father laughed and said okay, but you might be broke. I shrugged my shoulders and kept writing at our home PC.

In high school when it was time to decide on a future career, I chose to pursue an Honours Degree in Criminology at the University of Ottawa, but at the back of my mind, the dream of writing for a living persisted.

Fast forward fifteen years, and as a happily married woman and proud mother to two children and four dogs, my dream came true.

www.michellegodardricherauthor.com

Thank you for purchasing
this publication of The Wild Rose Press, Inc.

For questions or more information
contact us at
info@thewildrosepress.com.

The Wild Rose Press, Inc.
www.thewildrosepress.com

Printed in the USA
CPSIA information can be obtained
at www.ICGtesting.com
LVHW021500070924
790238LV00002B/253